Friendship Fragments

Chantal Bookal

To my friends, from near and far to past and present:

Thank you inspiring a story of growth, happiness, nostalgia, chaos and downright fun. Without our moments of chosen sisterhood, this story would not have been created. This is for you.

Prologue

2014
   Graduation Day

Yasmine, Jordyn, and Amari had spent nearly every waking moment of the last four years with one another. And this would be their last morning together as undergraduate students with adulthood waiting for them on the other side— ready or not.

Being the early riser she was, Yasmine dramatically jumped out of her bed to obnoxiously bang on her late-rising friends' Jordyn and Amari's doors while blasting R&B music from their surround-sound speakers in the living room. They lived together in a three-bedroom duplex near campus, where they were close enough to the mix of college social life but far enough to separate themselves if necessary.

"Yasmine, it's too early for your shenanigans," Jordyn stated, still rubbing her eyes by the time she opened her bedroom door. Amari crossed her arms as she stood by her door confirming her displeasure with both Yasmine and her Spotify playlist being her alarm clock for the morning.

1

"Everyone lighten up. You'll miss it when I can't brighten up your mornings with my energy," she responded.

"I have a feeling we will survive. And turn that music down," Amari urged, turning backward to close her bedroom door, but not before Yasmine held it in place.

"Shouldn't we all have a mini-brunch before we head to graduation?" she inquired.

"I kind of agree. We have a couple of hours to get ready before we head to the stadium. Let's do it. I'll make the waffles!" Jordyn exclaimed.

"Now that's more like it. I'll make the eggs and bacon," Yasmine confirmed.

"Fine, fine. I can make the mimosas," Amari obliged.

Grabbing her less-than-enthused hands to dance, Yasmine announced, "Yay! Now it's really a party."

With little time to spare, they ate a quick bite before parting ways to prepare for their pomp and circumstance.

* * *

Although the piss poor weather tried to literally rain on their parade in the days prior, the weather was perfect on the day of the Wynters University outdoor commencement with clear blue skies and the sun shining beautifully over the football stadium.

As they entered to find a space where they could sit together, the air itself was filled with happiness and excitement, but was also coupled with an undercurrent of melancholy. Their pre-emptive tear-filled eyes, as they gazed at the swarms of graduates around them, symbolized far more than being proud of their accomplishments.

They would now be leading separate lives, with the hopes of the connection between them staying exactly as it was. But that wasn't realistic. Jordyn decided to stay in Atlanta, where Wynters University was located, to stay with her college sweetheart, Malik. Yasmine was heading back to New York to start her career as an assistant buyer, leaving her college beau, Xavier, in their college town. Amari was going back home to Silver Spring, Maryland to "find herself" and figure out what she wanted to do next in her career.

They held hands as their commencement speaker gave them words of wisdom to help carry them into their new chapter of life. His speech emphasized that while they carved irreplaceable memories during their college experience, there was still much more life to be lived afterward with even more lessons to be learned.

"I will miss y'all so much," cried Yasmine, through the darkly-tinted sunglasses she wore in an attempt to hide the stream of tears beginning to fall from her face. The thought of functioning on a day-to-day basis without her girls was something she dreaded for months leading up to this very moment. She didn't want to.

"We'll be just one phone call away from each other. We'll try to talk every day," Amari affirmed, clasping her friend's fingers with her own.

"Well ... you two are the ones leaving me here, remember?" Jordyn mentioned. She always knew how to ruin a moment, if you let her.

"I'm going back home where we both came from, unlike you, missy," responded Yasmine. If it weren't for the sunglasses conveniently covering her face, her exaggerated eye roll would not have gone unnoticed.

Yasmine and Jordyn knew each other the longest. They met in their second grade class when Jordyn debated with their teacher on her space in the line. She made a convincing argument about being taller than Yasmine and therefore, must stand behind her. At the time, their heights were fairly similar, which made for a ridiculous argument. Yasmine would later learn this to be Jordyn's personality. She always needed to have her way. Yasmine offered up her spot in the line during second grade and eventually, they became conjoined, never leaving each other's side. They had been best friends ever since.

They attended the same middle school and high school, never being apart too long besides the occasional class. When picking what college they would go to, it was a no-brainer that whatever college they chose, they would attend together. It was beautiful to go through so many transitions in life and still hold on to their friendship. Not many people were blessed with such an opportunity.

"Yea yea yea. You'll be down here in no time to be back with Xavier. You two can't stand to be away from each other," Jordyn noted.

She was right. Yasmine didn't know how she and Xavier were going to spend the time apart. When the girls weren't together, they were with Xavier and Malik, who were conveniently sitting in the row behind them for graduation. The men also being friends and roommates was the icing on the cake. Forever double-date partners was the plan.

Yasmine wanted to start working after graduation, then figure out the next steps for who would be moving where. Xavier's family also lived in New York, so moving back one day wasn't off the table as an option for him. They wanted a life together with a house, three kids, and two dogs. They would have to figure out how to make all of their plans come to fruition.

Once the commencement speech concluded, it was time for them to shift their tassels and do the notorious cap throw. Was it really graduation if caps weren't thrown in the air, only to have to search for them by whatever design was added to the top? Yasmine and her girls certainly didn't think so. After the ceremonious activities concluded, the ladies proceeded to take photos together, of one another, and with other classmates before meeting up with their families.

"Let's all catch up later when we're done spending time with our families," said Amari. She was going to a different restaurant than Yasmine and Jordyn. They tried to get her dad to switch, but it was a fruitless attempt since his mind was set on their own plans.

Yasmine and Jordyn's families took separate cars to meet up at an Italian restaurant. Yasmine was the oldest child in her family. She knew the burden of "setting the example," with no rubric from her parents all too well. Her younger brother, Anthony Jr., would be starting school in the fall. He wanted to stay close to home, so he decided on a local college instead of the route Yasmine took leaving the nest.

"You looked beautiful up there, angel," her dad said, simultaneously navigating the endless Atlanta traffic. Her mom nodded in agreement.

"Thanks, Dad."

Yasmine's dad, Anthony Sr., was a dentist who served in Flatbush, Brooklyn where she grew up. His family migrated the north from the Carolinas in the sixties and he planted roots there for their family. She was a daddy's girl through and through, spending every free moment she could with him since she was a little girl. She missed him so much when she left for Atlanta.

Her relationship with her mom, however, was a bit different. Bernadette was born and raised in Brooklyn, where she owned a hair salon. When her dad was busy, Yasmine spent her days afterschool with her mom until he could pick her up. Sometimes Jordyn would join to keep her company. Yasmine's mom wanted her to know the meaning of hard work and made her sweep the strands of hair and pass her products when needed. This lasted all the way until high school, when she got her own job to avoid spending time in the shop.

Between Bernadette not being around the majority of the time and teenage angst between mother and daughter, they constantly argued. Whether it was about her whereabouts, if she was dating, or what her plans were for the future; they never quite got on the right foot. Yasmine felt a sense of relief when she received the acceptance letter from Wynters. She wanted to be a flight away, where she would not be disturbed by her mother's constant nagging. They sometimes felt like they were strangers who happened to share the same blood.

"Yes we're so proud, honey. I just wish you wanted me to do something with that hair of yours. Most people would enjoy having a hairdresser for a mom," said Bernadette flatly. Yasmine deliberately avoided the eye contact her mom was trying to give from the side view mirror. She was perfectly content with the silk press she gave herself the night before.

Yasmine rebutted. "Can you just not? Not today, please." Her mom always knew how to set her off and Yasmine hated it. She was grateful when she let it go. They spent the rest of the ride in silence, listening to Earth, Wind & Fire until they arrived at the restaurant.

"Wow this lot is packed," Anthony Jr. remarked, noticing there were hardly any parking spots left for them. But it made sense since there were several graduations happening concurrently.

"Let me go in and tell them we're here for our reservation to expedite the process. Come take the wheel, my love," Anthony Sr. said to Bernadette, unbuckling his seatbelt to exit the car. Despite her own issues with her mother, Yasmine did enjoy seeing the love her parents shared with one another. They recently celebrated their twenty fifth anniversary in Anguilla. She could not wait to have her own celebration with Xavier twenty plus years from now.

"No need to do that, Dad. Jordyn and her family already checked our party in since they got here first," Yasmine confirmed.

"Oh great. Time to eat then," he responded.

They luckily found one of the last parking spots available. As they entered the Italian restaurant, the crowd inside certainly mirrored the outside. It was a decent-sized restaurant, but still cozy enough for a family to enjoy an intimate dinner. Jordyn gave the place such great reviews from dates with Malik, Yasmine thought it would be a perfect place for their joint celebration.

"So nice to see you!" Jordyn exclaimed, hugging each of Yasmine's parents. Yasmine returned the same gesture to Jordyn's mom and older siblings. Jordyn was the youngest of four, and she most definitely acted like it.

They chose the "Family Style" dining option in advance to make ordering for a group of eight seamless. From the classic Caesar salad to the garlic bread to the lasagna, everyone thoroughly enjoyed their meals.

Friendship Fragments

After dinner, both families went to a nearby bar and ordered cocktails to continue the celebrations.

By the time the ladies arrived back to their apartment, Amari was already showered and relaxing on their sofa with a glass of wine in hand.

"How was your night?" she asked as Yasmine and Jordyn joined her on adjacent armchairs in their living room.

The taped boxes surrounding the room, reminding them of their impending departure, was torture. Yasmine's entranced eyes bounced to each box in front of her, trying to stop the tears wanting to make another appearance.

"The food was good and our parents enjoyed themselves. Long day, though. How was yours?" Jordyn asked, trying to stifle her yawn.

"It was good. We went to a soul food restaurant my dad loves, then he and the rest of the family went back to their hotel," Amari responded.

"That's good." There was a bit of heavy silence in the room before Jordyn continued. "Can you believe it's our last few days in this apartment?"

"I know, it's so sad. I was being optimistic earlier, but we really don't know if and how things may change between us. How many of our parents are actually still close with their college friends?" Amari questioned.

"My mom does have a few, but I feel the same. We say we'll call and find time to see each other, but what if we don't?" Jordyn asked. It was a valid question. There were close friends from high school that she and Yasmine no longer maintained a relationship with. There weren't arguments to instigate the endings, but their relationships inevitably fizzled out regardless. The same fear started seeping in like a flood, especially since she and Yasmine never left each other's side since they were eight years old. What would the distance do to them?

"I think we should make a pact," Yasmine blurted out before fully thinking it through. Her mind was racing on ways to keep their friendship intact, and this was the first thing that made sense to her.

"A pact? What kind of pact?" asked Amari.

"Hmm. A vacation pact, I think. Life may get in the way; we already know that. We should make a promise to keep our connection alive by going on a vacation together every year. It could be local or international. But it would be time with just us girls, to reconnect? I don't know. It's an idea."

"I think it's an amazing idea. Let's do it. Where should we go next year? Jamaica? Let's do it!" Jordyn shouted, jumping out of her seat.

"That's a good idea. A vacation pact. I say, let's do it, too. Doesn't hurt to try," responded Amari.

"Ok, let's seal it in with a pinky promise," Yasmine said, extending hers out first. They combined their pinky fingers as a promise to keep their cherished bond strong for years to come.

1. Morning Woes
Yasmine

Present Day

Yasmine was sick of the constant bullshit. And today was no different. Her morning routine during the week was predictable, lending itself to New York City's notorious "all gas, no breaks" energy. But what happened when the gas fully exhausted itself and there was nothing left to give?

Every day, she would wake up, go to the gym, shower then prepare a quick breakfast before heading out. She needed to ease into her day before leaving her safe haven to face whatever the outside world would offer, whether she was ready to face it or not.

And let's not talk about the morning commute. She would leave to catch her train from Williamsburg into midtown, navigate the crowded city streets to enter her workplace, and repeat the pattern daily until the weekend.

Somehow, this particular morning was distinctively different from the start. Everything that could possibly go wrong did. As she squinted her sleep-deprived eyes against the sun beaming through her floor-to-ceiling windows, she struggled to untangle herself from her sheets, realizing it was far too late to take her time as she normally would. Yasmine rushed to take a shower, where she would soon find was freezing cold against her warm skin.

She didn't even have the time to choose the perfect outfit to say "I am the right person for this promotion" to her boss in their quarterly check in. The dress she pulled out of her closet would have to suffice.

As she hastily made her way to the door, she found her cell phone still uncharged, accidentally left in the living room where she laid the night before. Unlocking it to see if there were any missed calls or messages, the memories flooded back. The annoyance. The angst. The tears. Xavier. She recalled having yet another argument with her not-so-official boyfriend-ex before throwing the phone down, leaving it while she settled in her bed with a fistful of tears until she drifted off to sleep.

There was no time to focus on that now. She forced those emotions to the back of her mind, promising to return to them when she had the mental capacity to do so.

Her morning luck unfortunately didn't get any better. At first, when she entered the train station, everything seemed exactly as it always had. Although it was already warm outside, there was no comparison to walking into a sweltering New York City train station. The thick, humid air could be cut with a knife, paired with the nauseating stench of the trash and rodents that infested each location. The congestion from the amount of commuters on top of that would be enough to set anyone off.

Waiting for her train to arrive, she watched students in their preppy uniforms congregating in the same spot they did every day and couples dressed in business casual attire juggling coffees in one hand and their bags in another, but what caught her eye was a group of college-aged girls laughing right next to her.

It reminded her of her days at Wynters University nearly a decade prior. Back then, life had been much different. Simpler even. She was much different. She missed her friends from back then –

Friendship Fragments

Jordyn and Amari – more than ever. She yearned for the simple joys and laughter they shared in their college days. Their bond, forged in late-night study sessions, spontaneous trips, and shared dreams was the driving force of their youth.

Yasmine was snapped back to reality as a fellow commuter bumped into her without apology, pushing her right into the group that triggered her college memories. Straightening out her clothes and checking her bag to ensure she wasn't pickpocketed; Yasmine could not have imagined the unexpected turn that happened next.

Her face widened in horror as she watched a stranger, a shadowed silhouette amongst the morning crowd, step dangerously close to the edge of the platform. The sound of the approaching train grew louder and fiercer, honking to announce its arrival, but that was not enough to encourage this person to take a step back. Another commuter on the platform attempted to grab him, but it was to no avail. With an audible gasp, Yasmine covered her mouth, unable to shift her gaze away from what unfolded in front of her, in what seemed like slow motion.

"NOOOOO!!" The echoes of this simple yet powerful word filled the station, unclear of the direction it started from. She wasn't even sure if the words escaped her mouth.

In that split second, Yasmine saw someone's life vanish before her eyes, and the world around her erupted into pure chaos as people screamed in horror while others exasperated in despair. Not only was this a horrible tragedy to witness, but this would certainly delay everyone's morning. A New York City commuter's nightmare.

Yasmine quickly texted her boss to give him a heads up for her late arrival. Although this was out of her control, she couldn't help but to think about if the morning mayhem and regular tardiness because of the subway's untimely inconveniences would affect her chances at the new role she was vying for.

As the paramedics arrived to respond to this emergency, Yasmine couldn't help but feel a profound sense of sadness. Although she did not know the stranger who felt their life no longer was worth living for, she was overcome with emotion. She broke down into tears, releasing the weight of issues in her own life with them.

This incident served as a stark reminder of how overwhelming life had become. Yasmine's demanding job as a retail buyer required her to be back in the office daily, an increasingly unbearable shift to her routine. In this post-pandemic world, it was abundantly clear how much could be done within the confines of one's home without the distraction of outside noise and endless complaints. But she needed her job, so she reluctantly obliged.

As she made her way out of the chaotic station, Yasmine requested a taxi that would no doubt have a surge in cost, paired with an extended wait time. While trying to distract herself from the disruption to her day, Yasmine found herself in deep thought again about her girlfriends, reminiscing on simpler times.

The last time they were together was during their first home-coming after graduation, still on a high from the purgatory between high school and true adulthood. They spent the weekend as if nothing had changed— drinking and laughing and dancing until the sun came up. They promised to conquer the world together, but life split them into separate directions.

The years passed swiftly, and each of them embarked on their own unique journeys spread across the country. Careers, marriage, children – they were all at different points in their lives now. It became increasingly challenging to stay connected with navigating the complexities of adulthood, but Yasmine longed for the days when they were inseparable. It was nearly six months since they talked as a friend group outside of the occasional text to check in.

"Let's catch up soon," they would often find themselves saying to one another when an after-school or work activity took up an evening. It was difficult to get on one accord all at once.

Yasmine knew she needed a break, not just from her job but from the relentless pace of city life. The morning pandemonium at the subway station was a wake-up call and reminder of how quickly life could change. She didn't want to wait until it was too late to reconnect with her old friends. It was time to rekindle those once unbreakable bonds.

It was time to plan a long overdue reunion—in person. It seemed like the perfect time to make good on the pact they made so long ago. It might be a challenge with their busy lives and responsibilities, but she would be remissed if she didn't try.

2. Autopilot
Yasmine

YASMINE WAS STILL SHAKEN up while she stood outside of the train station. She pulled out her phone to send a text message to her old friends, suggesting a video call that very night. It would be great for them to reconnect and reminisce about the good ole days, when everything was a bit less complicated.

Yasmine

Good Morning Ladies!

Amari

Good Morning Y'all! How is everyone doing on this fine Thursday?

Jordyn

Good Morning! I just finished dropping the kids off at school, chile. I'm good, though. Amari, why are you up so early?

. . .

Amari

I get up at this time to start writing. Sometimes, I believe my body will never get fully adjusted to West Coast time. Lol. What's up with y'all?

Yasmine

Girl, a lot. It's been so long since we all chatted on the phone. Can we do that tonight? I miss you all dearly.

Amari

I miss y'all, too. Let's do it. Y'all know I'm 3 hours behind East Coast time, so what time is best for you?

Jordyn

The kids head to bed around 8:30. That would be an ideal time for me.

Amari

That's 5:30 here. That would work for me too.

Jordyn

Ok cool. Yasmine?

Distracted by the text messages from her friends and a notification of her phone dying at any moment, Yasmine didn't notice her taxi arrived over ten minutes prior, which led to a cancellation after not getting a response. She immediately called another one and waited to get settled in the car before continuing her text exchange.

Yasmine
Sorry! I'm in commute hell right now and on top of that, my phone is on its last leg. That time is good for me too. Let me focus on this day ahead. I'll talk to you all later. Love you!

Amari
Surely don't miss that at all. Love y'all too. Talk later.

Jordyn
Me either. Have a good day, y'all! Love you.

Yasmine's heart was full knowing later in the evening she would talk to her beloved friends. Even if her proposal for a trip didn't pan out, a conversation with them would be enough to fill her depleted cup. As the taxi pulled up to her work building, she exited the car with a renewed sense of determination. Maybe it would be her lucky day after all.

As she walked onto her floor, the nerves took over again with her heart pounding through her chest. Yasmine rushed to her desk and tried to get a grip on her composure before her meeting.

"You good?" asked Valerie as she walked over to Yasmine, temporarily distracting her from the speech she was preparing in her head.

Valerie was a designer for the brand and one of the first friends Yasmine made. They confided in each other about everything from work to people they dated. They never ran out of things to talk about. They didn't really do activities together outside of work, but their bond was just as strong as if they did. Valerie was one of those work friends Yasmine couldn't see herself doing day-to-day tasks without.

"I'm ok, but my commute was hell. It's always something."

"Don't I know it, girl? I was just stopping by to say hi, but could tell your energy seemed a bit off." Valerie made herself comfortable on the bench near Yasmine's desk for them to talk more discreetly.

"Yea between my hellish commute and this upcoming meeting with Jackson, my nerves are shot."

"Are you finally going to ask him about this promotion you deserve?"

Yasmine responded nervously, "Yes. And I know I am more than capable, but what if he doesn't think so?"

"If he doesn't think so, he's an idiot. I've seen you fight for every role since we both started. And you shouldn't have had to do that. Your work speaks for itself."

Valerie was right. Yasmine started her role at Haus, a popular contemporary women's clothing brand, fresh out of college. She started there as an assistant, building relationships with her cross-functional partners and making a name for herself where few people looked like her. She often felt like she needed to be the example for Black people at her company, letting her counterparts know she and anyone else who looked like her belonged in the same rooms, contributing to the decision making instead of only their bank accounts.

In a way, she always felt like she was on the battlefield. Some counterparts were in their roles for barely a year or two before their promotions, while she would have to wait for three or more. It wasn't fair and she knew it.

After consistently making her voice heard with the right answers in front of the right leaders in the company, they started seeing her true value. She eventually moved up to the associate level then to manager level with a smidge more ease than the assistant level. But since being at the manager level, it was a five-year uphill battle to get to the director role she desperately desired.

She felt out of place and started finding other passions outside of her nine-to-five, leaning more into interior design. It started off as apartment makeovers and designs for her friends, then through word-of-mouth, she eventually had a roster of clients who regularly sought her to decorate their apartments, homes, and even office spaces.

During the pandemic, business boomed for her due to people wanting to curate their homes they previously didn't see beyond the weekend. Since the world opened back up and more people were back in the office, business slowed down a bit. The costs for basic necessities such as food, rent, and car payments skyrocketed. The roster she meticulously built and could rely on started drying up, leading to her having to fully focus on her nine-to-five.

A new opportunity finally presented itself to Yasmine when her boss, Marie, left the company for a new role three months ago. She saw her Vice President, Jackson, interviewing other people from outside the company but knew she was the better fit. It was fair since, after all, she fulfilled her own job duties as well as the one above her since it was vacated. She managed five direct reports under her and handled all of her own responsibilities seamlessly. All she could hope was that Jackson understood her value on the team and rewarded her for it.

"Girl, I would love to chat more but I need to prep for this meeting. See you at lunch?" Yasmine asked, realizing she had less than an hour to review her notes.

"I get it, girl. See you at lunch!" Valerie responded, leaving to continue her workday.

With the power of listening to some Toni Braxton to calm her nerves and a subtle power pose, Yasmine was ready to face Jackson and shoot her shot for the director's role.

* * *

"Yasmine, it's good to see you. How are you today?" he asked.

"I'm well. Thank you for asking. I scheduled this time for our quarterly review so we can go over some of my accomplishments in the last year."

"Yasmine, I am well versed in your accomplishments. From diversifying our assortment to improved sales over the last year and cost savings with our vendors, we appreciate all that you do for the company. You have been an asset for years." As he listed her achievements, Yasmine smiled brightly, feeling like her hard work finally paid off.

"I can't express how hearing this makes me feel. Which brings me to my next topic."

Jackson raised an eyebrow before asking, "And what topic is that?"

"The director role has been open for months and I've worked hard to keep everyone afloat while also successfully managing my own workload. It's only right that I ask to be considered for the position." Jackson awkwardly adjusted his suit jacket as Yasmine revealed her intention.

Clearing his throat, he explained, "Sorry Yasmine, we acknowledge the great work you have done thus far, but we still think there is more work to be done before you're considered for a promotion. We're going to move Catherine to the director position, with you reporting directly to her. We planned to announce it next week, but since we're on the topic now, I can let you know in advance. You are definitely on our list for the next open director position."

Yasmine worked at the company for over a decade. She did the work, spent the hours, and also mastered code switching to not appear "too much" or "aggressive." Somehow working twice as hard still didn't get her anywhere.

While she had to prove her worth, once again, she was witnessing a co-worker who did the bare minimum rise to the position she deserved with minimal effort. And this idea of a role opening up soon was bullshit. It took forever for roles to open up these days, especially at the director level. It could take years to happen.

"Catherine is at the manager level like me. Can I get an example of something I would need to show or improve on in order to be considered for the position versus her? While you mentioned my accomplishments, the specifics are that I increased sales by over twenty percent over last year, there was a ten percent cost savings with my largest vendor and I expanded our market share in a challenging time for the industry. I have been working hard in this role and even took on additional responsibility while the position has been vacant. I don't want to have to wait three or five years for another role to open up for my potential chance." Yasmine took a deep breath to not fully explode from her building frustration. There was no way he could deny how successful she had been.

"Yasmine, I understand how you feel. The decision has already been made. You're on the right path, keep doing what you're doing. You're just not ready yet...."

Yasmine tuned him out as he continued to flower her with compliments about how great she was at her job. He added fluff about how much he valued her and her time would come. Eventually. While she was disappointed, she was not surprised. She felt deflated leaving the meeting, not knowing which route to take. She couldn't exactly quit, but she needed a plan. One that didn't include staying at a company that didn't think she was worthy enough to get an earned promotion.

Yasmine's only option to get through the day was to numb herself, communicating with her team and getting her job done as she would on any other day. Her only moment during the workday for reprieve would be when she met up with Valerie for lunch.

* * *

"How did it go?" Valerie asked as they sat down together to eat their salads.

Sighing, Yasmine responded, "Well he's giving the role to Catherine...."

"What?! That's bullshit and you know it. The girl barely does any work. Her team complains about her all the time."

"Oh trust me, I know. It's all politics here. I can't believe I thought I even had a chance."

"You're amazing and you know that. The people here don't deserve you. I always tell you that. What are you going to do?" Valerie questioned, always protective of Yasmine. Her words made Yasmine's throat start heating up. *Not again.*

"Honestly, I don't know. You know I have my interior design business on the side, but that's been slow. This pays the bills. I need to see what else is out there, but I'm just so frustrated with everything. I just need a break..." Yasmine's voice cracked at her final statement. Before she could say anything else, Valerie embraced her and allowed her to release tears for the second time in one day.

After lunch, Yasmine felt completely numb. She had nothing left to give. She ignored Jackson's fruitless attempts to crack jokes with her whenever he passed her desk. She finished her tasks for the day and put herself on autopilot until it was time to head back home.

3. Catching Up
Yasmine

AFTER THE DISAPPOINTING workday she had, Yasmine wanted nothing more than to go home, only looking forward to catching up with her girls. The peaceful train ride home rivaled the subway fiasco that transpired a mere nine hours prior. Yasmine mindlessly scrolled through social media and listened to her favorite R&B tracks to get her through. She felt a sense of relief when re-entering her apartment, finally able to remove her mask of trying to seamlessly blend in and instead, be her authentic self.

The relief quickly vanished when she was met with the same disarray she left her place in, mirroring the way she felt about her life at the moment. There were pots scattered on the stovetop, a sink full of dishes and she already knew her bathroom and bedroom would meet her with a similar level of disorganization.

In an effort to not be overwhelmed, she took a deep breath and tackled one thing at a time, not focusing on the next task until completing the one before. She started in the kitchen, knowing she would want to prepare dinner. Jordyn asked for their call to be shifted an hour for more time to put the children to bed, which gave Yasmine ample time to get some things back in order.

Friendship Fragments

By the time she finished straightening up and showering to wind down, it was already time for the call. With a decluttered space, Yasmine's mind was clearer and she was more than ready to chat with her girls. She grabbed a glass of Pinot Noir and made herself comfortable on the sofa. The Facetime call was long overdue and Yasmine's face lit up as soon as it connected, showing her friends on the screen.

"Hi ladies! It's been ages! How's everyone doing?!"

Smiling from ear to ear, Jordyn exclaimed, "Oh, I've missed y'all so much!" She was sitting up in her bed, ready to sleep immediately after the call.

Amari sat on the floor of her beautiful Los Angeles loft. "Same. It's been too long, ladies! I can't wait to catch up."

"I've been waiting for this all day! There's so much going on," said Jordyn, shaking her head and looking exhausted. It was possible they all needed the call.

"Like what, Jordyn? Talk to us." Yasmine asked, hating the sadness in her aura and wanting to get to the bottom of it.

Their lives were so different from one another now. Jordyn was building a life with her family and Amari was chasing her dreams in a brand-new state. Yasmine's life felt like it was at a standstill in comparison. What did she really have to show after all of their time apart? She was not settled down romantically, had challenges in getting where she wanted in her career and still lived in her tiny one-bedroom apartment in Brooklyn.

Jordyn sighed deeply before responding. "Balancing this job, the kids' school schedules, and being a wife is quite the juggling act. But I am grateful."

Jordyn recently also became an influencer by accident. After getting married at an early age and having two children back-to-back, she wanted to do something for herself. She was always great at cooking and one day, decided to set up a tripod and the rest was history. Across YouTube, Instagram, and TikTok she amassed hundreds of thousands of followers on each. She went on to explain how much she appreciated the partnerships she acquired with companies, but the pressure of meeting deadlines sometimes interfered with keeping her home life in order.

Yasmine empathized. "I wish I could hug you right now. You're a superhero, Jordyn. I don't know how you do it all, honestly."

Jordyn responded matter-of-factly, "Lots of coffee in the morning and wine in the evening, my friend. And I can't say we don't have help from my mother-in-law since she's moved down here."

"We're always here for you, Jordyn. You know I don't have a conventional schedule. You can call me whenever," Amari chimed in.

"You're right, I will do a better job at that. We all should," said Jordyn.

"We tried to make a promise to not let life get in the way, but look at us now," said Yasmine, laughing. This conversation was showing how much they were missing in each other's lives.

Amari asked, "Well Yas, what's been going on with you?"

Such a simple question ended up feeling loaded. Yasmine didn't know where to begin. Should she start with the subway fiasco that triggered her call request? Should she finally tell her friends about her secret rendezvous with her ex-college boyfriend, Xavier? Her friends certainly would not be happy to hear about his resurgence. Not after what he did.

Deciding to keep it as light as possible, Yasmine responded, "Where do I begin? My boss has been driving me crazy. He won't even consider giving me the promotion I've been working so hard for. Today, he told me a coworker who doesn't do half the work that I do would be getting the open director role instead."

Amari stated, "Ugh, that's frustrating, Yasmine. You're more than deserving of it!"

"Absolutely! Your dedication should be recognized after all of the years you've given to them," Jordyn echoed the same sentiments.

"Thanks. It sucks, but it may be time for me to consider other options. I want to feel like my work has value. I would love for interior designing to pick back up again to potentially pivot there full time, but I'm not sure if or when that would be possible."

Friendship Fragments

Amari nodded in agreement and explained, "I'm with you on not knowing exactly what's next, I've hit a bit of a creative roadblock lately. So, I'm thinking about moving to Houston for some fresh inspiration."

One thing about Amari– she was not against uprooting her life and leaving anywhere she felt constricted. She believed a change of scenery was what people needed to tap into their undiscovered greatness. Although most of the women had made some sort of move in their life, her free-spirited nature was admirable. She was a published writer, but moved from the DMV to Los Angeles to try and get into screenwriting. Yasmine knew a few details from Amari's recent visit a few months back, but didn't realize she was thinking of another move.

"Houston? That's quite the change!" exclaimed Yasmine.

"I get it. Sometimes you need to shake things up to get those creative juices flowing," Jordyn confirmed.

"That's exactly it. I'm ready for a new adventure," Amari explained.

Seeing this as the perfect opportunity to bring up her idea, Yasmine said, "Me too. You know what we should all do?"

"Oh goodness, what now?!" Amari jokingly replied.

"Here Yasmine goes with one of her bright ideas," Jordyn piggybacked. The ladies laughed, knowing Yasmine was usually the mastermind behind all of their plans— whether good or bad.

Yasmine needed this level of banter back in her life. Since all of her closest friends no longer lived in the same city, she did make one friend in her apartment complex, Brianna. As much as she loved the bond they continued to build, it didn't change how much she missed Jordyn and Amari.

"AHT AHT. Not too much on me y'all!" She smirked before proposing, "How about a vacation in mid-July? We made our pact at graduation and never did anything about it. Maybe now's our chance to finally make good on it and spend some quality time together."

Amari pondered for a moment then responded, "Ok I'm listening. Where are you thinking?"

"How about Jamaica like we always discussed?"

"July is around the corner, girl. But it is right before the kids restart school, which would be nice. I'll have to check with Malik to make sure this works for his schedule and the kids, but if it works, I am all the way there," Jordan explained. "I actually haven't been on a vacation without the kids since they were born and this could be good for me."

"This change of scenery and some quality time together might get all of our creative juices flowing again, too. Plus, I miss y'all very much," Amari admitted.

Yasmine agreed. "Miss you both, too. That's the spirit! Hopefully we can all make it work. I'll start planning right away!"

"I can help if you need," Amari expressed. "Just let me know."

As they chatted excitedly about their upcoming reunion and vacation plans, the bond between Yasmine, Jordyn and Amari felt as strong as it always did. Although life threw them curveballs, it was as if time hadn't passed at all.

4. Plans In Motion

Yasmine

NOT ONLY WAS the sun shining bright on a beautiful Saturday morning in Brooklyn, but it was also Memorial Day weekend. There was something about the air in New York City when the seasons shifted from winter to summer. It made people want to savor every moment as if it were their last, like the moment they stopped having fun, the cold would return to steal their joy. Yasmine planned to celebrate this unofficial start to the summer season with a brunch date with her girl, Brianna.

Despite her friendship reunion trip being less than eight weeks away, she was up for the challenge to make sure every detail was planned to perfection. Jordyn was the final puzzle piece, confirming she would be able to join. Malik agreed it would be a good idea for her to get a break before the kids started school again and his mother was more than willing to take over for the week.

While getting ready, Yasmine Facetimed Amari, wanting to pick her brain about some of her ideas for activities on the trip. Despite being friends with Jordyn since they were eight-years-old, Yasmine and Amari always shared a special bond. Even being miles away from each other, they always kept in close contact over the years. She also knew Jordyn had a lot on her plate, prepping for the first trip without her kids and didn't want to inundate her with the small details. She deserved to come on the vacation and not have to think — a gift not often granted to mothers.

"Hi, boo!"

"Hi, Yas, how are you? And why are you getting all dressed up?" asked Amari, noticing Yasmine putting on her makeup.

"Brunch, girl. I will be outside all weekend. Even more than that though, I'm so excited about our trip!"

"Girl, me too! I am ready to get away."

"Same, sis. It took a little digging to find the perfect space to accommodate all of us, but I have officially secured a huge ocean view villa suite at this all-inclusive resort called Moonstone Oasis. Since everyone is flying from different places, we're just telling Jordyn the dates, which are July eleventh through the twentieth, right?"

"Yes!"

"We should all have these flights booked within the next two to three weeks, even sooner if possible. I know it's tight, but I don't want the flight prices to go up too much," Yasmine explained. She was starting to feel the pressure of time working against them, but also remained grateful for her girls willing to come on short notice.

Everything will work itself out, she kept reminding herself.

"Makes sense. I think we'll be fine. I've researched some excursions we should do. I know we'll want to have relaxing moments over the week, but I think we should definitely do some activities, too. Have you heard of Dunn's River Falls?"

"Chile, yes I have, but doesn't that include climbing up rocks? I'm just a girl trying to be cute on vacation...but I am also a team player. We could add that to the itinerary. What else do you have in mind?" Yasmine was the friend who liked to dress up and lay out in the sun on vacation. Amari, on the other hand, loved adventures. It would be fair to plan on including both.

"How about a boat ride, a private one with only us on it?"

Yasmine sighed a breath of relief. "Now that's what the girls need! That was already on my list, girl. Bitches love boats. It's us, the bitches."

"Perfect! Do you need help booking anything else?"

"No, I'm already in communication with a company a friend recommended and they also helped us arrange a driver for our time on vacation, too. Let's hope they don't kidnap us." Yasmine chuckled, joking, but not joking at the same time.

"Girl, they won't. You are so dramatic."

Yasmine snickered. "Sure am!" Amari joined her in laughter, reminiscent of the light moments Yasmine missed with her friends the most.

"Agreed," Yasmine continued. "I do have one more thing to run by you though."

"Sure. What's up?"

"Soooo...I know Jordyn hasn't met her yet, but I was thinking of inviting Brianna on the trip. What do you think about that?" Yasmine was met with a brief, but noticeable awkward silence.

"...You know I wouldn't mind. But Jordyn can be very territorial and in fairness, the trip is supposed to be about us three reconnecting. It could cause some unnecessary tension. I don't feel like dealing with her shenanigans."

Yasmine was worried she might have that response. Amari knew the territorial version of her all too well.

* * *

Amari was admitted into Wynters University on the business school track. She wanted to be an accountant like her mother, who passed away due to birth complications with her. She later learned about the plan to honor her mother's memory by fulfilling the life she never was able to.

Yasmine and Amari met during one of their freshman year classes during their second semester, Intro to Business School. In this class, they were put into groups where they created a mock business and presented it to their professor at the end of the course. Each person had their own role from marketing to financing to accounting.

Yasmine and Amari quickly realized how similar they were to one another, being the more reserved people in their eclectic team. After one particular meeting with their group, Yasmine walked up to Amari and asked her what she thought of the meeting. There was a self-appointed group leader, Bryan, who mansplained everything about their project to them. Every time he spoke, Yasmine had to control the nagging urge to tell him to shut up.

"If I didn't already have my doubts about this career path, he surely would make me switch," Amari admitted, sending them both into a laughing fit. Over the next few weeks, they would meet up for lunch to go over their parts of the project separately. Then when they got back together with the group, they would smirk at one another with the inside jokes they shared about each member of their team.

Feeling like she would be the perfect addition to their little friend group, Yasmine tried convincing a very disinterested Jordyn to meet Amari for weeks with no success. Jordyn's perspective of the situation was that this new person was trying to be her replacement, which couldn't be further from the truth. Amari only wanted a sisterhood and Yasmine wanted them to be that safe space for her.

Yasmine eventually decided the only way to get her to cooperate would be by tricking her. She asked Jordyn to meet her in the newest dining hall on campus to check it out. What she didn't know was Yasmine and Amari would already be there waiting for her. To not put her off from Jordyn before actually meeting her, Yasmine conveniently left out the part where she had no interest in meeting Amari.

As Jordyn walked toward the table they were already sitting at, Amari stood up to greet her with a hug. "Hi, I'm Amari! I've heard so much about you."

"Oh. I've heard some things about you, too." Jordyn sat down, intentionally avoiding Amari's open arms. Seething, she refused to glance in either Amari or Yasmine's direction. She stayed silent while Yasmine and Amari joked about random topics.

Amari walked away briefly, giving Jordyn the opportunity to say exactly what was on her mind. "Why would you lie to me about the real reason for coming here?"

"I didn't lie to you, I really wanted us to check out the new dining hall. But I couldn't be 100% honest about Amari coming. I wanted you to see how great she was for yourself. She's my friend and you are, too. Maybe we could all—" Yasmine was cut off before she could complete her statement.

"No. I did not want to meet her. I don't care to be friends with a watered-down version of myself."

It wasn't until Yasmine's jaw dropped and Jordyn looked behind her, they noticed a tear-filled Amari standing right within ear's reach. No one could get a word out before she ran out crying. Amari made every attempt to avoid them both for a few weeks following that introduction.

In an effort to right her wrongs, the ladies met together to have what was later coined "The Sit Down" to address what transpired. Jordyn apologized for her behavior and worked to foster a relationship with Amari. There were moments where Amari still believed that if she were never caught, Jordyn would never have tried to be her friend. Yasmine always tried to quell those thoughts, but deep down, even she wasn't one hundred percent sure.

That was back then, though. Yasmine wanted to give her friend more credit and hope she matured from the girl she was in college. While her friends lived hours away from her, Brianna had become her ride-or-die. It was still possible for them all to reconnect and bring a new face in the bunch too, right?

"You can bring up the idea of Brianna coming if you want, but I hope she's not the same Jordyn from all these years before," said Amari, snapping Yasmine out of her internal thoughts.

"I'll bring it up in our group chat to see, but if it's a no, then I have to respect that." Yasmine felt a bit deflated although she knew Amari was right. She really didn't know what to expect.

"Let's see what she says. This trip will be amazing no matter what."

"I couldn't agree more! Let's get to planning, the trip will be here before we know it."

5. Neighborly Exchange
Yasmine

NEITHER YASMINE nor Brianna imagined they would have been friends after their initial introduction three years ago. They were invited to their neighbor, Diane's, birthday gathering in the building lounge. Yasmine had only lived in the building for a few months at the time, but never really explored beyond her apartment.

The theme of the birthday party was everyone's favorite era— the 90s. Yasmine decided to dress like Aaliyah, sporting a white crop top with baggy denim jeans, Air Force Ones, and a bandana with sunglasses to top off the look.

When she last visited the top floor lounge, it had chic contemporary decor, comfortable seating areas, and panoramic views of the city skyline. It could offer entertainment options for any celebration with TVs, speaker phones, a fridge, and a small stove. For this night's event, Diane completely transformed the space into a House Party theme, giving that nostalgic college feel. There was dim lighting, graffiti signs for each station from "Drink Station" to "Photobooth," and red Solo cups everywhere.

As Yasmine walked in, it seemed like the majority of the building was invited to the event, packed with people sporting their own themed outfits. Diane was dressed as Kid while her best friend dressed as Play, further contributing to the theme. Drinks, laughter, and chatter flowed throughout the room with an intense game of beer pong holding much of the attention.

"Hi, Yasmine, I am so glad you were able to join!" Diane exclaimed with a warm embrace. They knew each other from a weekly dance class they used to attend. Although they stopped going to the class, they always kept in touch. It was nice to have a familiar face in the building. They had the occasional conversation, but never really connected much on a deeper level outside of that. Friendships looked differently from person to person and Yasmine learned quickly to accept each person's purpose in her life, which included appreciating Diane's presence.

"Happy Birthday, D! You did an amazing job decorating this space."

"Thanks, girl. I wasn't sure how it would all turn out, but everything looks good. I'm impressed with how well y'all followed the theme, Miss Aaliyah," she said with a wink.

"Yes well—" Yasmine didn't get to finish her next statement to compliment Diane and her bestie's outfits because more guests came in stealing her attention.

Yasmine found the nearest corner to observe from the sidelines, needing a little more time to warm up in newer environments before letting her personality shine.

The bubbly girl she later learned to be Brianna, on the other hand, was a social butterfly. She effortlessly navigated through the crowd with infectious laughter, drawing people into her orbit. This girl garnered a level of vulnerability Yasmine both cringed at and was awestruck by.

"Hi! My name is Brianna, what's yours?" Brianna asked, joining Yasmine in the corner she was nestled in, attempting to give her a hug.

"Hi, my name is Yasmine. Nice to meet you," responded Yasmine with her hand extended instead. A hug with a stranger was a little too intimate for her liking.

Brianna paused briefly and looked down at Yasmine's hand a bit before extending her own. "How long have you lived here?"

"I moved here recently."

"Nice! How do you like it so far?"

"It's spacious and quiet so far. Everyone is nice, too."

"I've lived here for almost two years now and I definitely agree. Want to join in on the fun?" Brianna's once open energy was now more hesitant than when she first walked over, the cautiousness in her voice betraying her ask. Yasmine started feeling bad, but the girl was also nagging her. She wanted nothing more than to be left alone.

"I'm good right now, thanks for asking. I'll join a little bit later."

"Ok. Well, it was nice meeting you, Yasmine. I hope you have a great evening," Brianna said, leaving to mingle with the rest of the crowd.

"Thank you," replied Yasmine, finally uncrossing her arms. She hated small talk. She was more into deep, authentic conversations. But small talk could be exactly what led to deeper moments, so it was a catch twenty-two. She was elated when Brianna finally took the hint and left her alone.

With her own friends, Yasmine was friendly and always had a great time, but so many years passed since they were together. She missed them even more during those moments alone at events with no one to share something she noticed after people-watching or laughing together about a distant memory.

After the birthday gathering, Yasmine and Brianna only crossed paths occasionally and exchanged neighborly salutations. It wasn't until a peculiar elevator ride almost a year later when the trajectory of their relationship changed. They were the only two people getting on the elevator and Yasmine noticed Brianna crying.

"Are you ok?" she asked, already knowing the answer. *Why do people lead with such a question when they don't know what to say? Do better*, she thought to herself.

"I'm fine. I will be fine," Brianna answered. The words said one thing, but the tears streaming down her face said another.

"If you need to talk to someone, I'm all ears. What's your number?"

"Oh. Um. Pass me your phone, I'll put it in." Brianna's tear-glistened eyes widened, seemingly taken aback as Yasmine passed her the phone.

"281?" Yasmine asked, raising her brow at the strange area code in her phone. She was now standing between the open elevator and Brianna's floor, in an attempt to not have the doors close on her.

Brianna smirked and said, "Texas. I was born in New York, but I moved to Houston when I was really young. I came back after college."

"Nice! Well, I hope your day gets better. Even if it doesn't, I will text you to check in," said Yasmine while giving Brianna a tight side hug, which triggered more tears before the doors closed.

Worried about the girl she learned was likely in the city all alone, Yasmine tried arranging for them to have brunch the following weekend. Brianna wasn't available and they met the first weekend of the following month at a recently opened restaurant close to their apartment building.

"How are you?" asked Yasmine as they waited for their drinks.

"I've been better, but I'm getting there." This version of Brianna was far more subdued than the version Yasmine first met.

"I am all ears if you want to share, but it's totally fine if you don't want to."

"No, it's fine. I should talk more about it."

Brianna went on to explain how her brother died in a car accident back in Houston. They were best friends and inseparable their whole life until Brianna decided to move back to New York. On top of mourning the loss of a loved one, she also felt burdened with guilt. She wished she didn't leave him back at home. She wished she could have told him to not get into the car. That was the thing about grief.

Always wondering what could have been done differently, wondering if it would have changed the outcome.

"I am so sorry for your loss. Grieve how you need to and I am always here if you want to chat."

"Forgive me, but your kindness comes as such a surprise to me. You weren't exactly welcoming when we met at that birthday party."

Yasmine's cheeks heated with a combination of embarrassment and the mimosas hitting her. "Well yes. I'm sorry about that. I am a bit shy and standoffish in new environments. Once I warm up, though, I'm likeable. I think I am, anyway."

"No, you totally are. Sorry if I offended you. I just thought you met me and decided you didn't like me. That happens sometimes."

"You are quite the social butterfly it seemed. I felt a bit envious of that, but it wasn't you, I promise."

"Glad to hear it. Let's make a toast to start over and really get to know each other."

After their brunch, they did just that. Yasmine became a confidante for Brianna and their bond grew even deeper over the years. Texts and calls turned into movie nights, which turned into more brunch and dinners. After getting to know each other, they realized how similar they were. Yasmine didn't think she could have another friendship like the one she shared with Jordyn and Amari, but somehow Brianna fit like a missing puzzle piece.

6. Liquid Courage
Yasmine

AFTER HER PHONE conversation with Amari, Yasmine immediately brought the idea of Brianna coming on the trip to the group chat. Jordyn was seemingly open to the idea, saying she was more than welcome, quelling the fears Yasmine and Amari shared. Now, she could officially extend the invite to Brianna at brunch. They planned to meet in their lobby to get in a taxi to Kokomo Restaurant.

"Hi Bri! How are you?!" asked Yasmine, embracing her in a hug. Although they lived in the same building, they could go weeks without seeing each other because their schedules didn't align. Other times, Brianna's job as a travel nurse kept her away for weeks at a time.

"Hey girl! I am in need of a mimosa ASAP."

The girls spent their ride catching up on building and work drama while their driver bobbed and weaved through Brooklyn's endless Saturday traffic, from double parked cars to bumper-to-bumper traffic on local streets.

Although not planned, Kokomo was the perfect place for them to brunch, given its Caribbean cuisine and lively atmosphere. It would be the perfect place to extend the invite for their trip to Jamaica.

38

It was buzzing with tons of people, per usual. Tables on the outside and inside of the restaurant were filled with people laughing and enjoying their time together. This certainly wasn't a location to show up to without a reservation. Thankfully, the ladies were aware and reserved their table ahead of time to avoid the long wait for last minute brunch goers.

"Do you ladies need some time to review our menu?" the waitress asked, pouring the ladies water at their table.

"Not at all. Can we order Kokomosa Flights? We already decided on our way here," responded Brianna without even a glance at the menu.

The waitress warmly smiled at the quick response. "Well, we can appreciate people knowing exactly what they want. I'll get those prepared for you immediately. As you decide on food, let me know if you have any questions. I'll be back shortly."

The drinks came out quickly and the ladies ordered their meals. Brianna ordered the infamous oxtail flatbread, while Yasmine opted for the plantain pancakes with the fried chicken add-on.

"This location is actually the perfect spot for what I want to ask you today," said Yasmine, trying to savor the last bits of her meal.

"Oh goodness, what's going on, Yas?"

Yasmine laughed at her friend's flair for the dramatics as she put down her phone and chugged one of her mimosas. "It's nothing serious, Bri. Do you have any upcoming work or vacation plans?"

This was important to ask because of Brianna's job. During the pandemic, she saw how lucrative it was as a travel nurse, along with the flexibility and had been doing it ever since. It tied in her passion for nursing with her passion for traveling. It was never a surprise when she posted being in another country on social media. Yasmine often admired her for living on her own terms, which reminded her to figure out what was next for her own job, whether it be interior designing or something else.

Brianna let out a deep sigh before responding. "Oh girl, that is an easy question to answer. I'm going to Mexico next week. I'll be gone for a week. Then, my next nursing assignment is not until the beginning of August. Why do you ask?"

"My close college friends and I are planning a trip to Jamaica. We haven't all been together in a while, so we want to reconnect. I wanted to invite you because I consider you one of my close friends, just as I do them. Obviously you already know Amari, but my other friend I've mentioned to you, Jordyn, will also be there. I would love for them to grow to love you as much as I have."

"Yasmine, I'm not even drunk yet. Don't make me cry. This sounds great. If Jordyn is anything like Amari, I'm sure I will love her, too. How is Amari, anyway?"

"Amari is good. With Jordyn, she's had moments where she was territorial over me in the past, but that was years ago. When we asked if she was comfortable with you joining, she said you are more than welcome. Thank goodness for growth."

"Haha definitely. Thank you for the heads up, though. We're all grown now. No need to be territorial at this big age."

"Agreed, sis."

"Well, it's always a yes for me when it comes to Jamaica. We've never been on vacation together before and Amari is also great. Thank you both for including me."

"Anytime, my friend."

The ladies continued discussing details about their upcoming vacation, television shows they were binging, and dating fails. It was unclear how much time passed at brunch, but they knew they overstayed their welcome when the waitress came by to announce the next reservation needed to be seated.

Feeling liquid courage from the mimosas, Yasmine knew it was time to have the conversation she had been avoiding.

7. Puppy Love
Yasmine

XAVIER. Yasmine met him at Wynters University freshman year.

The Wynters' campus was gorgeous with beautiful brick buildings, towering columns, and sculptures throughout. There were beautiful nooks located all around where students could be found studying on a long bench or on the lush grass. Students from various parts of the country came together to this one location as a fun purgatory before real adulthood began. The college dream.

Yasmine and Xavier lived in the same dormitory, Levittson Hall. The boys and girls lived on opposite sides of the hallway, but always mingled together in the lounge. From movies to game nights, some of Yasmine's best memories were made during those weekends in their quaint lounge.

"Girllll, we have not seen all of the fine men yet," said Jordyn, plopping herself onto Yasmine's bed as if it were her own. After a few flirty exchanges, she went on a dining hall date with one of the guys on the floor, Malik.

"Oh yea? Tell me more."

"Well, you already know about Malik. He's perfect." She blushed. "But on our date, he introduced me to his roommate, Xavier, and WOW." By the exaggeration of Jordyn's facial expression, one would have thought she saw Morris Chestnut roaming the campus.

"How could there be a fine man on our floor and I haven't seen him yet? There's been so many moments we've all been together so far."

The floor's resident advisors held an ice breaking mixer during move-in week, but Jordyn went on to explain that Xavier moved in some time after that, just in time for classes to start. And for some reason, he chose not to hang out in the lounge when everyone else on the floor did activities. He had an older cousin on campus and preferred to be with him and his friends off campus.

"Hmm, well I guess I'll have to meet this Xavier person one day," Yasmine replied. Living on the same floor, but never seeing this mysterious person made him sound like more of a myth than a real person. Yasmine didn't give it much attention after their conversation about him.

For games involving alcohol, students would cram up in a designated dorm room to avoid being reprimanded by their resident advisors for underage drinking.

During an otherwise eventless weekend in November of their first semester, Malik announced that he and Xavier would be hosting a game night in theirs. Yasmine almost opted out, too tired from the week, but curiosity got the best of her and she prepared herself for a fun night out. With Malik mingling in the background, it was clear who the other gentleman that opened the dorm room door was. Scanning him from head to toe, Yasmine quickly realized that Jordyn did not do his description any justice.

Xavier stood at six-foot-three, with Hershey brown skin, perfectly complemented by his sparkling white teeth. His broad, muscular shoulders rivaled the most athletic men on campus. And his scent?! The muskiness of his cologne was a sensual invitation to whatever he was selling. Yasmine was ready to buy whatever it was.

She envisioned him looking more similar to Malik, who stood at no more than five-foot-ten with golden, caramel skin. He was handsome also, but in a dorky way. The type of handsome you marry. Xavier looked like the type of guy your parents gave warnings about. There was no comparison when looking at the two friends. Not for Yasmine, anyway

"Now what is your name?" Xavier asked, holding the door open for both her and Jordyn to enter. He extended his arm for a handshake, grinning like a Cheshire cat.

"Yasmine, are you going to walk in?" Jordyn asked, nudging her friend back to reality. The mere presence of the man already put her in a trance.

"Ah so that's your name. Come in and stay a while, Yasmine." The way he enunciated every letter in her name made her feel things she had yet to experience at eighteen-years-old. Yasmine was a virgin. She never wanted to give her body to just anyone, regardless of how many other people in her life did. Or how many guys tried to persuade her it made no sense to hold onto her virginity. She wanted to save herself for someone special.

"Su..sure, thank you for the warm welcome," she stuttered, keeping her eyes fixated toward the ground instead of being further distracted by his cocoa brown eyes.

The first thing she noticed in their room was that for boys, it was shockingly neat. It was decorated with posters of 90s movies like Boyz N The Hood, Juice, Friday, and House Party on one side. The other side was decorated with sports memorabilia like football helmets and trophies spread throughout.

As everyone sneakily made their way into the dorm room, they were separated into boys versus girls for a game of Taboo.

"Ok, everyone should know how to play, right?" Malik asked.

"Duh, Malik, who's never played Taboo?" Jordyn responded, playfully slapping his arm. For people who had only been dating for a couple of months, they bickered like an old, married couple. But they seemed happy. Everyone could tell by the way they looked in each other's eyes.

"Shit, I don't know. But just in case, saying any of the words or phrases at the bottom of the card is taboo and y'all will lose the round— "

"And have to take a shot," Xavier concluded, smirking mischievously. Everyone in the room exchanged playful words, ready to make their opposing team lose.

As the game was underway, the boys were decent, but nothing in comparison to the girls with a secret weapon. Each other. Yasmine and Jordyn were the only people in the room who knew each other from back at home, making clues easier to solve.

Yasmine stood up once it was her turn again, where Xavier watched over her card to make sure she didn't slip up and say a word to compromise their points. His close proximity made her heart rate increase, with the hairs on her skin rising in unison at military-level attention.

"Don't be cheating. I see what you and Jordyn are doing over there, Miss Yasmine," he whispered. His minty breath on her skin made her want him even closer, creating an undying craving for the taste of his lips.

Fighting against her intrusive thoughts, Yasmine responded, "Let's face it, we would all beat the guys regardless of if we knew each other or not." Looking up at him, her knees almost buckled from his intense gaze. Despite the interest between them seeming reciprocated, Yasmine didn't want to jump to any conclusions, unclear if her imagination was betraying her.

After five back-to-back rounds of the game, the ladies beat the men badly. They became belligerently drunk, with yelling and shouting from the room becoming so raucous, they were caught red-handed by their resident advisors.

"Freshmen, y'all know better than this. Everyone disperse immediately or else you'll all get written up," said one resident advisor. Everything happened so abruptly, Yasmine didn't get to explore more of what she was feeling with Xavier throughout the night. Afterward, everything reverted back to how it was prior to them meeting, with Xavier nowhere to be found.

Friendship Fragments

* * *

"Yasmine, this was under the door with your name on it," said Jordyn a week later, holding a white envelope with unfamiliar handwriting in her hand. Surprised since she didn't know many people on campus and wasn't expecting anything, Yasmine jumped out of bed, grabbing the letter to read what it could be.

Blushing from the note, Yasmine must have missed when Jordyn asked her for details. Jordyn grabbed the letter out of Yasmine's hands to see for herself.

Yasmine,

I loved our vibe when we met the other day. How about I take you out on a date to dive a little deeper? Text me if you're interested: (917)333-0112.

-Xavier

"Woah, this is from Xavier. A handwritten note, Yas. You better text him right now," Jordyn demanded. She always had a convincing way about herself. Both ladies possessed strong personalities in their own right, but Jordyn's was far more intense. At least that's what people always said. For Yasmine, Jordyn was just Jordyn. Her strong willpower got her almost anything she wanted and Yasmine often wished she could be the same.

Yasmine ended up texting Xavier, but she waited until the next day not to seem too eager. Consistent text messages turned into Facetime calls, which turned into movie nights in their floor's lounge. After two weeks of realizing they wanted to get to know each other further, Xavier surprised her with a more intimate plan. All she knew was to meet him in the lobby by seven in the evening and to "wear something sexy."

As the elevator doors opened, he waited at the entrance with a

45

bouquet of two dozen red roses and reached out to loop her arms with his. They walked to a parking lot, where he drove her to Applebee's in his cousin's car.

What may be deemed a cheap date now years later, meant the world to Yasmine at the time. Most dates freshmen went on were in dining halls and local restaurants near campus. Xavier made an extra effort to do something different and it didn't go unnoticed.

"Not only are you beautiful on the outside, but you're even more beautiful on the inside. I'm a lucky man," he said.

"We'll just have to see about that, sir."

They learned how much they shared in common as their bond grew deeper. They grew up similarly, being the eldest in their families, which carried a burden to always do and be great. Their main goal was to make their parents and siblings proud. They left their first date feeling even closer than she anticipated.

Singular dates turned into double dates with Jordyn and Malik. The girls loved having another aspect of their lives binding them together. It was perfect.

Xavier's mysterious personality often made him the talk of campus. The men wanted to be his friend and the ladies wanted to take him down. He never seemed to pay much attention to it though, only giving Yasmine his undivided attention, or so she thought.

During their junior year, there were mumblings of him taking freshmen on dates, but Yasmine always thought people were envious of their relationship, wanting to use any excuse to break them apart. He was her college sweetheart and she planned to be with him forever. No one was going to change that.

Jordyn and Malik also were together all throughout college. They planned to double-date the rest of their lives and even become the Best Man and Maid of Honor at each other's weddings. After graduation, Xavier ended up staying in Atlanta while Yasmine decided to go back home to New York to start her career.

They were supposed to find a way back to one another, but the long distance was hard on them. They went from spending time together twenty-four seven to squeezing in small moments to talk and taking the occasional trip, but it wasn't enough.

"Yas, I have something I need to talk to you about," said Jordyn over their weekly Facetime call a year after graduation. She set her phone down, pacing, unclear of how to approach whatever it was she needed to share. Yasmine assumed she might have been pregnant.

"You're scaring me, Jordyn. What's up?"

"Alright, you know how there's always been rumors about Xavier?"

Yasmine was starting to feel like a burning lump was stuck in her throat. "Yea, I never let that faze me. He's an attractive man, I get why people would want to start rumors." The nauseous feeling settling in her stomach betrayed her confidence.

"Well, I hate to be the one to tell you this, but it's not a rumor. Malik and I were eating at a steakhouse last night and saw him tonguing down another girl in there."

"It probably wasn't him, Jordyn. Don't be ridiculous."

"It was, but I took a zoomed in picture for proof...right before I went over to him and cursed his ass out. I'll send it to you." On cue, Yasmine's phone buzzed with a text from Jordyn.

"What are you telling me?" Yasmine stared at the photo she sent in disbelief..hurt..anger.

"Fuck him, Yas. And fuck Malik, too. I know he knew this whole time and said nothing. He's unbelievable."

"I...I..."

"It's ok, Yasmine. We'll get through this," were the only words Yasmine remembered before completely breaking down with hurt. The life Yasmine envisioned was shattered, leaving small scars as reminders of the imprint he left on her life.

8. Rekindled Confusion
Yasmine

YASMINE'S present romantic life was still as confusing as it was all those years before. She entertained meaningless situationships with people she met on public transportation, through mutual friends, and on dating apps. You name it, she tried it. Sadly, no one could have a hold on her heart quite like the charming boy she met freshman year.

She wanted the marriage, the house, and the kids, but life didn't quite work itself out in the way she envisioned. She often wondered if it ever would. In many ways, Jordyn's life mirrored the exact path Yasmine pictured for herself, but she was not envious of her friend. It made her heart full knowing that Jordyn found her happy ending. At least someone in her life did.

Xavier moved back to New York over the last year to take care of his mom, who was recently diagnosed with cancer. Yasmine only knew because he posted about it on social media. She didn't follow him, but she *followed* him. The girls who get it, get it.

She sent him well wishes when he first shared the news, but didn't delve deeper about their past or reconnecting. It didn't seem like the right time, nor was she sure she wanted to. While residual feelings for him lingered, so did hurt.

Friendship Fragments

Yasmine was visiting family in her childhood neighborhood in Brooklyn one hot, summer afternoon in August. Flatbush, baby. Kids could be seen rolling around on scooters and others waiting in line to score an ice cream cone from Mister Softee.

As much as she loved her new building, she often missed home, where its melting pot fused various cultures together. The streets pulsed with diverse cuisines, music, art, and traditions. It screamed heritage and community. She hoped gentrification didn't completely wash it all away one day.

While taking in her old neighborhood, she felt a tap on her shoulders; her body stiffened at the intimate touch.

"I know this ain't who I think it is," the familiar huskiness in the voice could not be denied. Yasmine turned to meet the same cocoa-brown eyes of the man who stole her heart all those years ago. Her stomach felt like it plummeted straight to the sidewalk, mind drudging through abandoned emotions trying to force its way to the surface.

He looked good, perhaps even better than her memories and social media combined. He was more muscular now with a full beard. The boy she fell in love with became a man.

"Xavier. W..what are you doing here? How are you?" she asked, returning the embrace he didn't hesitate to initiate before they began walking together, their direction aimless.

"Well, you know I'm in town for my mom. I have some cousins that live nearby, so I stopped by to visit. You know I don't come to Brooklyn unless I have a reason to."

"Oh, how could I forget," Yasmine joked, rolling her eyes at him. He was born and raised in Queens and when they were together, he would always find a reason to remind everyone of it. Their banter felt familiar yet foreign, but his gaze still made her nervous. The last time they had a normal conversation with each other, they were still dating. In love. So much had changed since then.

"What are you doing the rest of the day?"

"Probably heading back to my place to chill. How about you?"

"You hungry? Let's grab a quick bite then I can drive you home."

Their impromptu run-in turned into lunch and then some drinks. Their chemistry surprisingly didn't fade over the years. They exchanged old college stories, updates about friends and family, and endless laughter. Unfinished business lingered in the small crevices of silence they encountered throughout the evening. It was only fair for them to completely see it through, right? Even if only for one moment.

"I can't lie, I missed you, Yas. My pride prevented me from telling you this out loud, but I am sorry for the way I hurt you. You never deserved that," he confessed. Tears welled up in Yasmine's eyes at the words she never thought she'd hear aloud.

When she initially confronted him about cheating, he was more concerned with why people were trying to ruin their relationship versus his actual actions. His admission of guilt didn't happen until she showed him the photo evidence of his wrongdoing. But no apology. No reason why. She never reached back out to him. He never reached back out to her. They never spoke again until she heard about his mom one year ago.

"I can't express how much I appreciate you telling me that. I didn't realize how much I needed to hear this from you. It seems like you've matured."

"I have. If you're single, I'd love to take you on a real date whenever we're both free next. It would also be nice to get my mind off of everything with my mom."

Attempting to hide her giddiness at the possibilities, Yasmine simply responded, "That would be nice. Keep me posted."

Over the following months, what Yasmine pictured as the potential rekindling to the relationship she never fully got over, slowly became a haze of confusion. Not only was the broken trust from his cheating hard to repair, it also seemed like the two were on separate pages.

Yasmine wanted to pick up where they left off as a continuation from where things went awry. Xavier, on the other hand, wanted a clean slate. Besides the years-late admission of his wrongdoing, he wasn't interested in discussing their breakup beyond his lunch date apology. He believed that brushing past their issues was the only way they could move forward. She was all too familiar with his dismissiveness. Maybe he hadn't changed as much as she thought. Young Yasmine let his nonchalance slide way too often. Grown Yasmine was not impressed by his behavior.

"What is done is done. We can't change that now," he'd argue, slanted eyes urging her to let it go.

"But you know you hurt me and we have to acknowledge what went wrong. I don't want us to repeat the same mistakes," Yasmine rebutted.

The same conversation would go in circles for weeks before Yasmine decided to play it his way. She didn't want the only person she ever loved to slip away from her again.

When he wasn't busy with family affairs, they spent their evenings at dinner and their late nights making sweeter love than she ever experienced. Xavier was not only her first, but she hoped he would become her last.

Yasmine hesitated to update her friends, knowing exactly what they would say if she shared the news. Especially Jordyn. She was in a state of bliss and didn't want anything or anyone to interfere with it. Xavier agreed to do the same, waiting to share with his own close friends and family until he was ready. They didn't want their highs to be clouded with pessimism before giving themselves a real chance. Brianna was the only person who knew any details about them, at least until their relationship was confirmed.

Nine months went by before their conversation on the morning of the train incident.

"Yasmine, I don't have time for this. You know I have a lot on my plate," he urged on their FaceTime call.

"I definitely do, Xay. I just need to know if we'll officially be together again. I always planned to spend my life—" Yasmine's next words were immediately cut short by Xavier's scoff. If the weather weren't nice out, Yasmine would have thought the sudden chill in the air was coming from outside.

He closed his eyes for a few seconds, seemingly calming himself down from annoyance before responding. "If you think I am considering anyone else's life right now besides my mom's, you're wrong. I can't do this. Not right now. I'll talk to you later."

Yasmine's words were wrong. The timing too. She didn't have ill intent, but didn't fully think through how to approach the situation. She became frustrated with their direction. They were still keeping their relationship a secret. And she was tired of it. His lack of effort in progressing made her feel like he was using her as a temporary band-aid, while everything else in his life went haywire.

It felt eerily similar to other situationships she found herself in previously and although she loved Xavier, she would be doing a disservice to herself continuously avoiding a hard conversation. Walking on eggshells around the person you loved was not the life anyone should have to live.

They spent the rest of the night arguing through text, no side willing to hear the other out. Yasmine went into her bedroom and cried her eyes out, unsure of how the next steps between them would play out.

A few days passed before her brunch date with Brianna, neither Yasmine nor Xavier reaching out to one another. Wanting to break their past patterns, and system filled with champagne, she was finally ready to clear the air. As she neared her apartment door to make the call, she felt more nauseous than brave. The phone rang twice before he picked up.

"Hello, Yasmine." Xavier's annoyance was clear in his flat tone.

"How are you? How's everything with your mom?"

"She's ok. Right now, no news is good news. But there hasn't been significant improvement since she started this last round of chemo. We'll be talking to the doctor early next week." He was physically in the conversation, but mentally he was elsewhere. He focused on whatever he was working on, the sound of clattering of items and shutting of doors loudly interrupting their discussion. Chores maybe?

"I'm sorry to hear that. I hope things do turn around for the better soon. Are you busy right now?"

"I hope so, too. I'm running some errands, yea. What's up with you?"

"I'm decent. I just came back from brunch with Brianna and wanted to check on you."

"Ah ok. Yea I am good."

An uncomfortable quietness occupied the call before Yasmine mustered up the courage to ask, "So where are things with us? I know our last conversation didn't end on the right note. I had no ill intent and understand the pressure you're under right now. I want to apologize for my approach, but I also hope you understand where I was coming from."

"I do, Yasmine. I care about you. You know that. I really just need a break from this to figure out what I want right now. Can you give me the space to get both of us some answers?"

"Absolutely. I understand that you have a lot going on. I am always here if you want to talk."

"Thank you. I have to finish these errands. Can I call you back?"

"Sure!" The line went dead before she could say another word.

The enthusiasm in Yasmine's last words rivaled how she truly felt; her composure waning with the click of the phone, shifting into a puddle of tears.

Xavier's cold demeanor left frostbite over any warmth or progress Yasmine hoped for in their conversation, putting her guard back up to where she felt safe. If time and space would confirm what was meant for them, she was up for the challenge.

* * *

Yasmine went into the next month laser-focused on her trip ahead. Friendship was always the cure for any minor or major inconvenience. She was ready for her heart to be filled by her chosen sisters.

9. Disconnect
Jordyn

THREE WEEKS PASSED since Yasmine's spontaneous plans for a girls' trip came about. While Jordyn was initially excited for the chance to get away from her hectic life in Atlanta, she started feeling apprehensive as the plans became more solidified. She mulled it over in her mind while doing weekend chores, blasting New Edition through the speakers to set the mood. Her current task was folding clothes in the laundry room, simultaneously hiding from her screaming children upstairs. Their grandmother would have to find a way to keep them occupied because she needed a break.

When she wasn't cooking or cleaning, she was driving the kids to and from school. If she wasn't doing those chores, she was making content for her social media pages, which added some income to their household. When she wasn't trying to work, she needed to be present for a husband who spent most of his days working as a surgeon. She needed a break from it all. And Malik knew it, which was why he was ecstatic when the idea came about.

"This is just what you need, babe," he confirmed.

"Are you sure?" Jordyn asked, worried about leaving her little family home without her.

"Definitely. You spend nearly all of your time catering to us. And I know you miss your girls. Take the break, have some drinks, and we'll be right here when you get back," he confirmed with a kiss.

But why did Yasmine suddenly want to fulfill their pact after all of these years? It was not like her and Amari took the extra effort to visit Jordyn in Atlanta. Sure, Yasmine flew down for the impromptu wedding, the baby showers, and a homecoming here and there, but it never seemed like she wanted to visit to spend quality time with her dear old friend. There always needed to be another reason why and Amari almost never visited at all.

On top of everything else, the trip was for the college friends to reconnect, but somehow a new friend of Yasmine's was also invited? Jordyn heard about her here and there, but didn't realize just how close they became. Furthermore, Yasmine was well aware of how Jordyn could be around new people. Why would she suggest inviting a stranger?

Jordyn never felt more disconnected from Yasmine than she did in the current chapter of her life. They didn't talk on the phone as much as they used to— much less see each other.

Sometimes she felt like it was because of Malik and his friendship with her college sweetheart, Xavier. But she shouldn't be punished for their friendship. They were friends first. She knew that.

Or maybe because Jordyn accidentally became the catalyst for the end of Yasmine's relationship. It wasn't her fault Xavier was caught red-handed with another woman. One of many, if they accounted for all of the other accusations she chose to ignore.

To add insult to injury, Yasmine was secretly seeing him again for months now. Malik was trying to keep his friend's secret, but she eavesdropped on their phone conversation a week ago. When she confronted him, there was no choice but for him to be honest.

"Jordyn, please don't make a big deal about this. And please don't tell Yasmine you know," he urged.

"It's like we're not even friends at this point in our lives. She asked me to come on this trip, but didn't have the decency to tell me what else was going on in her life when I asked," she argued.

"You have to give them time to figure it out. Xavier has a lot on his plate and is figuring out if and how the relationship fits anyway." Malik always wanted to put things into perspective and even though Jordyn loved her husband, she hated this part of him at times. She wanted him to see things the way she saw them. Point, blank, period.

"Yea. He probably needs to figure out if he'll cheat again, too. At least he's speaking to you about it. She's hiding all of it from me. What else could she be hiding? I don't even know who she is anymore and I've known her longer than I have anyone else in my life, outside of family." Jordyn pressed her tongue to the roof of her mouth, attempting to control the waterworks that wanted to make an appearance. Her feelings were hurt. Badly.

"I'm not going to address your comments about Xavier because I know how you feel about him, but I do want to remind you that he *is* my friend. As far as Yasmine, you have to give people time to feel comfortable sharing things about their own life. Maybe she will talk about it on the trip. Maybe she won't. But you can't cast judgment when you don't have all of the facts. Have you thought about the pressure on both of them since the relationship didn't work out before?"

"Malik, I don't think we're going to see eye-to-eye on this. I also don't even know if I am going on the trip, to be honest. Let's table this conversation for now before it goes in an ugly direction."

He sighed deeply, kissing her forehead before exiting the room. Jordyn was fuming. But she also didn't want to let those problems affect them. There was enough of their own shit they were working through in therapy.

They loved each other as much as they did when they met at Wynters University, but his demanding job in surgery took away from them spending one-on-one time together, especially with the kids. His mom moved in to help them out, but it still didn't change the nights he was too tired to go out to dinner with her or go to one of their kids' extracurricular activities. They compromised to have one night a month dedicated only to them and for the most part, it was successful. She was truly grateful that after all of their time together, they were still each other's favorite person. Her personality could be a lot for some people, but he handled it with such grace - unlike her family.

Jordyn was the youngest in her family with her oldest brother, Byron, being twenty years older than her. She had two other sisters, Londyn and Falynn, over a decade older. The age difference was so big, it was challenging to connect with them on a deeper level. She often felt like they were a second set of parents, always trying to tell her what she should or shouldn't do. Her mom was too old and too tired to reprimand Jordyn's actions, so her siblings took her place. It created a resentful and rebellious relationship on both sides.

Although too young to know it at the time, meeting Yasmine made her feel more welcomed than she ever felt in her own home. Their second grade banter gave her the closeness she often wished she had with her siblings and she kept a tight grip on their connection straight through college. She never wanted anyone to get in between the bond they shared. Jordyn never pictured a life where Yasmine didn't exist in it until recently.

She was going to need to do some soul searching to decide if she wanted to go on the trip. If Yasmine didn't bring Xavier up, was she supposed to pretend like she didn't know? And it's not like Jordyn could call Amari to vent to her about any of it. For one, Amari would likely have a positive spin like Malik did. No need to piss herself off twice. For two, Amari was always closer to Yasmine because they met first. For all she knew, Amari probably already knew everything going on. Only Jordyn was in the dark, like always.

10. Vacation Prep
Yasmine

"Toothbrush, toothpaste, lotion, perfume, deodorant..." Yasmine whispered to herself as she began doing the final check of her toiletries. In the blink of an eye, the trip was somehow two days away. Between work and summer events kicking into full gear, time flew by swiftly.

A frantic knock at her door startled her from her focus. She was not expecting visitors. Yasmine let out a sigh of relief as she glanced through her peephole. It was Brianna.

"GIRL, why are you knocking on my door like you're the damn police?"

"Sorry, girl. The trip is basically here and as I started packing, I just realized my passport expired." She walked in, immediately pacing back and forth to calm her nerves.

"WHAT? How did it expire when you were in Mexico recently?"

"It expired like a week ago. I didn't notice until I went to check into the flight. This is so annoying."

"Let's not panic yet. Do you think you'll be able to get one expedited?"

Yasmine couldn't believe she forgot to check this vital information before booking the trip, but it was also a semi last minute plan, so she tried to extend her grace.

"I'm already on it, I have an eight am appointment tomorrow at the Passport Agency. Wish me luck. Have fun without me if I don't end up being able to come," Brianna replied, looking down and twiddling her fingers. Yasmine saw through the brave face she was trying to put on.

"We're going to put it into the universe that everything will work itself out. Did you finish packing, just in case?" she inquired, wanting to give her friend hope.

"I'm going to head up and do that now. I've been on the phone all morning trying to get an appointment and as soon as I got one, I took the elevator and came up here immediately to loop you in."

"Totally get it. Let's hope for the best."

"Well while I'm here, how are things with Xavier?" She sat down on the sofa, making herself comfortable.

Brianna had an uncanny ability to bring up topics at the wrong time. Yasmine didn't update her after their brunch date. Mostly because she didn't want to talk about it, but also because she was embarrassed. Her heart broke every time she looked around her apartment. The fresh memories of his presence there haunted her in every room like an unwelcomed ghost. Yasmine was already feeling emotional about the situation hours before.

"Well, I haven't shared this with you, but we're on a break. It's been a month," she finally muttered, avoiding any eye contact that could trigger more tears.

"Oh wow. I'm sorry, I didn't know. What happened? It's ok if you don't want to talk about it, too. I'd understand."

"I can talk about it. I shouldn't keep things bottled up like I normally do. I asked him about the direction of where things were going. It's been nine months and I was tired of feeling like an option instead of *the* option. He asked for a break instead, feeling overwhelmed with everything he had going on."

"Oh no, sorry to hear that. Have you spoken at all since this break?"

"A short text here and there, but not really."

"And you still want to be with him, right?"

"Yes and no. I'm not one hundred percent sure. He was my first true love and after all those years, that doesn't completely fade away. But our trust has been broken in the past. And he has a lot on his plate right now. I don't know where we go from here, to be honest."

"I understand. Take it one day at a time. But I want you to believe that you're deserving of someone who knows they want you." Brianna's words were equally as hurtful as they were thoughtful. Yasmine knew she deserved far more than what she was receiving, but wasn't sure if she'd ever receive it from any man if her track record was any indication.

"You're right, Bri. Thank you. Can you do me a favor and not bring him up to the girls when we're on vacation? Because of our past, I'm hesitant to share anything until I fully know what's going on between us. And they've seen him hurt me before. I'm not ready to deal with their judgment."

"You got it, girl. Your secret is safe with me. I'm going to head back and continue packing. I'll keep you posted on what happens with my passport situation," Brianna replied, hugging Yasmine before heading to the door.

"Please do." Even though she was irritated by the topic of Xavier coming up, their conversation made Yasmine feel lighter. She needed to get those feelings off her chest.

The conversation also made her think of the one person who was there for their relationship from the beginning. She felt guilty for not wanting to share their reconnection, but she knew she couldn't. Jordyn wouldn't want to hear anything about Xavier, nor support it. Not after how deep those wounds cut. She called every day after the breakup, letting Yasmine vent about her feelings repetitively, casting no judgment.

But she couldn't tell her about him being back in her life presently. Not yet. The least she could do was check in to see how her vacation prep was going. They hadn't talked one-on-one in a while, and she knew a phone call was long overdue. Yasmine anxiously waited for the other line to pick up, hoping her friend was available to talk. Finally, after a few rings, Jordyn answered.

"Hi, Yasmine," Jordyn said, flatly.

"Hey, Jordyn!" Yasmine replied cheerfully. "It's been way too long, hasn't it?"

"Yea, it's been pretty long," Jordyn replied in an irritated tone.

"You good? Excited for the trip?"

"I almost wasn't going to make it. Now that it's here, I guess I have to be, right?"

"Oh no. Why did you almost not make it? I thought you said Malik wanted you to go."

"He does. And so does my mother-in-law. You know how she is. They probably want to break from me, actually," Jordyn joked; her initial ice-cold energy melted.

Yasmine chuckled. She remembered Jordyn's mother-in-law all too well. "I can only imagine. But I hope she's been helping out, especially with you preparing for our trip," she replied, also making a mental note of Jordyn not responding to her previous question.

"Oh, she's been surprisingly supportive about me getting a break. She says I deserve it, and I know she'll take good care of Junior and Amina while I'm away. She loves them so much."

Her oldest son, Malik Jr., was seven and her daughter, Amina, was four. They looked like the perfect blend of their parents with caramel-colored skin and almond shaped eyes. Malik Jr. was more of a calm introvert like his dad. Amina was certainly the star of the show like Jordyn, outspoken and all. They created miniature versions of themselves, personality included.

Yasmine's heart swelled at the thought of her godchildren. It had been two years since she last visited them and there was no reasonable excuse. Life got in the way, but it shouldn't have been so long. Her next trip after Jamaica needed to be visiting them.

"This is great to hear, Jordyn. I wanted to check in and make sure you're not feeling too overwhelmed. Especially with this being your first vacation leaving them at home."

"Thanks, Yasmine. It means a lot to me. I'm about as ready as I can be."

"Take it one step at a time. But it sounds like you have things in order to me."

As they continued chatting, Jordyn couldn't help but drift into memories of their childhood. "You know, Yasmine, it's funny. Malik Jr. is almost the same age we were when we became friends."

"I remember those days like they were yesterday. I can't believe we've been friends for over twenty years. Time really does fly, doesn't it?"

"Sure does. It also seems like he was born yesterday. I can't believe how much he's growing up."

"I know! I saw some recent photos you posted and I could not believe it myself. I hope he maintains meaningful friendships like ours throughout his life. It's so important."

"Well, we can do better so I hope he has better relationships than ours," said Jordyn.

"I can understand why you said that. We'll have time to get back on track during and after this trip, though. I just know it."

"Yea, we'll see. You did invite an additional guest who isn't a part of the group. We'll see how that goes," Jordyn responded.

"Don't do that. Brianna is really nice; I think you'll like her once you get to know her."

Awkward silence enveloped the call. Since they knew each other for so long, Yasmine was typically good at diffusing these conversations with her friend, but it didn't seem to be working in this situation.

Jordyn chuckled, responding. "I feel like such an outcast sometimes, you know? It's like y'all intentionally leave me out."

It pained Yasmine to hear those words, feeling somewhat responsible for Jordyn's feelings. As much as it was hard to admit, the distance naturally made them grow apart. In addition to Jordyn's sometimes unpredictable behavior.

Yasmine pulled back over the years. Small moments to take a break used to last a day, but they've now extended into weeks. Months. She felt like Jordyn couldn't relate to her in the same ways as some of her other friends did. And vice versa, Jordyn seemed to pull back, too, but she also was busy with everything on her plate and Yasmine never questioned it.

Yasmine wanted to reassure her. "I can see how you might feel that way. You're at a different stage of life, but we love you just the same. I can speak for myself when I say I need to do much better with visiting and calling. Sometimes, I feel like I'm intruding on your family life. I'm sure there is a lot we both need to catch up on when we see each other in person."

"Definitely never intruding. I'm happy we get to spend some quality time together over this next week. Let's make the best of it. I gotta go, but I love you."

"I love you, too."

Day 1: Ar[rivals]

11. Travel Chaos

Yasmine

TRAVEL DAYS TENDED to bring some level of chaos and disorder no matter how much preparation occurred in advance. After staying up late to finish packing everything needed to make the trip a success, Yasmine nearly snoozed through the incessant sound of her alarm clock, forgetting they needed to make it to the airport on time.

While Brianna was able to get her passport expedited in time for the trip, she also found herself in a race against time after oversleeping. After several unanswered calls, Yasmine's last resort was to go downstairs and knock on her door until she finally woke up. They frantically gathered their belongings and rushed to the airport, hoping they wouldn't miss their early morning flight.

Yasmine added another layer of unexpected pandemonium once they arrived. As she reached the check-in counter, her overweight bag became the next hurdle to face. With limited time to spare, she began hastily redistributing some items into her carry-on.

"Need any help?" Brianna offered.

"No, I'm good," Yasmine responded curtly, not wanting Brianna to see the few surprises she packed for everyone on the trip. Her mind couldn't process where anything was in the panic of the moment and opted to sort it out on her own.

She shifted enough items before rushing to the security line. Despite them having TSA Precheck, the line was equally as long as general boarding, adding to their heightened mountain of stress.

"Think we'll make it?" asked Brianna, anxiously standing next to her.

"No idea, sis. Let's hope for the best at this point."

With limited time to spare after getting through security, they ran to their gate, which inconveniently was in the furthest corner of the terminal. By the time they finally reached the boarding gate, arriving just before the cabin doors of their aircraft closed, they were drenched in sweat with their hearts pounding through their chests.

The flight was packed, aisles filled with people excited for their destination to paradise. Being the last ones on the aircraft, there was no space in the overhead bin for Yasmine's carry-on, with the only option for it to get gate checked and they felt horrible asking the man in the aisle seat to stand for them to settle into their window and middle seats.

"We made it!" Brianna exhaled sharply as they made themselves comfortable in their seats.

"Barely, but we did. What a morning," responded Yasmine before the flight attendants began their routine pre-flight announcements.

The morning madness was so intense, they drifted off to sleep before takeoff. They were awakened by claps as the pilot made a smooth landing. As annoying as that post-landing gesture was, nothing was more irritating than when people stood up before the plane reached the gate. Getting luggage from the overhead bin in advance wouldn't somehow make them teleport past the rows of people in front of them also preparing to depart the aircraft. Yasmine and Brianna tilted their heads sideways and looked at one another, telepathically sharing their thoughts on the matter.

* * *

When Yasmine checked Amari's flight status while in the customs' line, it showed her red eye flight landed also, timed perfectly to arrive around the same time. The airport was packed from end to end with travelers and it was hard to spot if she was ahead of or behind them.

Yasmine and Brianna were waiting by the baggage carousel for their luggage when they heard a familiar voice.

"Hi y'all! How was your flight?" Amari asked, heading over to the ladies with her luggage in tow.

"Hi boo! We were wondering where you were," said Yasmine, greeting her longtime friend with a tight hug. Amari returned the gesture with the same amount of love.

"I may have landed before y'all," she responded before looking in Brianna's direction. "And you! How have you been?"

"Good, girl. Can't complain. Ready for a drink."

"Amen to that," Amari responded. The ladies nodded their heads in agreement.

"What time did Jordyn say she was arriving?" Amari asked.

Pulling her phone out of her bag, Yasmine confirmed, "It looks like Jordyn gets here around three pm. I know she tried to change for an earlier flight, but couldn't. The driver already knows he needs to come back for her."

"Not a problem at all. But we're getting her drunk upon arrival. She better be taking a nap right now. I know I'll need one."

They giggled as they headed for the exit to meet the driver, Delroy, who they booked for their transportation needs throughout the weekend.

"Hughes Party!" a man with a heavy Patois accent shouted from the "Arrivals" section of Sangster International Airport. He was holding a sign in his hand with Yasmine's last name.

"That's us! You must be Delroy," said Yasmine, walking up to greet him. Amari and Brianna followed behind her, where he led them outside of the airport.

Friendship Fragments

Stepping further outside, the warmth of the Caribbean air wrapped them like a warm embrace, mirroring the reconnection Yasmine envisioned having with her friends on their trip. A gentle breeze blew the trees in the surrounding area, teasing the salty fragrance of the nearby ocean. The soft sounds of live reggae music set the tone for the enjoyment to take place.

"Now this is what I'm talking about," Brianna said, facing the sunny sky. New York, on the other hand, was having a rainy summer and the ladies were desperate for some sun and clear skies. It was the perfect temperature to start their vacation.

"Yea mon. Follow mi."

The term "Yea Mon" was a phrase commonly used on the island. It could be used as confirmation, encouragement, acknowledgment, or in agreement. Growing up in Brooklyn, Yasmine was well versed in common Jamaican phrases and terms but was happy to experience it on island versus from her old neighborhood and pictures online.

"Stay right deh so. I will pull up di van fi help wid di luggage."

"What did he say?" Brianna asked, turning to Amari.

After Brianna moved to Texas, she didn't have as much exposure to Caribbean culture as she would have if she stayed in New York growing up. Both of Amari's parents were Jamaican, so if the girls ever needed some translating while on vacation, they would likely defer to her.

"He's grabbing the van then helping us with our luggage. How about we grab a drink and some patties from Margaritaville really quickly?" she replied.

Margaritaville was right outside the airport, allowing visitors to get a taste of Jamaica before or after their flights. The ladies ordered what they wanted, then met Delroy back at the van with frozen drinks in one hand and a perfectly golden, flaky patty in the other.

As they made their way to the van, Brianna whispered, "Y'all....I might not know what he is saying, but he's fine as hell."

Yasmine and Amari nodded in agreement, but didn't say too much being within an earshot of him. When letting them into the van, they noticed chilled water bottles with plantain chips in a basket.

After he put the suitcases in and re-entered the van, Yasmine asked, "Is this basket for us?"

"Yea mon. Tek whatever yuh want. We can make stops fi any treats yuh want, too," he offered. The girls started to see exactly how Stella decided to get her groove back. He was already making this experience an enjoyable one with his kindness. They echoed their thanks to him in response.

"Not ah problem. Heading to Moonstone Oasis Resort, right?" Delroy was looking on his phone for what seemed like an itinerary as the ladies nodded their heads. "And yuh all want mi fi guh back fi anotha friend lata, right?"

"Yes, you will. Jordyn is arriving around three pm. Do you have all of the flight info I sent over?" Yasmine questioned.

"Yea mon. Just ah double check in case anything changed."

"I appreciate that. We're good to go for today, but if anything else changes during the week, we will send you a text in advance."

"That would be perfect. Thank yuh," he confirmed.

The ride to the hotel was forty minutes and the ladies tried to chit chat for the first half of the ride. Still tired from their morning travels, they each slowly drifted back to sleep, recharging for the rest of the day ahead.

"Excuse mi ladies, we are pulling into di resort now."

12. Play Nice

Yasmine

THE MOONSTONE OASIS RESORT looked like an absolute tropical heaven, exceeding the expectations the ladies anticipated prior to their arrival. As Delroy steered the van into the resort, a breathtaking sight unfolded before the women's eyes.

"WOWWW," said Amari, unable to contain her amazement.

Despite seeing pictures on the official hotel's website, pictures really did the place no justice. The beauty had to be appreciated in person. As the van entered the gates, there were towering palm trees lining the pathway.

The hotel lobby could be viewed from the outside with the indoors effortlessly mimicking the beauty of the island itself. There were tropical plants everywhere with the focal point being a mini waterfall cascading from a beautiful, stony wall. The hotel was already living up to its name. It truly looked peaceful, like an oasis.

"NAHHH, y'all did a good job. This place looks amazing!" Brianna exclaimed.

"Thank you so much! This hotel is newly renovated and recently re-opened. The initial reviews have been great. I hope it can live up to the hype," said Yasmine. She anxiously hoped every aspect of the plans for the week would be satisfactory for both her and her friends. Little Miss Type A always moved the bar further for herself.

Distracted by the resort's beauty, the ladies forgot Delroy was removing their luggage from the back of his van. "Alright, here yuh are. Mi wi come back lata with unnu other friend. Any plans fi di evening where yuh all would need mi for?"

"I think we're keeping it simple today to get settled in, but we'll definitely be ready for some activities tomorrow," explained Yasmine.

"Ok, not a problem. Whatsapp my number if yuh end up needing anything."

"Will do. Thank you, Delroy."

The hotel staff greeted the friends with tropical drinks as they checked in. They joked and laughed all the way to their suite. When trying to find the best resort option for their stay, it was important to have a suite option with multiple rooms. Everyone could be in the same common areas but had enough space to feel comfortable. Gone were the days of four people sharing one double occupancy room.

A refreshing ocean-like aroma greeted the women as they entered the suite, followed by the bright sunlight from outside. There was a kitchenette with a refrigerator and bar area near the front. Two rooms could be found to the left. Further inward was a double sofa bed with a television facing it. The floor to ceiling windows led to an ocean-front balcony where the pool's design created the perfect illusion of it connecting to the ocean. The ladies were in awe at the beauty before them.

"This view is perfect. Yas, I hope you added some beach time onto that itinerary of yours," Amari joked. Yasmine knew there was some underlying truth to the remark, though. They would be thanking her later for the attention to detail. The joke would certainly be on them, if anything.

"There's a few open blocks where we can do whatever we want. We can definitely go to the beach at any of those times. We can't come to an island and not go to the beach. That's blasphemy," she finally replied. They laughed in agreement. No need to start things off on the wrong note.

While Amari and Brianna sat down on the balcony to catch up, Yasmine saw it as the perfect opportunity to get her welcome bags together.

"I am going to get showered so we can head to the pool," she mentioned before heading back inside. Amari and Brianna were in such deep conversation, they never acknowledged her statement.

The room arrangements were Amari and Jordyn in one room with Yasmine and Brianna in the other. This made the most sense since Yasmine brought Brianna on the trip and wanted her to feel comfortable.

Yasmine snuck all the surprise items into the bathroom with her. She turned on the shower water, not to seem suspicious to her friends, then got to work.

She ordered custom welcome bags with their names on it and purchased hangover items to put inside— Tylenol, IV Hydration Packets, Wet Wipes, and Makeup Remover. She also added each person's favorite liquor in a mini size and water shoes for any excursions or other water activities they might do.

Yasmine took a shower immediately after to wash off the ick of the airport. When she was ready for the pool, bathing suit and all, she noticed Amari and Brianna were still talking on the balcony, having what looked like an intense conversation. They met once, but not to the extent where they could be in such a passionate debate, right?

As she opened the balcony doors to make sure everything was good, she was met with a deafening silence and startled looks plastered on their faces. *Strange.*

"Is everything ok out here? It looks pretty intense," she asked.

Awkwardly laughing, Brianna responded and showed an image on her phone. "We're debating about these sneakers that just dropped. I hate them and Amari thinks they are the best Jordans to come out this year, which couldn't be further from the truth."

"Yea, Brianna clearly doesn't have good sneaker taste. That's all I know," said Amari in agreement, avoiding any immediate eye contact in Yasmine's direction.

Yasmine knew as much about sneakers as she knew about the proper precautions to take in the event of the earthquake. If there was something else going on, it was a good way to divert. Or maybe she really was imagining things?

"Ok well, I may not know much about sneakers, but what I do know is y'all need to get ready. I am ready for the pool!"

Both ladies agreed and left the balcony to get ready in their respective rooms. While they showered, Yasmine turned on some music and prepared the shots for everyone to take. They also each brought their own full-sized bottle of liquor in case they didn't like what the hotel was offering.

By the time Yasmine sat on the sofa scrolling through social media, the ladies were finally dressed for the pool.

"Alright y'all, it's shot-o-clock!" she said, passing the shots out before they could rebut. "We can take these, then head to the pool. Jordyn should be here in the next hour or so."

The ladies took their shots then vibed out to the R&B music playing in the background.

"One more shot before we leave?" Brianna asked.

"Absolutely," responded Amari. Whatever tension Yasmine may have sensed dissipated.

The resort had a few pools, but they wanted to explore the one nearest to the lobby, where it would be easier for Jordyn to find them when she arrived. They sat at the pool's bar and ordered more drinks, listening to the music the live DJ was playing.

They were about three drinks in when they heard, "I know y'all didn't get the party started without me!" Jordyn stood at the edge of the pool, already in her swimsuit. She must have gone to the room and got herself settled in.

Yasmine was so excited to see her friend that she almost submerged her entire body in the water when she jumped off the stool to run and hug her.

"Jordyn, I've missed you so much," she said, hugging her friend tightly.

"I missed you, too." The ladies hugged for what seemed like an eternity. It wasn't until a wet finger tapped Yasmine's shoulder for them to notice Brianna and Amari also had come out of the pool.

"Nice to meet you, Jordyn. My name is Brianna," she said while reaching out to hug her. Jordyn gave her a peculiar look, deciding only to extend her hand out in return.

"Nice to meet you, Brianna. Looking forward to getting to know you," Jordyn responded dryly, which annoyed Yasmine. It wasn't completely unlike what her friends expected from her, but it was unnecessary, especially during an introduction. Yasmine also couldn't be a hypocrite because she technically did the same thing when she met Brianna, but seeing someone else doing it made her cringe.

Mental note: Be more friendly when meeting new people.

With everyone together, the ladies lounged on their pool chairs. They grabbed a drink from the bar for Jordyn, then laid out to sunbathe and catch up. With the sun shining even brighter than when they first landed, everyone's melanin would be perfectly sun kissed in no time.

Jordyn started venting. "Y'all, my flight was a mess. I left my kids, only to be surrounded by screaming ones on the way here. I am glad we're at an adults-only resort."

"Yes, girl, the only way to vacation," said Yasmine, reaching her cup out to take cheers with everyone.

Amari interjected. "And that driver, Delroy?! He was a snack and a half. Great eye candy."

"Sure was. We gotta find out if he's single," Brianna mentioned.

"Speaking of that, is anyone here single? We need to know all of the tea as we start this vacation." Jordyn dived right in. No need for small talk, huh?

Brianna quickly chimed in. "Me and Yasmine are. I've heard you're married. Amari, how about you?" Yasmine shuddered, knowing Brianna speaking for almost everyone would rub her the wrong way.

"Girl, now you know I'm single. Mingling, yes, but still in these streets," responded Amari with a side-eye.

"I'm not sure if anything changed since the last time I saw you, it's been a while!" Brianna responded.

Jordyn's defensive body language, even with her sunglasses on, made her annoyance clear to anyone paying attention. Yasmine decided to pull her to the side because this was not the way to start a trip.

"Jordyn, let's go grab some more drinks so you can catch up to us!"

"Yasss, that's what I'm talking about." Jordyn got up to put her coverup and slippers back on. Her friend looked amazing for having two kids, but she always had a great physique. She stood at 5'4" with caramel skin and hazel eyes. She had the biggest curly hair and a smile so beautiful that the strongest person felt inclined to do anything she asked. After all these years, her magic didn't seem to fade one bit.

"Do y'all need anything while we're over there?" Jordyn asked the group.

"We're good for now! After the amount we have drank already, I'm gonna pace myself, especially if y'all want me to last through tonight," Amari responded.

"Very understandable. Take a nap if you need to, sis. I took one on the flight."

Feeling familiar yet distant, Yasmine and Jordyn held hands while they walked over to the bar, just as they always did since second grade.

"I am so happy to see you, Jordy."

"Me too, Yas."

The ladies ordered their drinks and shots to help Jordyn catch up. They sat at the bar for a few before Yasmine decided to express what was on her mind.

"Listen. I know you don't know Brianna very well, but can you please do your best and play nice to make sure she feels comfortable?"

"What did I do? I've been talking to the girl," Jordyn responded with an eye roll.

"Babe, from your initial interaction to a few minutes before I suggested we get drinks to your overall body language, it isn't very welcoming. I'm not trying to bicker; I want everyone to have a good time this week."

Jordyn sighed before responding. "I will do my very best. You know it takes me a while to get comfortable with people. I've been gracious with her taking my place as your roommate for the week. Cut me some slack, Yas."

Yasmine grabbed her friend's hand and placed it on her lap. "I know, and I appreciate you for trying. If the shoe were on the other foot, I would do the same for you."

Mid-conversation, she glanced at Brianna and Amari to see if they were ok. It looked like they might have fallen asleep, reclined in their seats with sunglasses on, but it was hard to tell.

"I love that we did this. I needed this. We needed this," Jordyn said with tears welling in her eyes. She seemed visibly lighter or drunker by the time they headed back to where their friends were.

"What y'all over here talking about?" Yasmine asked as they re-joined their friends, who were not taking naps after all.

"Oh nothing, Yas. We were over here talking about how we would love to see some eye candy on this resort while we're here," Amari explained.

"Now *that* is something I think we can all agree on. I love my husband with all of my heart, but I can most definitely use my eyes to admire a fine specimen or two," Jordyn said, high fiving Yasmine. Everyone laughed in unison.

This was the side of her friend she knew and loved. They stayed by the pool and chatted until it was nearly six in the evening, when it was time to get ready for dinner.

"Y'all, I think we should head back to the rooms to start getting dressed for dinner. I am so hungry right now," Amari mentioned, standing up to put her shorts back on.

"What's the plan for the night?" Brianna inquired.

"There's a few restaurants we can try, but since we didn't make any reservations, tonight will be the buffet then we can make a reservation for another day while we're here," Yasmine explained.

"Yes, sounds like a plan. This mama likes her sleep, so—"

Before Jordyn could finish her sentence, Yasmine cut her off.

"AHT AHT, there's no sleep tonight. We're catching up, bonding over some games, and drinking. Maybe you can get some sleep after those activities."

"We'll see about that, Yas," Jordyn playfully responded.

13. Dress To Impress
Yasmine

SOMETHING about the first night of a vacation enticed people to want to dress their best, as a metaphorical precursor for the rest of the fun to ensue during their time. While Brianna showered, Yasmine took the opportunity to have more one-on-one time with Jordyn.

"Let me show you some new pictures of the kids," said Jordyn, pulling out her phone and scrolling through endless photos.

"They look so big now!" Yasmine exclaimed.

"Girl, don't I know it?! It feels like they were just babies. They surprise me every day with how smart and independent they're becoming," Jordyn echoed in a teary-eyed response. A softness always took over her spirit when she spoke about her children. Yasmine loved seeing that side of her friend.

They were still catching up when Amari came out to signal Jordyn's time to head into the shower. Time was swiftly passing by and they didn't know exactly what to expect at the buffet for dinner.

Having the more relaxed style, Amari wore a green ombré two-piece pant set with some white Air Force 1s. Somehow she could make the most simple of outfits look stylish. She put her beautiful locs in a low ponytail.

"Damn girl, you look good," Yasmine said to Brianna as she walked back into their room to get ready. Brianna had on a hot pink bodycon midi dress, with orange heels to match. Standing at a mere 5'0," caramel-skinned with her sleek bob, Brianna always stood out in a room. If not for her looks, it was for the confidence she exuded when in her presence.

Brianna was always so busy with work or travel, working out was never on her agenda. Good thing for her was she looked like she never missed a day at the gym.

"It's from gymnastics taking over my life until I graduated college. Blame my parents," Brianna always said.

Yasmine, on the other hand, worked out five times a week to maintain her ever-changing figure. She also looked great, but if she looked like her friend did, she likely wouldn't work out either. But health was wealth, as they said. Whoever *they* were.

While Yasmine showered, Brianna left the room briefly to take photos. She walked back in to put the final touches on her makeup.

She paused before saying, "Yasmine. I know Jordyn is your friend, but I hope she can change her energy from what I was met with earlier at the pool. I hope she doesn't plan to be unapproachable the entire week. We all came here to have a good time."

Proud of her proactivity from earlier in the day, Yasmine explained. "I mentioned this to you prior to the trip, but she can be standoffish at first with new people. Seems that aspect of her hasn't fully changed like we hoped. She's really nice once you get to know her though, I promise. Give her a chance. As you know, I was the same when we first met. Look at how far we've come from there."

"You're right. When I first met you, I would not have imagined how close we would become. And you're one of the sweetest people I know and I can't picture my life without you in it at this point. I'll give it a chance," Brianna responded before they walked out to meet up with the rest of their friends.

"Ok, Yas, I see you," Amari said, standing up to spin her in a circle. Brianna clapped in agreement with her comments.

Friendship Fragments

If there was ever a dip in one of the friends' confidence, Amari constantly reminded everyone of their beauty. Yasmine missed this about her friend. It didn't have the same effect with them living on different sides of the country.

Yasmine wore a backless apricot jumpsuit to complement her rich chocolate skin. It was from an up-and-coming brand she found on Instagram named KAPHILL. If the clothes weren't already show-stoppers, the designer's messaging to "take up space" and "stand in your truth" sold her even more. She was happy to finally wear a few of the pieces on the trip.

She stood at 5'7" with legs and curves for days and was not afraid to show them. The gym was working because as she put her knotless braids into a top knot, the reflection in the mirror showed definition in her back, exactly where she wanted it.

"Alright, sorry for the wait y'all. Jordyn, are you almost ready?" Yasmine asked, knocking on her bedroom door.

Opening the door to join them, she responded, "Why yes, yes I am." She bowed as she joined the ladies, making them laugh.

Jordyn walked out in a form-fitting pale orange maxi dress with matching sandals. Hot mama did not come to play tonight.

She took a closer look at Yasmine's outfit before confirming.

"Well would you look at that? The telepathy still works, huh."

"It sure does," laughed Yasmine. Them wearing the same color was always funny. This would happen a lot during their college years. They would get dressed separately for an event then still end up wearing the same color or type of outfit.

"Does anyone want pictures before we head out?" Brianna asked, interrupting Yasmine's thoughts. If anyone needed photos taken throughout the trip, she would be the girl for it. Brianna loved to capture a moment.

"I would love that, but right about now, I would love food even more. Let's take some after dinner," Amari vocalized. Her thinning patience was more than reasonable since she had the longest travel and was the first to be ready for the night.

"Very fair. We can do that. What are we doing after, anyway?" Brianna questioned.

"We said we'd drink and play some games. Definitely catch up and also get to know you some more, Brianna," Jordyn chimed in.

"Sounds like the perfect evening to me. Shots for the road?" Yasmine asked that question rhetorically because she started handing them out before anyone could respond. The friends took their shots and headed to the buffet to eat.

The buffet was buzzing with people and every cuisine possible. There were American, Italian, Asian, Seafood, Vegetarian and of course, Jamaican dishes to choose from. It was the perfect balance between a visitor's comfort zone and new options to try. It also represented the various types of restaurants they could experience on the resort, which gave the ladies an idea of where they might want to go to explore more throughout their stay.

While everyone was still eating dinner, Yasmine deliberately finished early and mentioned needing to go to the bathroom. When the ladies asked if she wanted them to join, she said she'd be fine.

What she really wanted to do was sneak back to the suite and lay out the welcome bags she put together for everyone. She decided to put them all on the table in the common room to be the first thing they noticed when returning to the room to end the night. She worked as fast as she could to not be suspicious.

When she got back to the restaurant, the ladies didn't seem to realize how long she was away, fully engaged in their own conversation.

"Girl, what took you so long?!" Jordyn asked before Yasmine could even sit back down. *Welp, that theory was quickly debunked.*

"Yea and why do you seem out of breath?" Amari asked, suspicion filling her squinted eyes.

"Chile, I started talking to some other guests for a while and then I went to the bathroom in our suite. My bad. What'd I miss?" she responded, hoping her argument seemed convincing.

Brianna chimed in. "Well, I just found out Jordyn dated one of my cousins back in high school!"

"Unh unh, which high school bae is this? I know it ain't who I think it is." Yasmine turned to face Jordyn, both with eagerness for her answer but also happy with her friends opening up to each other.

"Mhm girl, she's Terrance's cousin. We randomly started talking about high school and when his name came up, we realized they were related," Jordyn said matter-of-factly.

"What a small world," Yasmine replied before telling Brianna, "No offense, but he's not my fave person at all, but Jordyn is happily moved on so the past is in the past."

"No offense taken, he is the family fuckboy and it hasn't changed in all of these years. He's still as much of a mess as y'all might remember him to be. Good luck to that man," responded Brianna. At least she wasn't aloof to his behavior.

Jordyn followed up, "Speaking of fuckboys, yours was in college, Yasmine. Well, he was really moreso one afterward. Xavier. I wonder how he is. Have you spoken to him?" The sound of his name made both the hairs on Yasmine's arm raise and chest to tense up simultaneously. She tried her best to maintain her composure, despite her increased heart rate and the trickle of sweat betraying her as it trailed down her back.

Her fear of him coming up on this trip was coming true. She didn't want him to be the topic of discussion at all, especially with the way things had been recently left with them.

"Yea. I saw online where he moved back to New York to take care of his mom," Yasmine explained, trying not to give too much away.

"Well, that's sweet, he always spoke highly of his mom. It's been so long since you two broke up. I hope he's doing well," said Amari.

Everyone looked at Jordyn after she almost choked on her drink.

"Hmm well, that's nice. I don't. I'm not even sure why Yasmine still knows what is going on in his life after everything he put her through," Jordyn remarked.

Yasmine grabbed her drink to detract from the anxiousness she was engulfed with. She felt guilty but couldn't let her friends know anything until she was sure of the direction they were going. Whatever direction it might be.

Sensing her friend's discomfort next to her, Brianna stepped in.

"Alright y'all. Enough about these men. Let's get this party started, it's our first night in paradise."

Yasmine squeezed her friend's hand under the table, a silent thank you for diffusing the awkward moment.

Dodged that bullet.

14. First Night In
Jordyn

JORDYN DELIBERATELY CHOSE to be quiet on their walk back to the suite. It took everything inside of her not to blow up Yasmine's spot at the dinner table. The conversation at dinner was the perfect segue for her to finally be honest about what was going on in her life, yet she chose to continue being deceitful. While she probably was partially telling the truth, partial wasn't good enough. Omitting information still equated to lying and Jordyn did not like it one bit.

"Jordyn, you good?" Amari asked as they were about to enter the door.

Forcing a smile, she responded, "Yea I am. Feeling a little tired." *Tired of being lied to.*

Jordyn wanted to make a conscious decision to enjoy herself, but how could she when the one person she thought would never lie to her suddenly was?

"Well, it's time to turn up so wake that ass up," said Yasmine, seemingly oblivious to her friend's dismay. Her and Brianna were dancing as they moved closer to their suite. As Amari opened the door, Yasmine took a suspicious step back, letting the rest of the ladies in before her.

"Ooooh my Goooood, Yas, this was your little "bathroom break," huh?" Amari asked, air quoting in her friend's direction.

They were able to identify their bags by the names printed on them, each with differentiating colors. Wide-eyed and amazed, the ladies squealed with excitement. All except Jordyn.

Fake it for the sake of a good night, Jordyn thought to herself.

As the ladies perused through the inside of their bags, Yasmine announced, "I wanted to make our trip even more special, and I thought these welcome bags would be the perfect touch. You can choose to bring the bag itself to the beach, but there are also goodies inside we could use to help us throughout the trip."

"Yasmine, this is incredibly thoughtful and kind," noted Brianna, gently nudging her arm. It took everything inside of Jordyn not to roll her eyes. The dramatics were pissing her off.

"Definitely, you didn't have to do all of this. But we appreciate the gesture," said Amari.

Jordyn was actively trying to find kind words to say when Brianna continued. "I was wondering why you were being awkward earlier when I was trying to help you with your bag in the airport."

"Yea, I didn't want you to see anything and get suspicious. Sorry about that," Yasmine replied.

"No worries at all."

Finally finding some words, Jordyn said, "Yasmine, this is nice. Thank you."

"You sure, Jordyn? You don't seem so happy," Yasmine rebutted.

"I'm fine. Let's not do this, Yasmine," Jordyn retorted.

"Ok, well since everyone is happy, I'm happy y'all like them. Now enough sappy stuff, shall we make the most of our first night here?" Yasmine asked, acting innocent like she wasn't trying to start an argument.

"Yasss," Brianna replied.

Yasmine walked toward another bag tucked in the corner of the lounge while the rest of the ladies made themselves comfortable on the sofa. Jordyn sat in the furthest corner so she didn't have to be next to Yasmine.

"Games, anyone?" Yasmine asked, holding up "We're Not Really Strangers" as an option.

"Can we save games for another day we're here? I'm not sure I have that type of energy tonight," said Amari.

"I feel the same, actually," Jordyn confirmed.

"That's understandable, want to find a movie to watch instead until we're all ready to sleep?" Yasmine proposed.

"Sure, let's do it," Brianna responded.

They endlessly scrolled through Netflix on Yasmine's iPad before they decided to AirPlay *Two Can Play That Game* to the suite's television. They laughed at the early 2000s classic, connecting on the fact that the teenage versions of themselves thought it was the perfect rubric to securing the love of their life.

"I re-watched this right before Wynters so I wouldn't get caught up out here," Yasmine admitted.

"Only for us both to get cuffed up without the playbook first semester," Jordyn reminded her.

"Yea y'all were married in college. I, on the other hand, had quite the time," Amari said.

"Oh we know. Amari had people wanting to fight each other on campus for her love," Jordyn stated, playfully tapping on her friend's arm.

"You think you're me, huh? Because same!" Brianna declared, high fiving Amari.

"I got locked down quickly in college, I really haven't been able to explore. I envy that," Jordyn admitted. While she loved her husband dearly, she often wondered if she jumped into things too quickly. Maybe she didn't give herself enough time to experience more things before committing to Malik and starting a family.

Everyone had their own journey to take in life of course. People often mentioned wanting the "picture perfect" life she had. But whenever she heard stories about how much other people had explored in their lives, she sometimes wished she had the opportunity to take a walk in their shoes. Funny how that all worked.

Brianna replied, "Listen. We all have our own paths in life. No judgment on either end. But if you ever want a tip or trick on how to bounce on some dick, I may be able to help." The room erupted with laughter before they continued watching the film. She might have been trying to take her place, but Jordyn had to admit—even if only to herself—the girl was funny.

As the night went on, Jordyn watched as Brianna leaned a tired head on Yasmine, furthering her discovery of just how close their bond had grown. She wondered if Brianna knew about Xavier. That would be a problem.

Everyone began dozing off before Amari said, "Alright, I love y'all, but today has drained us. Tomorrow is a new day and we'll have more energy after a good night of sleep."

"Honestly, you're right. Let me pull out this itinerary to see what we're doing tomorrow," Jordyn responded. Yes, she was tired. But she also needed some time to herself to figure out how to approach the situation with Yasmine. To her knowledge, they had never kept secrets from one another, but maybe they did?

"Yea, what's the plan for tomorrow?" Brianna asked.

"Since we all arrived today, tomorrow morning and afternoon are open. If we wanted to go to one of the local clubs at night though, we can. Up to y'all. The itinerary is a guide, but we can do whatever we want," Yasmine announced.

"Sounds like a plan. Let's see what tomorrow brings us," Jordyn responded, walking toward her and Amari's room.

"Alright y'all, goodnight. Also, don't wait for me in the morning. Feel free to grab breakfast and I'll join y'all when I get up," Amari mentioned. It was no surprise since she was a late riser. When they lived together in college, she liked to wake up and do her own thing, whether that was sleeping in or doing some writing. Jordyn was also a late riser herself before motherhood changed it all for her.

Friendship Fragments

Before drifting off to sleep, she gave Malik a play by play of her day, including the Xavier lies. He reminded her to prioritize herself during the time away. He was right. She deserved the time off, away from her responsibilities at home. The drama would have to sit on the backburner. For now. Time to have fun.

Day 2: Getting [Re]Acquainted

15. Morning Bickers
Yasmine

IT NEVER MATTERED where in the world she was or what time she went to bed the night before, Yasmine always awakened with the rise of the sun, ready to face whatever the day would offer her. It was the first full day on vacation, after all.

She glanced over at Brianna, still fast asleep and opted not to disturb her. Instead, she showered and put on a simple maxi dress before sitting on their balcony. The morning crispness, coupled with the calmness of the ocean dancing with the sand, made her feel a sense of calm she was missing back at home. Between her job and the drama with Xavier, her mind could never find a moment to be still and not think about anything else. The endless amount of open tabs in her mind felt clear. For once.

The sounds of movement behind her interrupted her calmness, but she was happy to see Jordyn and Brianna chatting in the common area.

"Well, good morning, ladies!" she exclaimed as she walked back in to join her friends. They smiled and echoed their good mornings in response.

"So, we're going to eat and then come back to get dressed for the pool, right?" Yasmine inquired with more of a statement than a question.

"Yes, girl! I also have to come back and check in on my babies. I already miss them so much," Jordyn admitted.

"How old are they?" Brianna asked, attempting to bond with Jordyn as they walked out of the suite.

"My oldest son, Malik Jr., is seven and my daughter, Amina, is four. They really are the best thing that filled up my itty-bitty world." Tears welled in Jordyn's eyes at the thought of them.

"She really does have the best kids. And I'm not only saying this because they're my godchildren," Yasmine responded with a wink, leading Jordyn to squeeze her hand.

"That's beautiful. Looking forward to having my own family one day," Brianna declared.

"Some days are better than others but as long as you lead with love, it will be worth it," Jordyn said.

While they walked to get breakfast, Yasmine chose not to interrupt her friends as they continued to get to know one another. It was a short journey between the rooms and the main hotel area, where the dining hall was located. She shifted her attention to the beautiful blue skies and warm Caribbean breeze surrounding them.

* * *

The buffet was just as impressive for breakfast as it was for dinner the night before. From omelet and waffle stations to the traditional Jamaican cuisine of ackee and saltfish, porridge, and fried dumplings, the options for food were limitless and the women were in heaven.

The ladies enjoyed their early morning breakfast, and were about to leave when they saw Amari walking toward them with a plate, not noticing when she walked in.

"Good morning! Did y'all enjoy your breakfast?" Amari asked, sitting down to join her friends. Something about her energy seemed more sullen than the night before. Maybe she was still tired?

"It was good, but I definitely need to be patient and wait on the omelet station line tomorrow because these scrambled eggs are not my favorite," Brianna noted while showing the table her watery eggs. "Everything else was good, though."

"Agreed! And the traditional Jamaican breakfast was good, too. Can't go wrong with ackee and saltfish. It is most definitely better than what we have in Brooklyn," Yasmine said.

"Ooh, I'll have to try it tomorrow. I haven't had it in such a long time. Atlanta has Caribbean food, but it doesn't begin to compare to what we have in New York," Jordyn expressed.

The waitress came over and started clearing the plates off the table before checking in with Amari. "Anything I can help you with? Coffee? Hot water for tea?"

"May I have hot water and a peppermint tea bag?" Amari requested before continuing to enjoy her meal. "By the way, I'll meet y'all at the pool. I already put on my swimsuit. I can see y'all need to head back to the suite first."

"We sure do. Let's hurry and get ready so we can find a good spot for us all to sit at," Yasmine suggested, as she began to stand up. Jordyn and Brianna followed suit.

They walked by the pool area and saw it was beginning to fill with other guests ready to soak up the sun, signaling their sense of urgency to get ready quickly if they wanted seats together for the group.

* * *

"How do I look in this?" Jordyn asked, entering Yasmine and Brianna's room.

Yasmine grabbed her friend's hand and affirmed her. "You look beautiful, Jordy. Do you think something looks wrong?"

"I don't know. I could be in my head. It's my first real vacation since having the kids. I'm still getting used to this new body." Jordyn's eyes slowly looked down at her body with disappointment.

While Jordyn definitely didn't look exactly as she did in college, she still looked great. She had lost a significant amount of weight since the last time Yasmine saw her in person around two years ago. She was a bit thicker than college days, but it was in all of the right places. Who was still their college weight over ten years later anyway?

"As someone who never met you before yesterday, I have to agree. You look great. I wouldn't know you had kids if you didn't mention it," Brianna said, giving Jordyn additional words of affirmation.

Jordyn smiled at her with appreciation. Before she could say anything in response, Amari opened the door, double fisting a mixed drink in her hand.

"Damn, why couldn't you bring us drinks, too? Or even ask if we wanted something," Jordyn hissed. Yasmine squirmed at her sharp remark.

"I didn't know y'all weren't at the pool yet and only came back for sunglasses. Feel free to go to one of the several bars around here and get some for yourself if it's that big of a deal to you, Jordyn," Amari snapped back, annoyed by her statement.

"Amari, all of that attitude is unnecessary. But OK," Jordyn responded, storming out to the balcony while Amari went into their room.

Amari was not usually the type to feed into the dramatics of the friend group, but this time she did. Yasmine wasn't sure how to navigate her out-of-character situation, but knew she needed to check on both of her friends.

She knocked on Amari's door before peeking in. "Are you good?"

"I'm fine, but Jordyn can be annoying sometimes. It's bad enough we're rooming together with her messiness," replied Amari, pointing out the mess that was taking over their room. "Then she made so much noise when y'all were getting ready to head out. My first day of vacation is not starting out on the best note."

From living together in college, Yasmine was well versed in Jordyn's lack of organization. It became one of their points of contention and led them to live apart briefly during their sophomore year.

By the looks of the clothes and toiletries scattered in front of her, some things hadn't changed, which was a valid reason for Amari's annoyance.

"I understand your frustration. I'm not used to you reacting in that way. I'm here if you need to talk," Yasmine responded, heading to the door.

"I'll be fine, Yas. Just give me a moment."

"No problem. Take your time."

Jordyn was staring out at the ocean when Yasmine interrupted her on the balcony. "Hey Jordyn. I'm checking in."

"I don't know what her deal was. Obviously, I know there's several bars here. I only asked why she didn't ask us if we wanted a drink. It wasn't that serious."

"It wasn't that serious to you, but we also told her we would meet her by the pool. Maybe she didn't expect us to still be in the room. It seems like a misunderstanding that we can move past, though. What do you think?"

"I think her statement was unnecessary. We just got here; I don't have time for the antics. I was trying to have a good day." Jordyn shut down and was beyond the point of listening, but Yasmine refused to let their first full day on vacation start like this.

"She probably felt the exact same about yours. From the outside looking in, it could have been *how* you said it versus the actual words you used."

"Whatever, Yasmine. You would say that."

"What exactly do you mean by that, Jordyn?"

"You defend everyone except me anyway, so I'll just be quiet."

"Ok. I don't know where all of this is coming from, but I want us all to have a good day. I'm going to gather everyone for drinks, then hopefully we can turn this day around. It's still early enough." The statement didn't lend itself to a response, nor did Yasmine want one. She turned to make her way back inside instead, where she saw

Amari and Brianna laughing. At least one of them was trying to shift their mood.

Yasmine grabbed the nearest bottle of alcohol and some shot glasses before joining Amari and Brianna's conversation. "What are y'all over here laughing about?" Despite introducing them to one another, Yasmine was ashamed to admit, even to herself, she felt a bit jealous of their closeness. Wasn't this what she wanted? People getting along on vacation?

"Girl, we're over here going over the time you introduced me to Amari and she got so drunk she started dancing with the homeless woman on the subway platform," Brianna chuckled.

"Listen, the woman had moves, ok?! Don't knock it until you try it," Amari responded.

"How could I forget, that day was so fun!" said Yasmine.

Amari came to New York last summer to visit family. There was no better time to visit the city. The weather was perfect for outdoor activities, people were out and about, and everyone was in a good mood. Yasmine knew Amari would be visiting, but it wasn't clear if she would be able to spend any time with her.

Amari texted her on Saturday to say her afternoon was free. She joined Yasmine and Brianna at brunch, which turned into bar hopping for more drinks into much later that night. It was the perfect impromptu summer night. Although meeting for the first time, Amari and Brianna hit it off immediately. For a brief moment, it reminded Yasmine of their college days with Jordyn. She imagined that she would have enjoyed herself as much as they did.

They all drank far more than they should have. While waiting on their train, there was a nearby drummer playing. In typical New York City fashion, the subway platform was filled with commuters and homeless people alike.

Amari, being the kind-hearted person she was, never let other people's circumstances affect how she interacted in the world. She saw a woman dancing near what looked like her belongings and went to grab her hands to dance with her. The entire station filled with applause and cheers as they danced until the train arrived.

That subway moment was a sharp contrast to the one Yasmine was exposed to at the start of the summer. She wasn't sure if the person was homeless, but she often wondered if there was someone in the stranger's life who could have changed their mind. To let them know their life mattered.

She immersed herself so deep in her memories, Amari asked, "Yasmine, are you good?"

"Yea, my bad. I hope we have as much fun on this trip like we did on that day."

"Of course we will, Yas. The day is still young!" exclaimed Brianna.

Yasmine affirmed. "Indeed it is. Let's make the most of it. Y'all ready for the pool?"

16. Poolside Confessions
Yasmine

THE POOL AREA was teeming with people by the time they arrived. The ease at which they found four pool loungers the previous day was proving to be more of a challenge with the weekend crowd arriving at the resort, especially after the morning bickering set them back a little bit. Yasmine, Amari, and Brianna finally found three chairs with an extra seat for Jordyn in case she decided to join them. She stayed back in the suite, despite Yasmine trying to convince her otherwise.

Brianna chose to sunbathe while Yasmine and Amari found an empty corner in the pool not taken over by other nearby guests.

"Same ole shit, right?" Amari smirked, taking a sip of her rum punch.

"It's so annoying. From her weird energy yesterday with Brianna to her attitude today, I wish she learned how to let things go after all these years."

"I totally get it. I can't believe she hasn't changed after all of this time. Then, the mess in the room this morning added insult to injury for me. It's hard for me to function in that level of chaos."

"She should know better. I don't want to keep pulling her to the side every second to ask her to fix her attitude."

"You shouldn't have to. What did she say when you spoke to her?"

"She was hung up on your response. I can agree you snapped a bit, but so did she. It all felt like a big misunderstanding."

"Yes, I admit I could've responded better. We all came on this vacation for some time away from our realities and any drama coming with that. I hope she can get it together for us all to have a good time. If I need to apologize to smooth things over, I will."

"That's a great idea. She also makes it seem like I'm such a horrible friend. She said I defend everyone else but her. After all of this time, she still creates these narratives in her head that we don't like her, but it couldn't be further from the truth. Explaining it over and over can become exhausting. The more I think about it, that's another reason why I've distanced myself from her over the past couple of years."

The revelation was something Yasmine never admitted aloud. She knew deep down that her friend's negative tendencies kept her away, but it also didn't change her feeling guilty for not being around as much. Jordyn was always stubborn and it never felt like Yasmine could express her frustrations without it turning into an argument or be blown out of proportion.

"You and I both know how much you've gone to bat for her when she's rubbed people the wrong way. And don't feel bad about the distance, you're not alone. We have so many days left on this trip. On one hand I'm like, 'Ah this is why I stay away' and then on the other, it's like I miss y'all so much. We should be savoring every moment together."

Since Amari usually kept her feelings close to the vest, Yasmine never realized they shared similar feelings about Jordyn. Did she also like being at a distance from Yasmine? Maybe time would tell. Or maybe she should outright ask? Not today, though.

"So, how's everything in LA? Your writing? Screenwriting?"

Yasmine asked, attempting to shift gears from her mind starting to spin.

"Well, the screenwriting itself has been great. I've been networking and getting to know more people in the industry, which has been great."

"That sounds like good news! Why do I sense some hesitation on your end?"

"Well, I am a little embarrassed to say I've been secretly messing around with a screenwriter I met at one of the networking conferences. It's very casual and not serious at all. He's been my mentor and is helping me get in contact with the right people. Things are good, but sometimes I question if I would get some of my opportunities if he wasn't around assisting me."

"There is nothing wrong with a little help. You don't need to feel guilty about that. When you're in the position you want to be career-wise, you can also pay it forward to someone else. Does he make you feel that way or is it you?"

"Hmm, I'd have to say it's me. He seems happy to help, however I need him to."

"Amari, you have gotten this far in your career long before whoever this person is even came into the picture. You're a talented writer, and your success is not dependent on anyone else. Remember that."

Amari nodded, feeling grateful for her friend's support. "You're right, Yas. I just need to believe in myself more."

Yasmine smiled reassuringly. "Exactly, girl. You've got all the talent and determination you need. And if he's the right one for you, casual or not, he should never make you feel less than the amazing person you are."

Amari sighed, appearing lighter. "Thanks boo. You always know how to put things in perspective. But can you do me a favor? Please don't mention my situation with Lawrence to any of the other girls. I don't want to be judged."

"Oh, that's his name," she replied flatly while grabbing her friend's hand under the water. "Don't worry, I won't. Your love life is your business, and I've got your back. And it's a man this time around, too? You know I can't keep up with you, chile." The ladies laughed because as long as they've known each other, Amari could be dating a man or a woman when she was ready. Love had no gender for her.

"Yes, girl. He's cool. We'll see where it goes."

"Well, your secret is safe with me. Let's focus on having an amazing time here and making unforgettable memories with our girls."

The ladies were so deep in conversation, they didn't notice Brianna walking up to them. "What y'all over here talking about?"

"You know, the sun, clouds and amazing ambiance of this beautiful establishment," Amari jokingly responded, pointing out their surroundings.

"Ah ok. I'll just assume that's code for Jordyn." They laughed in unison, leaning into the light moment for a release.

"But seriously. We've been talking about a little bit of everything. Catching up after all this time," Yasmine explained.

"We've been over here for a while. Maybe we should head back to check on Jordyn and grab drinks," Amari suggested.

"She actually came to sit by me while you both were talking," said Brianna, pointing her chin in the direction of their loungers. Jordyn was on the phone, sipping a drink in her hand.

"Let's go join her then grab lunch. I might be due for a nap before tonight," said Yasmine, pressing her lips together in a fruitless attempt to mask the yawn trying to force its way out.

The ladies grabbed more drinks before sitting down near Jordyn. Amari said something inaudible to her before they both stepped away from the group.

"I'm so excited for a night out. I feel like we've had enough resort time now. We need to see what else the island has to offer," Brianna noted with a cute little shimmy dance.

"Yes! I texted Delroy earlier to pick us up by eleven to head to a nearby nightclub," Yasmine confirmed.

Friendship Fragments

"Woot woot, finally time to turn up tonight! I don't have another movie night on vacation in me," Brianna admitted.

Yasmine smirked. "I know, I know. I hope everyone is more energized from here on out. How are you feeling, Bri? I know this is the first time you're meeting Jordyn. Second time meeting Amari."

There was a contemplative pause before her response. "Well, there's no dull moments so far, I'll tell you that." They laughed.

"Yes! There were a couple of awkward moments, but you've been a team player so thank you for that."

"Anything for you, girl. You're my friend and it hasn't been excruciating. Who can complain on an island this beautiful?"

"This is very true."

Amari and Jordyn were laughing when they came back toward the group. They picked up small bites for lunch then went back to their suite. Yasmine and Jordyn opted for naps while Amari and Brianna stayed up. Amari went out on the balcony to do some work while Brianna stayed in to read.

Afternoon well spent.

17. Anything But Clothes
Yasmine

THE LIVELY DINNERTIME energy among the group far outshined the rocky start to the day. Everyone spent some time apart, recharging in their own way before coating their stomachs for the night ahead.

"That nap was everything. What's the vibe for tonight? Are we getting extra sexy?" Jordyn asked, eating her last bite of dinner.

Brianna chimed in jokingly. "I sure hope so. All I brought to wear is string in the daytime and mesh at night. It's giving anything but clothes."

"Oh my God, do you remember the 'Anything But Clothes' party our sophomore year," Jordyn teased, bumping Yasmine's elbow.

"Please don't remind me," Amari interjected.

"Don't remind YOU. Imagine my horror." Yasmine shuddered at one of her many embarrassing college moments. But who didn't have those?

The "Anything But Clothes" party was a themed event often on college campuses where attendees created and wore outfits using unconventional materials. Partygoers crafted attire out of items not typically associated with clothing such as: duct tape, garbage bags, newspaper, balloons, leaves, or food items like plastic wrap and aluminum foil.

During sophomore year, the girls decided to go for a caution tape meets TLC vibe. Yasmine gave Chili with her silk press and yellow headscarf to match her caution tape dress. Jordyn was T-Boz with her short cut at the time and Amari gave Left Eye with a yellow condom placed over her right eye. They were showered with so many compliments on how good they looked as a unit.

Yasmine became so drunk over the course of the night; she couldn't lift her dead weight off the sidewalk after she took a seat to stop the room from spinning. It took both Amari and Jordyn's strength to carry her into the car by her arms and legs. When they got her inside, she peed on herself then threw up. Her friends never let her live the horrible experience down, forever etched in all of their memories.

"HA. HA. HA," Yasmine responded dryly as they explained the story to Brianna. "Now y'all know that was embarrassing for me, but if I really think about it, we might be in need of a night exactly like that one. Without me being the butt of the joke this time, of course. Let's turn things up a notch."

"I agree. Time for more shots!" Brianna shouted as they exited the dining area, ready to have a good night.

* * *

As usual, Amari was the first to get ready. She let another thirty minutes go by before she became anxious about how behind the rest of her friends were. "Alright, it's ten thirty. Delroy will be here soon. We've got to speed up this getting ready process, beauty queens."

After a quick text to update Delroy on their tardiness, the ladies finally finished getting ready just before midnight. They walked out to meet him by the van where he held the door open for each of them to get in.

"Hi ladies, nice to finally see unnu again," he said kindly to the group.

There were water bottles waiting for them on the seats, similar to when they first arrived from the airport.

"How was di first day pon di island? Are yuh all enjoying yuhself so far?" he asked, gauging if the ladies liked their time so far.

Each of the ladies chimed in about their day, but also mentioned how excited they were to finally get off the resort. They continued pregaming in the car and vibed out to the music playing from the speakers.

The ride to the nightclub was less than twenty minutes away with light traffic. There was a small crowd outside, looking like a mixture of locals and tourists— young and old— ready to relish in the night.

Holding the door open and helping each lady out of the car, Delroy said, "This club is very nice. I will be nearby. Just text mi around fifteen minutes before so I can pick yuh all back up on time."

"Will do, Delroy," Yasmine confirmed.

Walking inside the club, light beams of green, gold, and red took over the dance floor, adding an energetic feel to the environment. The rhythmic beats of dancehall music were led by a DJ at the back center of the room, skillfully blending each track and "riddim" for the partygoers to enjoy. The club was engulfed with the sights of smoke, which by the smell of it, was most definitely due to the island's notorious ganja.

While the crowd inside was a bit larger than the one near the entrance, it was still quite empty with the occasional sprinkle of partygoers in different corners of the room. They had enough time to settle in with a drink or two before it got packed. *Shot o'clock!*

Yasmine could tell when Jordyn started feeling her alcohol by the way she let loose, grabbing her hand to head to the dance floor. Soon after, Amari and Brianna joined in, creating their own dance circle where everyone showed off their moves.

What was supposed to be a small moment between the friends

unintentionally created an even bigger circle with more partygoers joining in on the fun. It was clear when the locals started dancing because groups of men and women came together with synchronized dance moves, seemingly competing with the group before.

Amari wasn't one to dance much, but she was showing a different side, dancing with one of the groups in the center of the circle. She grabbed Brianna's rhythmless self to make her feel more comfortable on the dance floor.

Yasmine stepped back to watch in awe at her friends having a great time. A little drunkenness was all the ladies needed to reset and have a great night. Yasmine joined Jordyn at the bar to check in on her.

"How are you feeling?" Jordyn hadn't been out much since having the kids and she wanted to make sure she wasn't going over her limit.

"I'm good, why do you ask?"

"Do you think you should take a little break? Or are you good?"

"I'm fine, Yas. Let's have some fun," Jordyn said, grabbing Yasmine to dance again. Although she didn't want her friend to get too drunk, she liked this version of her far better than the one earlier in the day. She was letting her hair down, not sweating the small stuff.

They re-joined Amari and Brianna, dancing the night away before deciding it was finally time to head back to the resort.

"Delroy!" exclaimed Jordyn, running toward the van that was ready for them as soon as they exited the club. She embraced him as if he were Malik and not the driver they met a day prior.

"Jordyn." The warning in Yasmine's tone was all she needed to hear to straighten up.

"Sorry about that," Yasmine mumbled to him.

"I can tell yuh all had a good time. If yuh are enjoying di island, that makes mi happy."

"Are you allowed to come out with us one night?" Jordyn inquired.

"No, I am not. But mi will mek sure fi keep unnu safe and neva will be too far from wherever I drop yuh off," he responded, ensuring their safety when they are with him.

"Boring," Jordyn muttered, leading Yasmine to pinch her elbow. "Ouch, Yas."

"We understand, Delroy. Thank you for your help," responded Yasmine. As she turned to check on the rest of her friends, Brianna was peacefully sleeping on Amari's shoulder.

Delroy drove them back to the resort under the night's sky, the silhouette of palm trees swaying gently against a backdrop of twinkling stars and fireflies dancing in the darkness like magical lanterns, leading Yasmine into deep thought. The night was exactly what she pictured for the entire trip and she hoped the trend continued for the rest of their time together.

As they pulled back into the resort area, Delroy confirmed the following day's schedule. "I know it's late, but we still good fi Dunn's River tomorrow?"

"I know we originally said eight am, but is nine am ok instead?" Amari inquired.

"It's up to yuh all, but it can tek one-and-a-half to two hours fi get there. I recommend heading there early so yuh can climb the Falls before it gets too crowded," he responded.

"Why'd you ask that, Amari?" Yasmine questioned. They were doing this adventurous excursion because of her, after all.

Amari expounded. "Knowing how late it is already, I wanted to see if we could get more time to sleep. But since the ride is long, we can always sleep in the car, too."

"Definitely! When unnu wake up in di mawning, just mek mi know di plan," Delroy requested, wanting to know how they wanted to approach the next day's schedule.

Yasmine stated, "Will do! Thank you, Delroy."

The thank you's echoed from the group as they walked into the lobby to head to bed. They each showered off the night and set their alarms for the long day ahead.

Friendship Fragments

Waking up for her nightly four am bathroom break, Yasmine was surprised to find Brianna's bed empty nor was she in their bathroom. She thought she heard muffled sounds coming from outside their room and checked to make sure everything was ok. Stepping quietly out of their room, she realized the sounds were actually low whimpers coming from the cracked balcony door.

She was mortified to find Amari neck deep in between Brianna's legs on the balcony floor. With every upward neck roll from Amari, Brianna's eyes rolled behind her head, biting her lips in an attempt to stifle a louder moan. Yasmine stayed out of view as she watched her friends' bodies entangled in coital bliss with one another.

With her hands over her mouth, to not alert her presence, she tiptoed backward into her room, hoping everything she witnessed was a dream.

Deep in her own thoughts, she struggled to drift back to sleep. *Amari and Brianna?* Amari was always open sexually. She could be dating a man for three years then turn around and date a woman for two. But she didn't know about Brianna's sexual preferences outside of men. Could they be something? How did she miss this? Didn't Amari just mention someone she was dating? What in the hell was going on?

Brianna returned to their room an hour later, took a quick shower, and slipped back into the bed, not realizing Yasmine was wide awake.

Day 3: Confused & Amused

18. The Climb
Yasmine

YASMINE HAD no concept of when she fell asleep or what time it was, but when she awoke to the sounds of Brianna getting ready in the bathroom, she realized the sun was already up, betraying her normal morning routine.

She desperately wanted everything she saw to be a dream, but she vividly remembered what she witnessed mere hours before and felt conflicted on what to do. She didn't want to necessarily out Brianna since she never knew of her different sexual preferences. At the same time, could she go through this entire trip without mentioning anything about it to anyone?

It was far too early to have her head spinning like it was, especially with a hangover threatening to push its way forward. She grabbed her hangover powder from the nightstand and quickly downed it in order to enjoy the long day ahead.

"Yasmine, why are you still in bed? You're usually the first one up," Jordyn mentioned, entering their room.

"I know. I must have been really tired," Yasmine fibbed.

"You slept so peacefully next to me the entire night," Brianna said, nudging her friend. Yasmine smirked back, not wanting to give away any hints of her being up during her twilight rendezvous.

Running behind schedule and needing to separate herself from the lies, Yasmine forced her way out of bed to get ready for the day.

"Ok, let me get sleepyhead Amari up. She somehow found herself sleeping on the sofa last night," Jordyn announced. Yasmine glanced in Brianna's direction to gauge her body language, which was stoic, impressively not giving anything away.

"I'm up, I'm upppp," Amari groaned from the lounge area. She walked by and said, "Good morning," then went to her room to get herself together.

* * *

Yasmine, Jordyn, and Brianna wanted to grab some quick pastries for everyone to enjoy on their ride to the Falls since there was no time for a full breakfast.

"What's up with you, Yas? You're being a little weird this morning," Brianna expressed, breaking the awkward silence encapsulating their walk to the hotel café.

"I'm fine. I think I might have a hangover," Yasmine said, covering her true feelings.

With a suspicious glance in her direction, Jordyn responded, "Hmm ok. Well, I need you to get it together on the drive there so we all survive this climb." They knew each other like the back of their hands, but Yasmine was grateful she chose not to pry.

The ladies laughed as they proceeded to get croissants, bagels, and coffee for their journey. By the time they got done at the café, it was already time to leave, and Delroy was prompt as usual. They ate their quick bites in the van then fell asleep shortly thereafter.

The only person who stayed up was Yasmine, haunted by the thoughts of the night before. She distracted herself with the island's lush greenery with every twist and turn, feeling like she was looking at a beautiful painting versus actually being there. Wherever there was a landmark or Jamaican fun facts throughout their journey, Delroy gave more island history— from highways being built to landmarks such as Rose Hall Great House, Hip Strip and Runaway Bay. The culture was so rich, how could anyone not fall in love with it?

She wished her friends were awake to enjoy the experience with her, but also enjoyed the temporary silence, unsure of what the day ahead would entail. Jordyn was the first to wake up and checked in on her husband and the kids. Amari and Brianna remained asleep for most of the ride.

"Alright now, we deh close now." As the words escaped Delroy's mouth, the view became breathtaking. Behind the mountainous terrain, there was a breathtaking glimpse of the Falls along with beautiful cerulean waters against the coastline.

"Woah, we're climbing that?" Brianna inquired with barely open eyes, pointing in the direction of the one-hundred-and-eighty foot fall peeking through the trees.

The contrast of Amari's excitement was comical. "Yes, this will be so fun!"

Attempting to quell any fears, Delroy explained, "Don't fret, unnu will be safe. Yuh cyant come ah Jamaica and nuh climb di Falls. Also, unless yuh all have ways to protect dem, leave your personal belongings in here so dem nuh get wet. I'll keep them safe."

A tour guide was nearby scanning tickets when the friends exited the van to walk down the steps and start the Falls from the beginning. In the midst of the rainforest, they could see cascading clearwater sloping over smooth, terraced rocks that created a natural staircase extending from the top to the bottom of the Falls. It extended to the beach, creating a breathtaking view for their journey.

Preparing for their climb up from the bottom, the ladies held hands, helping each person climb the terraced limestone steps, attempting not to give way to the occasional slippery rock with each level they followed him up to.

"Whatever you do, don't look back," Yasmine repeated to herself as she made her way to the top with her friends. It was the first thing the tour guide mentioned, and it carried her through the climb. Although it was terrifying at times, the ladies pushed through. They used great communication and teamwork to get all the way to the top, holding each other's hands and taking the occasional picture along the way since Brianna was insistent on capturing the moment with her water-protected phone carrier.

Soaked with water from the climb, Brianna shifted her wig into its proper place. "Besides getting soaked and my hair sliding back to show my Meek Mill braids, that wasn't bad at all." Everyone laughed as they walked past the street vendors offering souvenirs and photos to remember their time.

They made their way back to the van to meet Delroy afterward, wanting only one thing more than dry clothes. Food.

"Unnu had fun, right?" Delroy asked.

"Yes, definitely glad we ended up coming early like you suggested, it's definitely getting more crowded now," Amari confirmed, pointing to the large groups of people going in the direction they left from.

"Yea mon. I wouldn't lead yuh wrong. Where to next?" he asked.

"Food please!" Jordyn yelled before anyone else could.

"Yuh all like jerk chicken?"

After a resounding yes from everyone in the car, Delroy made his way out of the tourist-filled area. He went toward a nearby streetside grill, where the ladies could grab some food for the journey back to the resort.

Jerk chicken was not just chicken with sauce on it. It was a representation of the culture and identity, embedded within the island's rich heritage. While many people used a marinade mimicking the effect of "jerking" the chicken, the traditional slow grilling process over pimento wood contributed to the unique flavor of the meal itself. Paired with the island's hard dough bread and some cabbage slaw, it was a perfect meal to encompass the culture.

The smoke of the grill greeted them far before they parked on the curb. Two men manned the large, black barreled grill with thick

accents, speaking Patois so fast that no one in the group could understand. Not even Amari. Thankfully, Delroy was there to help with
their order.

"It smells so good!" Yasmine exclaimed.

Each of them made their orders then re-entered the van to
enjoy their authentic Jamaican food. Even Delroy got himself a
plate. It was by far the best meal they ate since arriving on the
island.

"What's the plan for tonight? Because I am beat," Jordyn stated.

"I wanted a different option than the buffet we've gone to every
night so I made a reservation at the Hibachi restaurant. Everyone
doesn't have to come, though. I know it's been a long day," Yasmine
responded, not wanting to put pressure on anyone who didn't want to
join.

"Sounds fun. Let's see how we feel when we get back and settle
ourselves back in," Jordyn responded.

The ride back to the resort was quiet. The jerk chicken-itis sent
everyone straight back to sleep, Yasmine included. The ladies were
eager to get out of the damp clothing they had on since the climb
once they returned.

* * *

Yasmine noticed Amari by herself on the balcony while Jordyn and
Brianna showered, making it the perfect opportunity to talk to her
one-on-one before the others could come out and eavesdrop. Perhaps
it would be the only moment they would have to privately chat. She
hesitated to say anything when she noticed her friend typing on her
laptop.

Yasmine was welcomed with a warm smile and Amari gestured
for her to sit, tapping on the seat near her. She closed her laptop,
turning to give her undivided attention.

"Am I interrupting you?" asked Yasmine.

"Not really. I do need to get some writing done because I'm

behind on some deadlines, but I have a bit of writer's block. I'll try again later, though. How are you feeling, Yas?"

"I'm good. Today was a good day, everyone was getting along. It was nice..." Second thoughts suddenly attempted to push forward in her mind, but faking the funk would be even harder. She needed to talk to someone.

"Agreed. Hoping it sticks through the night," Amari responded with a skeptical look cast across her face.

"I hope so, too..." Yasmine's voice trailed off as she finally addressed her friend. "Ok. Amari, I have something to ask you and I hope you'll be open to having this conversation."

"Sure. What's going on?" Amari's body language shifted slightly, bracing for the next words to come out of Yasmine's mouth.

Yasmine wanted to have the right approach to this discussion, knowing how avoidant her friend could be with conflict.

"Last night, I woke up in the middle of the night to pee—"

Before Yasmine continued, Amari's eyes widened with the realization of where she was going with the story.

"...I saw you and Brianna," Yasmine began babbling. "Obviously, I love you and support how you live your life. Seeing you both in such a compromising position was a shock, to say the least. With both of you being my friends, I just wish one of you told me what was going on..."

"Yasmine, it's not my place to share something Brianna hasn't shared with you herself. Yes, after we met for the first time, there was a spark. We flirted here and there. What you saw last night was the first time we ever acted on it—drunkenly. But that's all I am willing to say since it is not my story to share."

Yasmine was annoyed, but deep down she understood where she was coming from. As much as she wanted Amari to give her more information, she would have to wait until Brianna was ready to share. If that ever were to happen.

"I understand," was all Yasmine could respond before Jordyn yelled out from the common area.

"Amari, the shower is open!"

As Amari got up, she pleaded. "I am so sorry you found out that way. A little embarrassed, too, if I'm being honest. I'm not sure if you have shared this with Jordyn or anyone else, but if you haven't, I hope you can understand why this wouldn't be your information to spread."

With a nod, Amari squeezed her friend's shoulder and left the balcony. Yasmine stayed in place for a little before heading to her room for her own shower. She wanted to ask more. What about this Lawrence person in LA? Did she see a future with Brianna? Was it casual for the both of them? Would one of them break the other's heart?

She struggled to find resolve knowing her questions would not be answered in that moment, perhaps never at all.

19. Late Night Distractions
Yasmine

FEELING REFRESHED with enough napping after their daytime activities, everyone opted in to experience their first sit-down dinner on the resort. Yasmine kept replaying her conversation with Amari over and over in her head, understanding the hesitation, but wishing she would have opened up more even if only to express a crush on Brianna.

Brianna, on the other hand, always seemed like an open book prior to this situation. Yasmine was taken aback by her not feeling comfortable enough to share her feelings. At the same time, she understood the nuances of sexuality and how judgment often accompanied it.

Yasmine wished her friends knew her well enough to realize she wouldn't cast any judgment on either of them. Could she approach Brianna without making it seem like an attack? Should she take Amari's advice and leave it alone? She held onto hope that Brianna would open up to her, even if it happened after the trip.

On top of everything else, this was yet another secret being held within the group. Friendship was beautiful, but the truth of the matter was, sometimes there wasn't a comfort level to share every deepest, darkest secret. Not with every person, anyway. From the fear of judgment to not being sure how different life experiences would be received, the secrets on the trip were starting to feel like a cobweb Yasmine couldn't untangle herself from.

"Yasmine, you good?" Brianna asked, snapping her back to reality like a rubberband. She had a genuine look of concern when Yasmine's eyes met hers, walking a few paces ahead.

"I'm good. Why do you ask?"

Jordyn chimed in, "Well, we just asked you a question and you didn't answer. But also, you've been more quiet than usual today. What's up with you?" Amari shot a knowing glance in Yasmine's direction, eyes urging her to not share what she knew was on her mind.

Taken aback she missed the conversations right in front of her, she deflected. "Ugh sorry. I was randomly thinking about the promotion I told you guys I didn't get back at work. I need to figure that out. But let me be fully present here. What was the question?"

"It was about the group of fine men we just walked past. Finally some eye candy on this resort," she responded. "We were also trying to see if you liked the handsome one staring you down."

Yasmine turned around to see if she could catch a glimpse, but it was a little too late. All she could see were four shadowed figures heading in the opposite direction, but nothing else. "Damn, I have to pay more attention when I'm walking."

"You need to be more present overall, sis. Do we need to get you some more alcohol or something? Loosen up!" Brianna yelled.

Yasmine conceded, "I'm good. Promise."

Everyone continued laughing and joking around as they approached the Island Breeze Grill & Tiki Lounge, which was nestled in a more secluded part of the resort. The ladies hoped it lived up to the rave reviews they overheard from other guests.

Stepping inside, they were transported to an alternative yet captivating world where the island vibes met the artistry of Japanese cuisine. Bamboo furniture, tiki torches, and island-inspired artwork blended harmoniously with traditional Japanese elements. Large, open windows allowed the gentle Caribbean breeze to flow through the dining area, creating the perfect atmosphere for their evening out. The restaurant buzzed with the sounds of steel pans playing soothing reggae melodies, setting the mood for an amazing dining experience.

The waitress walked over to provide recommendations for food and drink choices. The cocktail menu featured clever concoctions, fusing both Jamaican and Asian cultures. The popular drink they offered was the Sunrise Sake, which contained Jamaican rum and sake with a ginger liqueur and fresh pineapple juice. The ladies all chose it as their first drink after hearing it was the most popular drink on the menu.

"I almost considered staying in tonight, but I'm so happy I didn't. This is quite the experience," Jordyn mentioned.

"I know, right. It really is gorgeous here, too," Yasmine confirmed.

"I can't wait to taste what the food is like. I feel like nothing can top the jerk chicken from earlier, though," Amari challenged. Everyone nodded their heads in agreement, the memory of its deliciousness still fresh on their tongues from the afternoon.

In typical hibachi form, the talented chefs prepared each dish with a flair for entertainment as they performed teppanyaki cooking at the table. The aroma of grilling ingredients and the signature Caribbean and Japanese spices infused the air with its mouthwatering aroma.

The ladies finished their dinner and drinks when Amari mentioned, "Ok. So tomorrow is the boat day, y'all. You know the girls love a boat situation."

"It's us, the girls," Yasmine chimed in, sharing a lighter moment with Amari than their intense conversation earlier in the evening.

"Yes. For me personally, I'm behind on some of my writing deadlines and plan to tackle that after dinner. But feel free to do y'all own thing tonight."

"Booooo," said Yasmine with a thumbs down.

"I am going to head back in too because I want to check in back at home, but also get some rest. I don't get much time to myself at home. Need to enjoy it while I can," said Jordyn.

"Well damn, does anyone wanna stay out a bit tonight?" asked Brianna, not bothering to hide her disappointment.

"I want to stay out longer, too. Let's get into some trouble," Yasmine replied, winking at Brianna.

"Roomies unite," Brianna chanted, extending her fist to touch Yasmine's. Through the corner of her eye, Yasmine noticed Jordyn roll her eyes, but chose to ignore it.

The ladies went their separate ways after dinner with Yasmine and Brianna deciding to walk around to explore the nightlife a bit more.

* * *

The resort transformed into a different vision of beauty at night. The pool looked ethereal, glistening as they walked by. Beyond the pool, the ocean mirrored the sky above with small glimmers of moonlight dancing with each wave.

There were different areas throughout the resort from entertainment to lounge areas. With drinks in hand, the ladies people watched the different types of people they came across. They noticed couples snuggled in hammocks, laughing and whispering sweet nothings between one another. Near the pool loungers, they found groups of friends clinking glasses to toast to the memories being made on vacation.

Yasmine was taking it all in when she heard a deep voice ask, "Hey, how y'all doing tonight?"

They saw a group of men sitting nearby, peaking Yasmine's curiosity on if they were the same ones her friends brought to her attention earlier in the evening. A soft but persistent elbow tap from Brianna confirmed her suspicions.

"We're good. Thank you for asking," Yasmine responded. Eyeing each of them from head-to-toe, she could confirm they were eye candy, indeed.

"Where are y'all other friends?" As the deep-voiced man stood up, Yasmine forced herself to keep her composure, not giving away her breath being taken away by his presence. This milk-chocolate man was above six foot three with tattoos all over his arms and the whiff of his woody scent put her under an intoxicating spell.

Get it together, Yasmine.

"Well, we had a bit of a long day today so they went back in for the night," she responded.

"Ooh ok. Where y'all from? Also, y'all can come sit over here if you want. We won't bite," another husky-voiced man said. This one's height could not be determined from his seat, but his skin was caramel and he had a laid back yet hospitable vibe. The ladies looked at each other for silent confirmation before making their way to the open seats next to them.

"Oh ok. I know it's rude to ask a woman's age, but you all look great. My name is Trevor, nice to meet you. This is David, Neil, and Chris." As the tattoo-sleeved gentleman introduced each of his friends, they raised their hand to confirm who was who.

The caramel-skinned man was David. He stood at five foot eleven with a short, kinky fro and luscious thick eyebrows. The other two men did not disappoint either. Chris was five foot nine with cornrows, football-wide shoulders, and an infectious smile. The last friend, Neil, had toffee-colored skin with a chiseled face that one would think Mary Edmonia Lewis herself sculpted to perfection with his perfect cheekbones and jawline. It was certainly a handsome group, each one's features standing out in their own way. Them having the same amount of people in their group as the ladies was the icing on the cake.

"Nice to meet you all. I am Brianna, and this is Yasmine. Our other friends are Amari and Jordyn. How long are y'all staying? Maybe you can meet them tomorrow." The way Brianna was spearheading the conversation with the men, Yasmine almost forgot the compromising position she was found in last night.

"We got here yesterday and don't leave until Tuesday. Where are y'all from?"

The conversations continued flowing with the ladies sharing where they were from and how they knew each other. The group of men was slightly younger, in their late twenties, compared to them in their early thirties. Similar to the ladies, they were single with the exception of Neil, who was the only one married out of the bunch.

They also lived in different places and came together as an "End of Summer" vacation. Trevor and Neil lived in New York while Chris lived in Houston and David in LA.

Yasmine and Trevor immediately started discussing their favorite restaurants in New York and realized they may have crossed paths previously without ever knowing. Brianna was in an all-you-can-date buffet between David and Chris.

Not registering it was already past midnight, Yasmine looked at her phone. "Alright, sorry to be the Debbie Downer, but I am exhausted after the long day we had. How about we pick this up tomorrow?"

"If you give me your number, I will make sure we find all of you," responded Trevor without hesitation, making his interest in Yasmine clear.

"What would be more impressive than me giving you my number is you figuring out how to find us without me making it that easy for you," she replied flirtatiously. Her interest was mutual despite playing hard to get, but she didn't want to give too much too soon. Her stance on men wasn't the most positive at the moment. Add meeting one on vacation to the mix and it sounded like a first-class ticket to hell.

Trevor helped her out of her seat while promising, "Oh don't worry, I will absolutely be on the lookout for you, beautiful." Yasmine rolled her eyes, a warm and fuzzy feeling betraying her on the inside.

The men were chivalrous, offering to walk the ladies back to their suite, but they declined. They didn't feel comfortable with strangers knowing where they were staying after meeting for the first time. The resort was safe enough to venture off on their own.

Yasmine and Brianna gushed about the men on their way back to the suite. Trevor made his intentions for Yasmine known while Brianna had first dibs on her choice between David and Chris. If they were all to meet up again, it wasn't clear if Amari would be interested in any of them, but Jordyn could always become pals with Neil since they were married. It would be a nice little setup, beneficial to everyone, if their paths crossed again.

"Trevor is fine as hell, Yas. I hope you stop playing with him," said Brianna.

"I'm not playing. I just don't know what I want to do yet," Yasmine replied.

"Does this have anything to do with Xavier?"

"No," Yasmine pondered for a second longer. "Well, I guess yes and no. I'm not sure."

While her and Xavier didn't have a title and were technically more of a sneaky link situation, she felt guilty about how talking to this new person made her feel, giving her butterflies she hadn't felt in a long time.

"Well, the good thing is, you've only just met Trevor. You get to decide what you want to do. And there shouldn't be any pressure with that."

Brianna was right. Yasmine was thinking way too hard about a fleeting moment with a stranger. And she needed to cut it out.

They found Amari dozed off on the sofa when they arrived back. Yasmine grabbed the laptop falling out of her hands and covered her with a blanket.

"Hey y'all. How was the rest of the night? Anything fun happen?" asked Amari, still half asleep.

"Go back to sleep, we'll tell you about it tomorrow."

20. Moment of Silence
Jordyn

JORDYN WAS RELIEVED when she finally separated from the group. With Yasmine and Brianna galivanting on the resort and Amari writing in the common area, she finally had a moment to breathe. Alone. The last couple of days were decent despite a few hiccups.

Dunn's River was a good bonding activity for them, yet she still couldn't shake the feeling of being replaced. It used to be J.A.Y. with her, Amari and Yasmine, but she felt she was being replaced by Brianna. The way Yasmine and her exchanged knowing glances, saying words without speaking at all. Moments like that used to be sacred for them two.

Starting in middle school, everyone had a sense of envy from their friendship. They had a secret handshake where they would give each other a double high five with a fist bump and locked their arms before ending with a pinky promise.

"Y'all are so annoying!" They would always hear from other students in their school.

"What's their deal?" Yasmine asked.

"They want what we have. But they never will because no matter what, it's just me and you, Yas. Love you to infinity and beyond."

"Forever and ever, Jordy."

When was the last time they even shared their handshake? Now, Yasmine also shared a special bond with someone else. Platonic cheating, if you will.

Yasmine's energy was also very strange throughout the day. Could it be the guilt from not being honest about Xavier? Was it something else? Her level of contemplation seemed almost like she was coming to terms with something, but she brushed it off as work on her mind. The lie detector test instantly determined that excuse was a bold-faced lie. Jordyn wanted to get to the bottom of it, but why should she keep overextending herself if Yasmine didn't meet her halfway?

And if the trip itself wasn't overwhelming enough, besides the initial text exchange with Malik two nights ago, not getting him on a call was starting to irritate her. Her mother-in-law would say he was busy at work or sleeping, but that was a piss poor excuse for not being able to Facetime his wife. Right? They worked so hard on making time for each other, but since she left for vacation, he acted like she was out of sight, out of mind. Their progress shouldn't regress just because she wasn't physically present. Being away from him made her mind spin. Was his level of devotion due to her always being in his orbit? What was he doing?

Jordyn

Babe. Can we Facetime soon? I've seen the kids, but I want to see your face too. I miss you so much.

"You good, Jordyn?" Amari asked, stepping into their room to grab a pen and notebook.

"Yea, just missing the family. I wanted this alone time and now I'm yearning to talk to them every moment. Does that make me pitiful?"

"I may not have a family of my own yet, but your feelings are absolutely valid. When I have my own one day, I'm sure I'll feel the same. Honor those feelings, but also try not to let it take away from your fun here if you can."

Jordyn's eyes widened at her friend's revelation. "I've never heard you talk about wanting a family."

"Well...that's because I wasn't sure I wanted one until recently. After my mom's birthing experience, I've always been afraid it would happen to me, too. Like a hereditary curse. But I want a legacy. Now I can't tell you if I want to have a child with a man or a woman, but what I can tell you is I want to grow a life from the inside out." Being the sappy mom she was, hearing anyone talk about children always brought tears to Jordyn's eyes. Beyond her hard exterior was a soft person who had so much love to give to the world. Being a mother was one of her proudest accomplishments, allowing her to be the authentically mushy version of herself.

"That is wonderful to hear, Amari. I'm sure it will happen for you, on your own terms," Jordyn affirmed before pausing. "...I do have one more thing that's on my mind to ask you, though."

"What's up?"

"Do you find Yasmine and Brianna's friendship to be off-putting? I feel like she's trying to be our replacement."

"Speaking for myself, their friendship doesn't bother me. Brianna likes to have a good time and doesn't bother anyone as far as I can see."

"There's just something about her. I don't know. Maybe it's my intuition, but something is off about that girl."

"Well, if you want my honest answer, Jordyn. You felt the exact same way with me and we turned out fine. Maybe do a temperature check within yourself to see if she's truly done something to you or if you might be projecting some internal feelings onto her. If anything, she's been around for Yas while the both of us have been away."

Well, what a sucker punch. Jordyn stayed in Atlanta because she built a life with Malik after undergrad. Yasmine could have done the same for Xavier. Or to stay with the friend she hadn't been separate from since elementary school, but she chose differently. Not Jordyn's fault.

She also knew she wasn't the most welcoming when she met Amari, but it's not some sort of character flaw. How many times did she have to apologize? What was the correlation to her current issues with Brianna? They were different situations. Even her closest friends didn't understand her, but she shouldn't be surprised. Jordyn played the villain role in their group, with Yasmine there to always save the day.

"Hmm interesting. Do you think I've been a team player on this trip, at least?"

"I think you have your moments, yes. But do I think you've fully allowed yourself to enjoy the trip? No. Do I think her being here has a part to do with it? Yes. But you agreed to her coming and you should make the best of it. For yourself, if no one else."

"Got it. I thought maybe you would see things from my side, but I'm not sure you do." *Don't cry. Don't cry. Don't cry.*

"It's not about sides. But I'm here if you want to talk more.... but for now, I'm going to head back to the sofa out there to hit some writing deadlines if that's ok." Amari stood from her side of the bed to leave their room before Jordyn could fully formulate a response. She was never good at having deep conversations or consoling her friends when they were down.

"No problem, Amari. I'm heading to bed. Goodnight."

Malik

Sorry, babe. I miss you too. I've been so swamped at work then crashing as soon as I get home. Are you free now?

With her last ounce of patience officially shattered, Jordyn curled up in bed and decided she wanted a moment of silence. From everyone.

Day 4: No New Friends

21. Boost of Confidence
Yasmine

AWAKENED by the bright sun peeking through the curtains, Yasmine felt an extra pep in her step. Although the chance meeting with Trevor and his friends could have just been a moment in time, it reminded her that there were more fish in the sea. And if Xavier couldn't recognize how amazing she was, someone else would.

She wanted to update Amari and Jordyn immediately, pulling off her bed covers to exit her room and share details about their night. When she noticed Amari on the balcony writing again, she went for Jordyn first, choosing to not disturb her peace.

"GIRL. Remember the group of men y'all were trying to show me last night on the way to the restaurant?" she asked, tapping a half-awake Jordyn out of her slumber.

"Now I know you didn't wake me up out of my sleep to ask me that, Yasmine. Go away," Jordyn groaned, turning to face her on the other side of the bed. Yasmine gave her the best pouty face she could give. The strongest of men had fallen victim to it over the years.

"Ok, ok. Fine. Yes, I remember. Why?"

Beaming with joy, Yasmine continued. "Well, on our post-dinner stroll, we ran into them near one of the bars. They were mad cool. And definitely as fine as y'all said they were."

"Oooh well that's great news. Did anyone special catch your eye?" Jordyn asked, sitting up to give Yasmine her full attention. "Was it the same guy staring at you before we went to the restaurant?"

Blushing, Yasmine gave all the details about Trevor and her playful way of telling him to find her without giving him her number.

"Well, this is exciting. This married old hag will be observing the love story unfold from the sidelines. At least there's another married person in the group. I'll hang out with him to not feel left out."

"Please do not call yourself old or a hag. You're neither of those things. Married or not, it's perfectly valid to look here and there. You said so yourself."

"True. After all these years, despite missing out on some of the experiences my friends have, I still can't see myself being with another man. I often wonder if Malik feels the same. Or if he thinks he missed out on anything." Despite her fiery personality, Jordyn kept everyone on a need-to-know basis about her relationship, but this comment seemed different— more introspective.

"If that's on your mind, maybe you should ask him. But I think the family you've created together is beautiful."

"Thanks, Yas. I'm going to take a quick shower, but y'all can head to breakfast without me. I want to check in on the house then meet up with y'all afterward," Jordyn stated.

"They must not know how to function without their Chief Mom-In-Charge. We can wait for you if you want."

"Agreed, just let us know, Jordyn," Amari replied, joining in the conversation as if she'd been there all along.

"I'm sure they would rather me stop being a helicopter mom from afar, but I can't help it. Thank you for offering to wait, but I'm good. Promise." Sadness was present, just beyond the plastered smile she forced on her face. Yasmine made a mental note to circle back with Jordyn later when they were alone.

Yasmine, Amari, and Brianna left Jordyn to get food . They caught Amari up on what happened the night before over breakfast. Yasmine paid close attention to Amari's body language when Brianna discussed her options between the guys, but she impressively seemed either unfazed or great at hiding her expressions.

"Wow, looks like I missed out on a lot of fun. But I won't miss out on any activities today. It will be a good one," she responded nonchalantly.

"So, where's y'all lil friends you met last night?" Jordyn asked, taking a seat next to them. Either she didn't get an answer or the phone conversation with her family was short. She appeared more at ease, which contrasted her earlier somber energy.

"Well, based on what Yasmine said to Trevor last night, it's giving hide and go seek. They're gonna have to find us," responded Brianna, sending everyone into a laughing fit.

Jordyn wasn't fully warmed up to Brianna, but it didn't seem like she was still icing her out either. Yasmine couldn't tell if it was all an act but appreciated the peace, if only for the sake of the trip.

The elephant in the room was the Amari and Brianna situation. Since it didn't seem to affect how they were interacting within the group, Yasmine decided it was best to leave it alone.

* * *

They were showered with compliments on their color coordination as they walked through the lobby, giving them an extra boost of confidence for the day. The shades of orange looked great on their skin tones.

"I told you I'd find you," a familiar deep voice greeted Yasmine before she saw the figure who gently touched her elbow. When she turned around, she wasn't surprised to see Trevor standing there with his mischievous grin.

Her friends stepped back for them to talk, giving her a playful look and nods of approval to entertain whatever the next words out of this man's mouth would be.

Trevor stepped back to take an eye scan of every inch of Yasmine's body from head-to-toe, where she avoided making eye contact with him, suddenly feeling bashful. "My my my. You are even more beautiful in the daytime than you are at night. I see y'all are heading out, but the boys and I would love to hang out with you and your girls later if you don't already have plans."

For the first time, looking beyond his gaze, she noticed the rest of his friends having their own conversation with the ladies.

"Yea. We're about to be on a boat for the afternoon. I'll check with my friends to make sure they're down. But by the looks of the chatter over there, your friends may have already gotten an answer for themselves." He followed her gaze in their friends' direction, laughing and engaging in their own conversation.

"Alright y'all. We gotta go. Delroy is here," Amari stated, annoyingly pointing in the direction of their driver standing outside his van.

Yasmine started walking away when she felt Trevor grab her hand, sending a shockwave through her body. "So, you're really going to make me beg for your number?" he asked. Between his freakishly good looks and irresistible smile, he was really hard to resist.

"Fine! For the sake of us letting you know if we can potentially link up later, I'll give it to you," said Yasmine, rolling her eyes at him for dramatic effect. Yasmine wanted this man and she wanted him badly. But he'd have to work a bit to hold her attention.

He passed her his phone to input her number before joining the rest of her friends, feeling his stare burn a hole in her back with every step she took to the van.

"Sorry, Delroy. Some new friends stopped us in the lobby," Yasmine said before he closed their door.

"Not ah problem at all, Yasmine," he responded.

"Friends, huh? The way the man was looking at you, it's giving he wants to be your future husband," Brianna said jokingly. Yasmine wasn't surprised her friends noticed what she felt on the inside. The man was doing something to her. And she was intrigued to find out exactly what that something was.

Curious about their conversations, Yasmine asked, "Alright alright. Enough about me. I did notice that the rest of the guys popped up to join y'all. What did they say?"

"Girl, he had you in a trance, huh? They just asked us if we wanted to hang out later. They seem cool, so we told them yes. We figured you wouldn't have an issue," said Jordyn, smirking. Yasmine was happy they passed the vibe check with her the most.

"Yea. I agree. They're a little young, but seem like they could be a good time," Amari expressed. Yasmine couldn't tell if Amari's analysis of them meant she really liked them or not. She was giving Jordyn vibes, with Jordyn giving the opposite. Strange.

"Well, we can talk about those men later. We're about to be on a boat, let's turn up!" Brianna said, passing out shots to everyone.

22. Rum Punch Bunch
Yasmine

With the cloud-free blue sky and the gentlest breeze in the warm air, it was an ideal day to set sail. Nestled behind a sea of other boats was their medium-sized catamaran. While they could have easily chosen to book a similar boat full of other vacation goers, there was nothing like letting loose with friends in a more intimate setting.

The scent of food being prepared enticed them first as the crew assisted them onto the boat.

"Wow, is this all for us?" asked Jordyn, used to being the caterer versus being catered to.

"Yea mon. We're preparing chicken for later, but there are also beef patties right there for yuh all to enjoy in the meantime."

They were so mesmerized by the idea of food; they almost missed the infamous red-hued carafes of liquor lined up by the bar. Jamaican Rum Punch. The rum punch on the resort wasn't bad, but they were pining for a stronger version than the gentrified version they'd been subjected to. Nothing compared to the authenticity from the sweet, tangy aroma of citrus juices melding with robust notes of Appleton and Wray & Nephew rums.

They also brought their own bottles of liquor and champagne as backup, in case they didn't like what was offered onboard. They could never go wrong with shots and champagne. A classique boat combination.

"Does anyone need Dramamine?" asked Jordyn, ruffling through miscellaneous items in her bag. All of the ladies ran to her to take one, just in case.

"Such a mom," Amari joked, nudging her friend's side.

"Listen, gotta stay ready so you never have to get ready. Kids will humble you."

"I can only imagine," responded Yasmine. Brianna nodded her head in agreement.

The ladies grabbed their drinks and shortly thereafter, the boat finally set sail. There was plush, cushioned seating on the sundeck inviting them to bask in the warmth of the sun and enjoy the view.

This group was ready to sing and dance their little hearts out for the three-hour sail. As if on cue, Yasmine noticed Brianna near the captain's booth, where she played "Pull Over" by Trina as the first track on the auxiliary cord. She could always be counted on to get the party started.

Gazing out into the open sea, Yasmine noted, "This is beautiful." The ladies nodded in agreement, taking in the view for themselves.

"Why are y'all still standing here?! Time to turn up. We're on a boat, bitches!" Brianna yelled, joining the rest of the ladies on the sun deck.

"You know what? You are absolutely right," Yasmine confirmed, standing up to shake a lil sumn.

"I put on my most ratchet playlist so Ima need y'all to turn up."

Jordyn and Amari followed suit. When they weren't dancing, they were taking pictures and videos to capture their memories together. Everyone was letting loose and having a great time—together.

The music being played ranged from old school hip-hop artists like Trina and Lil Kim to sprinkles of new school artists like Glorilla and Meg Thee Stallion.

They were having so much fun with drinks and dancing, they didn't even notice when they reached open water to swim. One of the crew men walked up and let them know, "Sorry to interrupt. If any of yuh want to go inna di wata, this is the spot."

"Oooh yes, let's!" Jordyn exclaimed as she took off her sunglasses and coverup.

When they noticed Brianna staying behind as the crew member, whose name they learned was Wilton, led the rest of the friends to where they should exit the boat, Amari asked, "Bri, you coming?"

"Nah girl, y'all have fun. I can't actually swim," she admitted, lowering her eyes in embarrassment.

Yasmine noticed her friend's energy change. "Girl it's ok. A lot of people can't swim. I learned last summer. You want me to stay on the boat with you?"

"Nah I'm good, thank you. I'll take the photos. Go have fun!"

The ladies followed Wilton to the steps that would lead them into the ocean when Jordyn pointed upstairs at the slide and inquired, "Can I dive off the top?" Yasmine was equally shocked and impressed at her friend's request.

"Well yes. But only if you're an experienced swimmer," Wilton confirmed with a smile.

"I am!"

"Ok then, you still need a life vest. Anyone else want to join her?"

"I actually will. Looks like fun," Amari noted.

"Well, y'all are on your own. I'm not trying to do that," Yasmine confirmed. She was not trying to take any more risks than she needed to. Learning how to swim was enough of an accomplishment for her. No need to try to be Simone Manuel.

"That's fine. Meet us in the water!" Amari exclaimed.

"Oh, I will. Don't you worry."

Yasmine met up with them in the open waters with Brianna instructing them to look in her direction for photos and videos.

Twenty minutes passed before it was time to head back onto the boat. The water activity worked up an appetite in the friends. Wilton let them know food would be ready for them when they returned to the deck. They noticed Brianna in a corner enjoying a patty as they sat near her.

"Don't mind me, I was having an appetizer while I waited for y'all to come back. Did y'all have fun?" she asked, wiping the golden crust off her face and swimsuit. Patties always made a mess. The taste was worth it, though.

"Yea it was nice. The water was so warm!" Yasmine exclaimed.

The scents of Jamaican cuisine danced through the air as soon as they stepped back onto the vessel. The fragrant blend of aromatic spices, smoky char, and succulent jerk chicken wafted from the grill area. After eating it the day before, they were eager to taste more authentic food from the island versus what was on the resort.

They enjoyed the freshly prepared jerk chicken, rice and peas, and cabbage in silence, confirming how good the food was. The taste of coconut from the rice mingled perfectly with the chicken. Every bite contained the perfect blend of flavor and spice.

"So y'all really trying to link with those men tonight?" Amari asked, breaking the food-induced silence.

"Yea, why? Do you not want to?" Brianna asked.

"I mean, I'll do it if y'all want. We just don't know them from anywhere."

"Amari, you're usually down for an adventure. What is this all about?" Jordyn asked with a concerned tone.

Yasmine's intuition told her it was less about the guys themselves and more so about Brianna's interest in them. Because she couldn't out her friends and still didn't have a full understanding of the true ins and outs of their situation, she kept her mouth shut.

Stumbling over her words, Amari responded, "I..Well..You know what, let's do it. It doesn't matter to me." Before anything else could be said, she stood up with her half-eaten plate and threw the rest of her food out and walked back to the sundeck.

Brianna almost choked on her chicken, not-so-subtly confirming

Yasmine's suspicions of the hesitation having something to do with her. If everyone were on the same page, maybe everything wouldn't feel as awkward.

"What is her deal?" Jordyn asked, confused about Amari's abrupt behavior.

"Not sure. Let me go check on her," Yasmine responded quickly before walking in the direction Amari did.

"Keep us posted," Jordyn requested.

* * *

"Are you good?" Yasmine asked, sitting next to a sunglass-covered Amari on the very front of the sundeck. She evidently didn't want to be disturbed, but Yasmine wanted to check in anyway.

Amari slid her sunglasses up onto her forehead, which revealed teary eyes. "I'm good. It's hard, you know. We're on this trip and I know we never implied if there would be true romance. I'm not sure if it is a romantic situation. It's confusing. We haven't had the chance to talk about what happened. I don't know what to do." Her voice cracked with those last words and she put her sunglasses back on her face.

Yasmine felt bad for her friend, but it was hard to even say anything to her or Brianna. They were not very forthcoming with what was going on before Yasmine quite literally saw it in her face. This emotion was adding an extra layer of confusion to Yasmine also. Did they have more than a sexual connection?

"I wish I had the words to say. You're both my friends. When you're able, let her know how you feel. But beyond that, let's try to have a good time. I know you want to respect if and when she wants to share her feelings, but I'm always here if you want to speak."

As she finished her statement, Jordyn and Brianna joined them on the sundeck. Amari wasn't one to show her emotions and didn't want to bring additional attention to herself. She squeezed her friend's hand as a silent promise not to mention anything to the rest of the women.

Jordyn, not reading the room as per usual, asked, "What y'all over here talking about?"

"We're here wondering why we haven't taken shots since we got back on the boat. Let's turn this thing up," said Yasmine, attempting to divert the conversation away from Amari.

Brianna volunteered to get more drinks then switch the music to reggae and dancehall. Even though Yasmine felt like Brianna knew exactly what might be going on, she was playing it off very well, opting to continue the good vibes on the boat.

Jordyn asked Yasmine to take some photos of her, but she knew it was a decoy. They were friends long enough for her to know all of her tricks. She did not like feeling left out.

"Ok, no one is listening. Talk to me. What's going on with Amari?" Jordyn whispered, pretending to review the photos Brianna took. As Yasmine glanced over at her friend still laying out on the cushions, her energy continued to be distant even with the sunglasses back on.

"She's just having a bad day. Let her be for now and hopefully her mood will change by the time we get back."

"You sure have a way of hiding things from me." *Ouch.*

Before Yasmine could ask what was being insinuated, Brianna came over with shots for the group. Everyone, including Amari, indulged. Afterward, between the sun and being full from their delicious onboard meal, they slowly drifted off to sleep.

Opening their eyes, they were met with beautiful golden-orange hues kissing the beautiful azure Caribbean waters, the scenic sunset rivaling the sky they started on the boat with. A vibration from her phone temporarily distracted her from the basking in the view.

Trevor
Hi beautiful. How was the boat ride? Having fun?

. . .

Yasmine

Hi there. It was good! We had a great time, food and all.

Trevor

Glad to hear it. Are y'all still up for a little game night tonight?

Yasmine

We are! Does 9pm work?

Trevor

9pm is perfect. See you then.

"Alright y'all. Everything is set with the guys. Let's get this night started."

23. Game Night
Yasmine

FROM HIGH SCHOOL to college and beyond, game nights always brought people together— friends and strangers alike— bonding over shared experiences and friendly competition with lots of laughter in between. Yasmine hoped for that exact vibe tonight with the guys.

Even though it was only a game night, the butterflies dancing inside her stomach were telling a different story. The guys seemed like a fun bunch, yes. But this up close and personal time could completely change her perspective of them. Of him. Men could go from appealing to repulsing in one New York Minute.

The friends all decided to dress cute for the occasion. First impressions mattered, after all. They put on their outfits and added final touches to their hair. As usual, there was someone running late. This time, it was Brianna.

"Alright, Bri, let's speed this up. Can we aim to leave here at exactly nine? I'm sure they can wait a few minutes for us," Yasmine noted.

"If he can't wait, then y'all can't date. That's Bible," said Brianna.

Jordyn backed her up saying, "I agree. Y'all know Malik has been waiting on my ass for almost fourteen years now." Yasmine and Amari giggled, knowing it to be true.

Even though Jordyn had her eye on Malik since the moment she saw him freshman year, she really did make him wait for everything. Everything they could control, anyway. She made him wait for her to respond to his texts, to answer his calls, for their first date, for their first time, for her to get ready for any event, and for her to move in with him. She wanted him to wait to propose until after medical school despite him wanting to do it after their graduation from undergrad.

Jordyn's goal was for them to be in a healthy place financially to afford the life they envisioned. Plans, though, sometimes go awry. She got pregnant halfway through his time in med school and they pivoted off script. They got married in a courthouse with the two people closest to them as their witnesses. Yasmine and Xavier. It was small, but it was perfect. They hosted another small gathering later with more family and friends to celebrate their marriage. They still were whole, despite a few diversions along the way.

"Tonight isn't only about me, though, y'all. They seem like a cool bunch so we should all let our hair down and have a good night. Wynters' style." Yasmine smirked, grabbing Jordyn and Amari's hands. Amari reached to grab Brianna, too, completing the link.

The music could be heard from down the hall before they reached the men's suite. Yasmine started feeling nervous and excited all at once. She didn't speak to Xavier much since she arrived on vacation, only a few text exchanges here and there. There was something about Trevor that took her mind off of him, and she liked it.

Chris opened the door quickly after the women knocked on the door. "Wow, Brianna. Don't you look like a vision." He kept his eyes fixated on her before adding, "You all look great actually. Welcome to our spot." He dramatically opened the door like it was an *MTV Cribs* episode to lead them inside. Their suite was a similar layout as the ladies, but with an extra room.

Yasmine could not keep her eyes off the fine ass man over by the bar. He was pouring out shots for the group while the rest of the men were chilling on the couch.

The way his muscles flexed in his black, silk button down shirt as he poured out the shots mesmerized her. His shirt perfectly clung to his chest and shoulders, accentuating the defined lines on his body. He paired his outfit with black denim, sneakers, and some sunglasses to match. It was dramatic in the best way. She started visualizing the many ways to take the shirt off and didn't hear when he asked what the ladies wanted to drink.

Jordyn slapped her arm. "Yasmine, what do you want to drink?"

"Tequila, if you have it," she responded, quickly composing herself.

He smirked as if he could read the thoughts in her mind. "My pleasure."

Mine too.

The men had everything possible from tequila, vodka, and cognac to gin and wine. There was also liquor available for them in their suite, but similar to the ladies, no one wanted the cheap stuff. Top shelf only. Everyone gathered around the sofa, shots in hand.

The introductions began. The men re-introduced themselves and explained how they knew each other. Then Amari and Jordyn introduced themselves to the full group for the first time. With music playing in the background and shots flowing, games began.

The evening unfolded with the men and women getting to know one another. The room was dimly lit, with the hum of chatter and music playing in the background, creating an atmosphere of excitement and anticipation.

After a while, they collectively decided to shift the energy to a more competitive one. They wanted to relive the college experience by playing classic games like Flip Cup and Beer Pong. The men were talking their shit, initially underestimating the women, but they quickly learned they weren't the ones to mess with. Round for round, they impressed the men by beating them in every game.

"Y'all practiced before you came tonight, huh," Chris joked.

"Is that your way of saying we're better than you, Chris? I really just think we're better at this than you," replied Brianna, playfully tapping his arm. Amari subtly rolled her eyes, but not before Yasmine noticed.

"You better tell them, Bri!" said Yasmine, egging her on.

"Now I didn't go to Wynters, but I will not have my girls go out bad. One thing about Yas and I though, at the game nights back at home, we never met a game of Taboo we couldn't win." Her competitiveness did not disappoint, matching the vibe of the Wynters Trio.

"Boom! Don't ever try to play me and my friends..." Jordyn continued. "But Brianna, Yasmine and I perfected our Taboo game in college. I'm glad to see the legacy being carried on," Jordyn snarked.

"Oh, I'm scared of y'all," Neil responded, diffusing the building tension in the air. He seemed to be a man of such few words, it almost shocked them when he spoke.

They went on to share stories of late-night adventures, wild parties, and unforgettable moments that took place during those carefree college years. Their laughter echoed through the room as they relived the past.

"Did someone mention Taboo?" asked Chris, bringing the familiar box from his room. This version of the game was Midnight Taboo, which Yasmine played in the past. The cards were spicy, but very fun to play with.

"Ok, now this party is really getting started," responded Jordyn, cracking her knuckles for dramatic effect.

"Is everything a competition with her?" David asked Amari.

"I would be lying if I said it wasn't," she responded, finally seeming to relax.

As Yasmine watched them seated next to her, she noticed David wore a blue linen button-down shirt with some white jeans and white

Air Force Ones to pair back with it. Ironically, Amari wore a blue denim jumpsuit that complemented his look well. The Cali vibes were present and they could probably really get along, if Amari allowed it.

Brianna started to deal the cards out when she mentioned, "I think we should switch this one up. Let's not make it men versus women. And Jordyn, I volunteer to not be on Yasmine's team so you can fulfill your former college glory." The warmth radiating the room quickly turned to ice. Brianna repaid Jordyn's earlier comment with the same level of petty.

"Lovely, let's do it," Jordyn responded, unfazed.

The game went from fun and light to being a silent competition between Brianna and Jordyn, over a shared possessiveness of Yasmine. It was ridiculous and uncalled for. Their niceties toward each other before this moment were now confirmed to be an act. Coexisting for one vacation shouldn't be that hard.

For Taboo, Team A was Brianna, David, Amari, and Chris. Team B was Yasmine, Jordyn, Neil, and Trevor.

Team A had a good groove with Brianna on their team. It didn't take long to realize the guys weren't as good at guessing nor saying the words as the women. Amari and Brianna were holding it down for their side.

Team B paid attention to Team A's disjointedness and used it to their advantage during their rounds.

Yasmine and Jordyn were professionals and quick to play off each other when guessing words. It was time for Trevor to give clues for the team when he looked directly at Yasmine. "It's what I'd like to happen before the end of the night, if you let me."

Yasmine was so stunned to speak, she almost let the time run out. Everyone darted looks between the two of them, waiting for her to say something. Anything. Jordyn jumped in on her behalf. "Kiss? Yasmine, please don't piss me off."

He smirked with confirmation of the answer and Yasmine unsuccessfully tried to hide her blushing, attempting to avoid eye contact with him as he sat back down next to her. They lost the first round, but it was well worth it for the flirtatiousness she shared with Trevor.

"Thank you for the save, Jordyn," said Yasmine.

"Mhm girl, don't let it happen again," Jordyn responded.

They played three rounds of the game before confirming Team B won two to one. Boasting at their victory, Jordyn emphasized, "So what were you saying, Brianna?"

Brianna mumbled something under her breath, but then audibly said, "A win is a win, you got it. It's not that deep." Jordyn smirked at her, adding insult to injury. Their win was due to the entire group having chemistry and not just Yasmine and Jordyn, but you could never tell her that.

As the night went on, the games slowed down and the men found themselves gravitating toward the women who captured their attention, attempting to connect on a more personal level.

Yasmine was of course with Trevor, Brianna with Chris, and Amari finally shifted her attention toward David. Being the married ones of the group, Neil and Jordyn naturally connected.

Between the games played throughout the night and more intimate conversation around the room, they didn't pay much attention to how much time had passed. A cascade of yawns signaled time to head to bed. Looking at the time on her phone, Yasmine realized it was nearly three a.m.

"So, what are we getting up to tomorrow?" Trevor asked the group, briefly stopping his private conversation with Yasmine.

"Oh, we're a 'we' now? Let me find out," said Yasmine, slowly letting her guard down. She could see her friends eyeing her with looks of approval.

Gently placing his hand on her knee, he clarified. "Well, we're definitely a *we*, but what about everyone else? Ladies, do y'all have plans?"

Amari chimed in. "We planned for a chill day tomorrow. We've had a couple of days of back-to-back activities since we've been here. What about y'all?"

"We were going to head to Rick's Cafe in Negril, about ninety minutes away. You can do what you want, either chill or participate in activities. They have good food and we can watch some islanders cliff dive. We could even do it ourselves if we wanted." Trevor nudged Yasmine. She was going to have to let him down softly about adventures not being one of her strong suits.

"Oooh I wanted to go there. And I heard the beaches over there are the most beautiful on the island," Jordyn squealed, excited about another potential adventure.

"Alright, so it's a plan then?" he asked.

"We didn't plan for Delroy to get us in the daytime tomorrow. How would we get there?" Amari asked hesitantly, hinting at her lack of interest.

"Our driver has more than enough room. If y'all are comfortable, you can come with us. We'll double check with him when we wake up if it would be ok, but I'm pretty sure it is," Trevor said, clearly the planner of their group. And a man with a plan was exactly what Yasmine needed at this point in her life.

"And so, we're set. Are you ok with that, Amari?" Jordyn asked, also sensing her reluctance.

"Yea, it's fine. Let's do it. I can nap on the way there," Amari responded. She was being a team player, if nothing else.

With Amari's support, the men confirmed they would follow up with the driver's response in the morning. The men walked the friends back to their suite, given the ungodly hour they were wrapping the night up.

"Wasn't that fun, y'all?" asked Yasmine as they arrived back at their suite, still reeling about the night.

"It was cool, they're cool. It's bedtime, though, y'all. Goodnight," Amari said, escaping into her room first.

As they returned to their individual room, Yasmine noticed Brianna silently preparing herself for bed, not being as bubbly as she normally would be. "Bri, you good?"

"I'm good, Yas. I'm used to Jordyn's sly remarks at this point, if that's what you're asking. I'm just tired. Goodnight."

"Ok, goodnight."

She wasn't in the mood to talk, and Yasmine respected her wishes to not pry any further until she was ready to share what was on her mind. Besides a few hiccups throughout the night, Yasmine went to bed hopeful for what surprises the day ahead might bring.

Day 5: To Be Quite Honest

24. Energy Shift
Yasmine

THE LIVELY ENERGY once taking up space in the ladies' suite was becoming increasingly more sullen as they entered the middle part of the trip. Yasmine tried to chalk it up to their long night out, but didn't know for sure. They were in for another long day ahead with Trevor's confirmation that the driver could accommodate both groups for Negril.

"Well, we know this day is going to be eventful, but at least the guys seem respectful so far. Let's make it a memorable one," said Yasmine, breaking the silence on their way to breakfast. Brianna stayed behind longer to get ready, but it was clear she still needed some space.

"Agreed. Mister Trevor is certainly applying pressure on you. You look good together," Jordyn stated, making Yasmine feel giddy inside, but she needed to shove those feelings away. Nothing was guaranteed. She also needed to sort out her own feelings. Did she actually like him? Or was he a Band-Aid for her heartbreak?

"I agree with the chemistry between you two. It's part of the only reason I'm taking one for the team and going out today. Y'all know I really would rather stay in," Amari noted.

"Thank you, Amari. You really don't have to come if you don't want to, though. I want everyone to fully enjoy their time," said Yasmine.

She replied, "It's cool. I don't want to miss out on a potentially good time."

The men were waiting for them by the entrance to eat breakfast together. If it were possible, they looked even finer than they did the day prior. 90s fine.

"Well don't y'all look fine as hell," Trevor said, eyes laser-focused on Yasmine and Yasmine alone.

"We were about to say the same thing about y'all," replied Yasmine, returning his gesture.

"Do you two need a room?" Chris asked, with a look of both disgust and amusement.

"Nah not yet," Trevor said, smirking as he opened the door for the ladies to walk in. His confidence made Yasmine feel tingly in places it shouldn't have. Not yet. She didn't need to look behind her to confirm what she felt. He was staring down every inch of her body.

They found two adjacent tables big enough to fit the group, and the men let the ladies grab their breakfast first before they traded places to hold their spot. With everyone moving in sync, it seemed more like a couples' vacation versus strangers who only met a few days prior. Brianna joined the ladies at the table while they waited for the rest of the men to return.

"Another long drive today, huh?" said Amari, less than enthused.

"Indeed. I can't help the length of the drive, but I do have what might be a solution to make the ride go by faster," David stated.

"Do tell."

"I'm not sure if y'all do edibles, but I brought enough for everyone to try. No pressure, though," he proposed, pulling out a jar of gummies out of his pocket.

"Oh, we're really taking it back to college days," Jordyn interjected. "Unh unh, leave me out of it."

"You don't want to relive your college days?" asked Neil.

She replied, "Absolutely not. The bad trip I had senior year was all I needed to know it wasn't for me. Y'all enjoy."

"Yea please don't. She guilt tripped us for weeks afterward. No need to relive the horror," Yasmine explained.

Neil responded, "Ah ok. That doesn't sound fun at all. I respect your decision. Bad trips don't happen all the time, but I agree that you shouldn't do it if you're not comfortable."

"Thank you for understanding," Jordyn stated.

"Well, I'm so ready, let's do it," Brianna said, turning to Chris to ask, "Will you?"

"Edibles aren't my thing, but don't worry, I'm bringing a lil something something to smoke when we arrive."

"I recommend you start with half to see how you feel first. If you take a piece now, it should hit midway through the ride on the way there, but you can always take it later, too. Up to you," David explained, passing them out at the breakfast table like they were Haribo gummies versus THC-infused ones.

Their driver, Peter, was already outside waiting by the time they finished up with their food. Brianna and Chris walked slightly ahead of the group through the hotel lobby exchanging jokes, unable to contain their laughter. She was friendly with the men, but kept a reserved distance from the rest of the ladies, which stung a bit.

"Hello ladies, nice fi meet unnu. I hear yuh all will be with us pon di journey today. My name is Peter and I will be your driver."

The men chivalrously allowed the women to get into the van first. Similarly to the previous night, each of them sat adjacent to the person they were interested in or with Jordyn and Neil's case, shared the most similarities with. They were busy talking about their spouses and children. With no one else on the trip who could relate to them in that regard, it was good they found comfort in one another.

"Alright, y'all. Let's make this journey a fun one and do some car karaoke," said Yasmine, pulling out a microphone from her bag.

"Who randomly walks around with a microphone in their bag?" Chris asked.

"Looks like I do, huh? I figured we needed something to pass the time," she replied.

"That makes sense. How about we make it fun?" Trevor proposed to the group.

"In what way?" Brianna interjected.

"We could go round for round with songs then whoever has the least amount of votes from the group for their choice loses and has to take a shot," he explained.

Neil suggested, "We're all becoming a little family here, right? Let's keep it simple and have the same teams as last night. We're mostly seated that way anyway."

"Welp, there goes my nap," Amari whined.

"C'mon it'll be fun," David stated, shaking her shoulders.

"Ok, ok. I'm down," Amari reluctantly replied.

They went toe to toe for seven rounds with prompts like "Best Song from a Male R&B Group" to "Worst Trending Song from the Tik Tok Era."

They got so caught up singing each other's choices and poorly attempting popular dances from social media, they almost forgot there were stakes at play. Redeeming themselves from the previous night's loss, Team A secured their victory for great taste in music.

"What were you saying again, Jordyn?" asked Brianna, obnoxiously holding a hand to her ear. After being standoffish all morning, she was locked and loaded to return the shade from their game night.

"Ok, Brianna. Y'all ate that lil one thing. Not too much on me, I'm tired this morning," Jordyn responded.

Everyone shook their heads at their never-ending beef before drifting into naps for the duration of the ride. The recharge was necessary to keep the day going.

25. Cliff Hangers
Yasmine + Brianna

Approaching the destination in Negril, their surroundings were vibrant, catching Yasmine's eyes as she opened them from her unexpected nap. Clear waters with gentle waves danced against the base of the cliffs, creating a breathtaking view for visitors. Palm trees bent and swayed in perfect harmony, like couples entranced in a romantic slow dance.

While taking in the scenery, Yasmine realized that more than anything else, she was beyond parched. Her mouth felt as dry as the sand their feet were about to be on.

The edible slowly crept its way into her system, her eyes feeling low and heavy, with a deep sense of euphoria taking over her body. She found a napping Trevor leaning his head on her shoulder with a hand resting on her thigh, surprised at the level of comfort they shared with one another.

"We reach, I will be nearby. Just text mi when unnu close to being ready," said Peter.

"Thank you, Peter," they all echoed.

As they walked to the entrance of the stony cliffside with wooden decks and bamboo-like rooftops, large groups of tourists of all ages and backgrounds could be seen throughout the vicinity. The live band played on stage, with sounds of Beres Hammond and Gregory Isaacs to set the tone of the day.

To their left, three levels of cliffs with stony steps to each could be seen where different people could dive into the beautiful turquoise waters, depending on their comfortability and skill level. To their right was a multi-level café where food and drinks could be ordered.

"I am not diving off any cliffs, by the way. I like to have fun, but this type of adventure is not for me," Yasmine mentioned, walking with Trevor.

"Not a problem at all. Whatever makes you comfortable. I'll meet up with y'all right after." He planted a slow, sensual kiss on her cheek before joining Amari, Jordyn, David, and Trevor. Between the body high and the intimacy they shared, she was holding onto the last bit of her composure by a thread.

They cheerfully watched their friends, jumping from both the high and midpoints of the cliffs and requested seats on the higher level of the actual café for a better view.

"How are you feeling, Brianna? Be honest with me," Yasmine whispered to her friend as they walked to their table. With half of the group gone, it was the perfect moment to check in with her.

"I'm starting to feel better. Thank you for asking, Yasmine. Jordyn was bugging me last night with this unnecessary drama. I came here to have fun and she keeps finding ways to interfere with that," she responded.

"I agree. I was hoping you both would start getting along by now."

"Don't say both. It's her energy. I notice when she rolls her eyes and gets annoyed when you and I joke around with each other. We can all be cool, if only for the time we're here. It shouldn't be that serious."

"I agree. I cannot control how she reacts to things, but I can talk to her if it makes you more comfortable. I'm the one who brought you here and we still have a few days left on the trip."

"I appreciate that. I think I'm ok. I don't want to stir the pot anymore. I do hope she gets her attitude together though. It can be very off-putting."

"I get that. Let's hope it's smooth sailing from here."

"So, Chris. Tell us a little bit more about Trevor," asked Brianna, walking up to lock arms with him. She tactfully switched gears from their conversation about Jordyn. Yasmine understood loud and clear.

He shrugged before responding. "He's a good dude. Been single for a little, but was in a long term relationship a while back. He would be ready to make a commitment to the right person at this point, though."

Rum punches were ordered as soon as they were seated to buy time while they waited for the rest of their friends to return.

"Damn, you're a good salesman. Did he give you a script of what to say?" Yasmine joked, secretly enjoying the insight she was getting into his friend.

"Nah not at all. We're all on vacation so you never know where things will go, but he's not one to fake how he's feeling. I can confirm that much," he responded.

"I can confirm that, too. Trevor is a good guy," Neil interjected.

Despite their encouraging words, Yasmine would have to get to know him more for herself. They only met two days ago, after all. The sounds of cheers from locals fearlessly diving off the cliffs with tricks averted their attention to the views.

"That was SOO fun, y'all," said Amari, as she and David joined the group. Yasmine noticed Jordyn and Trevor lagging behind, deep in conversation.

"She dived off the highest cliff like we were at the Olympic trials," David expressed with a curious look on his face.

"That was so fun! The edible started to really kick in after my first dive. I was trying to be careful," she responded.

David added, "If your antics were careful, I don't want to see what dangerous looks like." The group laughed while Trevor and Jordyn squeezed into the last two spots available.

"Yea she's a daredevil. That edible hit as soon as I hit the ledge and I almost said fuck it, but I held it down," Trevor explained as he sat down. What were him and Jordyn talking about?

"Alright, alright. Y'all are dragging it now," Amari confirmed.

With everyone at the table, they placed food orders with the waitress along with a bottle of alcohol for the group to split and make their own drinks. The food orders included lobster, escovitch fish, jerk chicken kabobs, and cajun pasta.

* * *

"Damn the food must be really good, y'all haven't said a word since the plates got on the table," said Chris. His intentions with Brianna were not clear yet, but their playful personalities complemented one another.

"I don't know if it's the edibles or what, but this might be the best food I had the whole trip," Neil noted.

"Honestly, we needed the switch up from resort food. Jerk chicken too at this point," Brianna explained. The ladies all nodded in agreement.

"Want to take a walk?" Trevor asked, facing Yasmine who just finished her meal. The rest of the group continued conversing.

"Sure, let's do it," she responded. The friends all made teasing comments as they walked away, but they ignored them.

* * *

"What made you want to pull me?" she asked when they were out of ears' reach. They went to a secluded pool area with less people and walked toward empty seats.

"I wanted a private conversation with you without everyone around. They crack a lot of jokes, but I am really drawn to you and want to dive a little deeper into that if that's ok," he replied, grabbing her hand.

"That's perfectly fine. Anything specific you want to know?" Yasmine asked, looking down at her hands laced with his, feeling both foreign and familiar.

"Hmm, firstly why are you single? You're beautiful, driven and so far, seem like you'd be a good partner to any man," Trevor asked.

"I'm not great at choosing, which still is a reflection of me in a sense. I've done a lot of inner work, so I feel like I'm at a better place to find my person."

"Well, that was very honest. Thank you for sharing that with me."

"No problem at all. What about you? Why are you single?"

"Well, I was in a five-year relationship a while ago, but she cheated and we broke up. Honestly, we should have ended long before we did, but like you, I've done some inner work to understand who and what I really want in a woman." *A vulnerable man, too.*

Their conversation never missed a beat. They shared a similar love for reading, going to museums, and doing other extracurricular activities than the typical party and brunch other people their age frequented.

Eyes glued on one another, they didn't notice how much time passed by until Jordyn strolled in their direction.

"Alright lovebirds. Enough. Let's hit the dance floor. We can't miss the sunset!" Jordyn urged, grabbing Yasmine's hand to follow her.

"My bad, I didn't mean to keep your friend from you," Trevor explained with his hands up playfully. He trailed behind them, allowing them to talk alone.

"Girl."

"Sis, you don't have to explain. You really like this boy. It's written all over your face."

"I think I might. But I'm still not completely sure yet."

"If he didn't already tell you, just know I threatened him—"

"Jordyn—"

"Oh hush. I told him you mean a lot to me and if his intent is to play with you like you're disposable, then I would beat his ass. It wasn't that bad." The ladies laughed. Despite the occasional bump in the road during their trip, Yasmine was happy to have her friend's unwavering support.

When they made their way back to the larger group, the café was full of people from end-to-end dancing and having a good time with the golden-orange sunset as the perfect backdrop for the evening. Yasmine and Trevor grabbed some drinks to catch up with their group.

Everyone was in their own world. Brianna and Chris were in the middle of the venue, dancing like no one else was watching. Neil and David looked like they were having an intense conversation. As Yasmine, Jordyn, and Trevor gathered the group to take shots, they noticed one person missing. Amari. Scanning the venue, Yasmine saw her walking in the direction of the bathroom.

"Be right back," she said to them before following behind her. If she didn't know any better, she would think Amari was walking as fast as she was on purpose.

"Amari, slow down, girl. You're walking too damn fast," said Yasmine, becoming breathless trying to keep up with her.

"Oh, are you done cuffing now? You were over there talking to your man forever," she responded, but didn't turn around to face her friend.

"Not my man, but there is a spark between us, you know? But as quickly as things can heat up, they can die down so I'm trying not to get my hopes up too high. You never know with men..."

"I get that. I definitely recommend you to take your time. I don't want to see you hurt." Finally matching Amari's brisk pace, Yasmine noticed Amari's eyes were red. *Was she crying?*

"What's wrong, Amari? Are you ok?"

"I'm fine."

"You don't seem fine, what's up?"

"Leave it alone, Yasmine. Please."

Ignoring her friend's request, Yasmine continued. "You know I can't do that. What's this about, Amari? Is this about Brianna? And Chris?"

Rolling her eyes, Amari explained, "A little. It's a lot seeing her connect with someone else like she did with me. Makes it seem like it was all an act. But there hasn't been time to discuss anything, including what happened with us the other night, so I'm not sure where her head is at."

"Oh no, I am sorry you're feeling this way. It's clear you're feeling a deeper connection with her. Maybe find a moment to speak alone."

Pointing angrily in the direction of the group, she stated, "We've been with these people the last day and a half, so how could I?" Yasmine could tell her friend was hurt and angry. She wasn't sure how to approach the situation. If they weren't her friends, she might have been able to give better advice. But now she felt like she was in the middle and even worse, Brianna still hadn't mentioned anything to her about it yet.

"I have a question, though, Amari. What about the screenwriter guy back at home you mentioned to me? Lawrence?"

"Yasmine, yes he's around. But like I told you, it's not serious. And there's a different level of connection with a woman. With how easily we bonded before and during this trip, I started to think I could develop something more serious with her. Clearly it was a fleeting moment on her part, though, and I misread the signals."

"I want you to take it easy. I don't want to see you hurt like this. From what you've told me, you and her just connected sexually for the first time on this trip. Maybe give her the time and space to see what she wants, too."

Clearly irritated at her friend's advice, she scoffed. "That's grand coming from you. You've been head over heels about a man you met literally two seconds ago."

"Amari, where is this coming from? All I am trying to do is make you feel better. That's why I came over here to check on you."

"Please save your superiority complex for someone else, Yasmine.

You try to save everyone else, but take a look in the mirror sometimes. I don't have time for your shit today."

Too stunned to speak, Yasmine took her turn in the bathroom. She was taken aback at the accusations thrown in her direction. She didn't want her friend to think she was better than her, but Amari found herself in a sticky situation. And why was she comparing it to the fresh situation with Trevor? Her disappointment in the Brianna situation was valid, but it didn't seem like a good enough reason to spew venom in Yasmine's direction. Especially when all she was trying to do was help.

She walked back to join the group and took another shot before grabbing Trevor to dance. He grabbed her by the waist and pulled her so close, their lips were mere inches apart. Yasmine's heart thumped through her chest as she attempted to finally make her wish come true.

"You good?" asked Trevor, ruining the moment.

"Just dance with me," she responded, trying to avoid tears welling up in her eyes. He obliged and thankfully let it go.

Out of the corner of her eye, Yasmine noticed Amari and Brianna having a heated exchange. It was about time those two sorted their differences out.

* * *

"Amari, why are you standing over here by yourself?" Brianna asked, finding her sitting alone at the bar. Brianna noticed her moping around after cliff diving ended, but figured it was because she really didn't want to do anything besides relax on the resort.

"Brianna, why do you even care?" Amari sneered in response.

"If I didn't care, I wouldn't be here right now. What's your problem?"

"Maybe you should go ask Chris that, Brianna. Please leave me alone."

Brianna's eyes widened in disbelief. "Are you serious right now?

You're mad at that? You've also been flirting with David. Have I said anything or made a big deal about it, no?"

"You're right. Me sitting over here minding my business is making a big deal about it."

Brianna took a step back, trying to control her building frustration.

"Amari. The last time I checked, I was very much single. And free to do whatever the fuck I want to do. If you would like to have a real conversation, I'm all ears. But I'm not fucking with whatever stink ass mood you're in right now."

"There's really nothing to discuss. Do you, boo."

With her last bit of patience dissipated, Brianna walked away before she said something she might regret.

26. Breath of Fresh Air
Yasmine

AFTER A FULL DAY SPENT TOGETHER, the light-hearted high energy between the group was replaced by an eerily quiet low on the ride back to the resort. Unbeknownst to the men who tried to crack jokes, none of the ladies were in the mood to chat.

Yasmine was still shocked about how Amari handled their conversation. Even more so since they never disagreed on most things since becoming friends. Her accusations seemed unfair. Did Amari always have those feelings about her? Was there something deeper going on Yasmine wasn't aware of? They would have to speak eventually, but right now, Yasmine just wanted some space. Amari's energy toward her since their conversation suggested she wanted the same.

"What are we doing tonight? Y'all want to hang out again?" asked Trevor, attempting to ease the tension he was likely picking up on. It wasn't clear if his fruitless efforts were for the sake of the total group or just Yasmine.

"Honestly, I'm still tired from us heading to bed late last night. Can we call it a night tonight?" asked Amari. Yasmine didn't give a damn what she wanted to do. She didn't want to be around her for any longer than she needed to.

"I'm cool with that. I'm tired, too. I want to check in on my wife anyway," Neil explained, probably tired of playing chaperone with Jordyn while everyone coupled off— mostly everyone.

"A family man. We love that. I'm down to call it a night tonight too," said Jordyn. They fist bumped each other, sealing in the wholesomeness of their connection.

"If you're down, I would love to spend more time with you," Trevor whispered to Yasmine. The mere feeling of his warm breath on her neck gave her goosebumps.

"I would love that. Text me when you're ready," she responded before laying on his shoulder to take a nap. Space from the group was exactly what she needed.

The silence between the friends continued when they arrived back to their suite. Between being tired and inner circle tensions building, they were all going to need to get back on track to enjoy the rest of their stay.

Brianna's energy was off since her heated exchange with Amari. Yasmine wanted to get the details on their drama but needed some space to figure her own shit out, too. It was starting to feel like the part of a girls' trip where everyone couldn't stand to be around each other. Three whole days to go. The horror.

"Damn, y'all really tired to the point where words are too hard to speak?" joked Jordyn, attempting to break the silence. Yasmine laughed at her friend's inability to read the room. Jordyn might have had annoying traits, but she was really good at providing comic relief in awkward moments. Brianna was, too, which was perhaps what drew Yasmine to her initially. It was a glimpse of her childhood friend she lost long ago.

"I'll have more words tomorrow. I'm tired, Jordyn," said Amari before disappearing into her room. Brianna rolled her eyes so far behind her head. And not in the way Yasmine saw a couple of nights ago.

"Y'all take it easy for the night. I'm going to head back out with Trevor," said Yasmine.

"Don't worry, we heard you lovebirds discussing it in the car," Brianna responded, mustering up a smile for the first time since they left Negril.

* * *

Yasmine was putting the final touches on her makeup when she saw a Facetime coming through. Xavier.

Wait, Xavier? What did he want? Quickly throwing on a sundress, she went to the balcony with her Airpods to speak to him privately.

"Damn, girl, you're looking extra fine with that sun kissed glow," Xavier said. He always knew the right words to say to make her feel good. He didn't look so bad himself; he was shirtless, revealing his lickable six pack relaxing on his couch.

"Thanks, Xay. What are you up to?"

"I'm good. You crossed my mind. I feel like you've been gone forever and wanted to check in on my friend. How's the trip so far?"

"So I'm your friend now?" she asked.

"Yasmine, don't start this." She could've taken heed to his warning to not go any deeper into the conversation, but needed answers. Connecting with Trevor made her see things differently. Maybe Xavier could finally provide the clarity she yearned for.

She continued. "Let me ask you a question, Xavier. Where do you see this going? After all of these years and us reconnecting, where's your head at?"

"This is where you're taking it already? We barely finished saying hi to each other."

"So, if you didn't want to talk, why did you call me?"

"Listen, I have a lot of shit going on in my life right now. And as much as I care about you and I probably always will, romance is not a priority for me at the moment. If what I can offer you right now isn't enough, I want you to find the love you deserve." He was expressionless as he concluded the final statement with nothing more to say on the topic. Yasmine realized everything he already said was more than enough.

"Xavier, I do know you're going through some things, but I also knew deep down, you never loved me the way I love you. Not the way you did in college anyway. I held onto hope when we reconnected, but I shouldn't have. I don't know why it's taken me so long to accept this." She shook her head as the reality of their situation fully sank in for her.

"Listen Yas, I don't want to upset you on your trip. Let's talk when you're back."

"Whatever you say," she replied, hanging up the phone without saying bye. Yasmine wasn't sure what would happen with Trevor, but she knew she deserved more than Xavier, even if it meant being alone.

Without saying words or bringing much attention to her presence, Brianna walked out onto the balcony and sat down next to Yasmine, who was trying to take deep breaths to keep herself calm. "Hey. Is everything ok?"

"I was talking to Xay. He just confirmed everything I already knew deep inside." Her voice cracked with those last words and she finally let the tears fall down her face.

"Aww babe. I'm so sorry," Brianna said, hugging her friend tightly while she quietly wept.

Yasmine let the tears out then they both sat in silence for a little. It felt like she was going through a breakup with him again. And this time, she had no residual hope of things heading back in the right direction. The one where they were truly, madly, and deeply in love. Their chapter ended. For good.

"I noticed you and Amari in a bit of a heated discussion earlier today. Want to share?" asked Yasmine, desperately wanting to change the topic from herself.

"Well, Yas, there's been something I needed to share with you," Brianna reluctantly expressed.

"What is it?"

"Firstly, please don't be mad at me."

"Oh please. Give a girl a chance first."

She babbled. "Ok. Well, Amari and I really bonded as friends after you introduced us. We would text here and there. It started to get a little deeper, but also would get a bit flirty. I didn't really understand my feelings because as far as I ever knew, I am a straight woman. Was? I'm not even sure at this point."

Brianna shared how she grew deeper feelings for Amari, but never planned to act on them. Their chemistry grew exponentially since reconnecting on the trip. She finally revealed the details of their intimacy with one another and how it also made her confused. Not because she didn't care about Amari, but because she could see herself doing it again.

Before continuing, Brianna paused, "Yasmine, you don't seem shocked by this big news I shared with you..."

"Well, I did not know the full scope of how you two began, but I did wake up a few nights ago where I saw you and Amari on the balcony. I snuck back to bed, but had been hoping you would share when you were ready."

"Oh..um..I'm sorry you had to see that. That's why you were acting cagey that day, huh?" Brianna asked, lowering her eyes in embarrassment.

"It was. But Brianna, there's nothing to feel ashamed of. Did I expect to see two of my close friends like that? No. But it hurt more that you weren't comfortable to share. At the same time, it sounds like you were figuring out your own sexuality, so I am not mad at either of you."

"Thank you for understanding, Yasmine. What's even more

confusing now is the guys being thrown into the mix. At first, Amari was getting jealous when she saw Chris and I connecting. Then as I saw her and David bonding on the cliffs, I was feeling a bit jealous, too. I was trying to check on her earlier and it was not very productive at all. I've also never seen the dismissive side of her and I'm not sure I like it."

Yasmine recalled her own conversation with Amari. "She was in no mood to have many conversations today, but it sounds like you two need another discussion. You should figure out what is more important: friendship or pursuing something more. Amari is bisexual and perhaps you are realizing you are, too. But you need to get on the same page about the direction y'all want to go in next."

Brianna was about to say something before Jordyn opened the balcony door and interrupted. "What y'all out here talking about?"

"Just recapping the day so far," Yasmine shared while getting up, "I need to hurry up and get ready. I told Trevor I would meet him by now and I haven't even figured out what I'm wearing."

"I know that's right, girl. Go get your man," Brianna said with a wink.

"And will!" Yasmine screamed, mustering up a reason to smile. Despite the off-putting conversation with Xavier, she was determined to have a good night. There was no guarantee Trevor would be "the one" or even someone she would date outside of the trip, but he was what she needed for the present moment. She wanted to lean into that.

"Have so much fun!" Brianna said when she noticed Yasmine heading for the door.

"Yes, give us all the tea when you return. Me first, though," Jordyn whispered as she hugged Yasmine on the way out. She couldn't help but still love her friend, antics and all. She returned her embrace tightly.

* * *

Trevor gazed at Yasmine as she walked toward him sitting by the bar. That smile of his melted away all of the evening's disappointments and she was ready to see where the night would take them.

He always looked so put together. His emerald green top went perfectly with the green high-neck dress she wore. How ironic for them to match without trying?

"You never have an off moment, do you? You look beautiful. And I see you're already trying to match me, too," he joked, pulling out her seat.

"I have my moments. But I definitely know how to look good on vacation, though. It seems like you're the one trying to match me, ok?!" They bantered back and forth for a bit before ordering drinks and small bites to start their night.

Even though Yasmine and her girlfriends didn't spend too much time outside at night since their vacation started, there was something inviting about the nighttime ambiance. The music played louder, drinks were flowing across different areas, and laughter surrounded the vicinity.

"What's on your mind?" Trevor asked after Yasmine was silent for a while, stuck in her own thoughts.

"I was taking in the resort's beauty. I do have a question for you, though."

"Sure. I love questions, let's do it." He was a sharp contrast to the men she was used to dealing with. Xavier would avoid challenging questions, saying she was thinking too hard or asking too many. He never wanted to give clear answers. Maybe Trevor's purpose in her life was to show her what she wanted in a potential partner wasn't too much after all.

"How would you like people to experience you?"

"Ohh we're getting deep early, huh?" he said before continuing. "I would say I want them to know me for my heart. As men, we're told we're weak if we aren't vulnerable or show our emotions. Thankfully, I grew up with an immense amount of love from my parents and family. I was taught that showing emotion is strength. I can be a man with the stigmas to that while also keeping some softness in my exterior, too. How about you?"

His response impressed her. "Well, that is quite the answer to follow up with. When people experience me, I want them to look beyond the exterior to realize there are deeper layers to be uncovered than what the eyes can see. I felt love growing up, yea, but I personally also was exposed to things that tainted my interactions with men, specifically. I want to move past those."

For the third time in one night, Yasmine forced herself to hold her tears back. She didn't tell too many people about her past experience where her older cousin took advantage, and sexually assaulted her. But in this moment, she felt comfortable sharing with Trevor.

In some ways, she always felt like it was her fault because women were taught to blame themselves, whether it be what they were wearing or who they put their trust into. She also felt like the men she attracted in her life were often a reflection of her past experiences. She subconsciously chose emotionally unavailable men due to her being an emotionally unavailable woman. She wanted to find her person and fully let her guard down— somewhere she felt safe.

Grabbing her hand, Trevor affirmed, "Please do not blame yourself. I'm sorry that happened to you. I'm sorry that so many women are taken advantage of. If I am ever blessed with a daughter, I hope I can do everything in my power to prevent it from happening to her." She felt the sincerity in his tone. *Was this man even real?*

They continued delving deeper into other topics like in-depth reasons why their previous relationships didn't work out, what their best and worst qualities were, and what they were looking for in a potential partner. They also went over fun things like what they had on their bucket list and favorite TV shows from childhood.

"Yasmine, if you're comfortable sharing, what was up with you and Amari earlier? Things seemed to get intense when you both went to the bathroom. It looked like you were arguing, but I didn't want to intrude."

"She was having a rough moment and I was trying to console her, but it felt like she was taking it out on me. I'm sure we will address it soon, but I did get irritated." Yasmine wanted to be honest in her response without giving too many intimate details about her friend's personal business.

"I understand. I hope you two get to have a conversation soon. No need for things to be awkward for the rest of y'all trip."

"I agree. We will."

"Changing topics, What do you think of me?"

"Well to be honest, Trevor, I don't know. These initial days have been great, but only time can tell where things will lead, you know?"

Speaking matter-of-factly, Trevor replied, "I agree. Yasmine, coming onto the trip, I really didn't plan to do anything besides reconnecting with my boys. A woman, especially one I would like to see outside of this vacation, was not on my radar at all. Meeting you has made this trip so much more and I'm not mad at it."

"I feel the same. We can take it day by day, but whatever comes of this, I hope we can stay friends. You really seem like a great guy," said Yasmine, echoing his sentiments while trying to stifle a yawn.

"We will. And you're an amazing woman. We had a long day, and I can tell you're tired. Let me walk you back to your room."

They held hands and laughed all the way back to her room. Turning from the doorknob to wish him good night, Yasmine was met with an intensity from Trevor's gaze, suddenly making her heart rate skyrocket. He placed his hand over hers, gently removing it from the handle and pushed her back against the wall. He bent down to kiss from her shoulders to the side of her neck, before nibbling on her ear.

Yasmine could barely keep her composure as he moved to tightly hold her by the waist and inched his way back down to softly lick and tug on her neck. She grabbed his face so their eyes could meet again. Their lips met, kissing slowly and passionately as if it were routine for them. He lifted one leg up to pin her further onto the wall, enough for her to feel the hardness of his entire body. Her hands examined his body, learning every muscular curve.

The tension between them was so explosive, she didn't want it to stop, pulling him in for a deeper kiss, tongues intertwined like there was no other place they belonged. Yasmine was ready to invite him in when he pulled back, biting his lips and said, "Mm. Have an amazing night, Yasmine. I hope I can see you again tomorrow."

Floating on cloud nine, she made her way back into the suite where her girlfriends were already asleep. The day was a roller coaster of emotions, but somehow she looked forward to the rest of the days to come.

Day 6: Sick Of It

27. Guilty

Jordyn + Yasmine

THE INCESSANT SOUND of Jordyn's phone woke her out of an otherwise pleasant slumber. With Amari unfazed and still sleeping peacefully next to her, she quietly exited the room to answer Amina and Malik Jr's call. The previous day was so busy, there wasn't time to check in on how they were doing.

"Where are you, Mommy?" Amina asked.

"I'm still on vacation, honey. Are you having a good time with your Nana?"

"Yes, it's fine. We want you to come home and play with us, though," she whined.

"I'm coming back soon. What are you doing today?"

"We want to go outside and play, but Nana said no," said Malik Jr, appearing on the screen with a pouty face confirming his disappointment. He looked exactly like his dad majority of the time, but his emotional facial expressions were his momma's.

"Maybe a little later, MJ. It's still too early for that. Maybe read a book or—"

"Good morning, kiddos!" Yasmine exclaimed, walking into the common area, cutting off Jordyn's impending mom speech urging them to read a book or clean up the toys they undoubtedly had thrown all around the house.

"Hi, Auntie Yas!" Amina exclaimed. Malik Jr. waved in the background, distracted by the television. Yasmine was happy to see her godchildren. She also didn't have many moments to speak to them since being on vacation. Jordyn would either take the calls in her room or when Yasmine was not around. Not on purpose though.

"Where's y'all daddy?" Yasmine inquired.

Malik Jr. responded, "He went to work this morning. He's coming home later." Getting him on the phone was harder than ever, but Jordyn often shared the same sentiments at home. Their progress from therapy seemed to have vanished in her absence, further increasing Jordyn's frustrations with him.

With puppy dog eyes, Amina asked, "Mommy, are you coming home soon?"

The question melted Jordyn's heart. "Yes, baby. In a couple of days. I love you and will call you later, ok?" Her kids missed her dearly and Mom's guilt was beginning to consume her. They echoed "I love you too's" to her before hanging up the phone.

"Never gets easy, huh?" Yasmine asked.

Jordyn admitted, "It doesn't. With Malik always at work and now me being here, I don't want them to feel like they're alone."

"I understand how you might feel, but please do not feel guilty for prioritizing yourself. I know this trip hasn't been perfect, but I hope you've at least enjoyed some time away from your day-to-day tasks. These days away won't change how they see or love you. You're an amazing mom." Yasmine was right. The trip was the recharge she needed to be able to give them her all when she returned.

"Thank you for that, Yas. I hope so," she responded. "Enough about me, though. How was your night?"

Yasmine explained the deep conversations with Trevor and how he made her feel, along with the intense feelings she was developing for a man she barely knew. They were knee deep in the update when

Brianna came out proclaiming, "I know there's not an update happening without including the whole team!"

"You know what? You're right, Brianna. Let me go see what Amari is doing," Jordyn said, beginning to walk toward their room door. She turned back around once she saw her still asleep in bed. Amari's energy had been strange for the last couple of days. Jordyn wished she was as comfortable with her as she was with Yasmine. To let her in more, but that wasn't the case.

"Damn, you're back quick. I'm guessing she isn't coming out?" Brianna asked when Jordyn re-joined them in the common area.

Jordyn shrugged then said, "It looks like she's sleeping in. We can get our day started then catch up with her later." Yasmine and Brianna seemed relieved by the idea and Jordyn couldn't help but feel like she was missing something.

Crossing her legs under her to get comfortable on the sofa, Yasmine began to recap her night. "Basically, my date was really good. Trevor is such a sharp contrast to the guys I normally date. He actually wants to talk about deep shit unlike these other men who keep everything surface-level. What I didn't share with Jordyn yet is when he walked me home …"

"—You gave it up filthy, right?" Brianna said, cutting Yasmine off.

"Damn, girl. Not yet. She has to let him work a little harder first," Jordyn interjected.

"You right, you right," Brianna agreed.

"You are letting him work hard, right Yasmine?" Jordyn gave her best serious mom face with a head tilt for dramatic effect.

Laughing at her friends' ridiculousness, Yasmine continued.

"Damn, y'all. Yes. Well…when we got to the door, he pushed my ass up against the wall and kissed me. Passionately. For a split second, I considered not letting him work any harder. But he's the one who pulled back with a smirk on his face before telling me goodnight."

"Alright now, Trevor. Sounds like the man knows exactly what he's doing," said Jordyn.

Friendship Fragments

"I love this for you, sis. What's the plan for today?" Brianna asked.

"It's an open day. We can do whatever we want, y'all. Much needed after the last few days."

"Facts. Let's grab something to eat." The ladies exited the suite, sending Amari a text to update her on their whereabouts.

* * *

"Is it just me or the energy in the suite is a bit more tense than it has been for the rest of the trip so far? What is going on with Amari, for example?" Jordyn asked midway through breakfast. Yasmine and Brianna glanced at each other, with guilty expressions plastered all over their faces.

"Wait, so y'all do know something I don't?" Jordyn asked, getting increasingly annoyed with every word coming out of her mouth. "This is why I stay to myself. There's always secrets and clique shit going on."

"Jordyn, please don't start. Not today," Yasmine responded, annoyance wiping the smile off her face.

"How am I starting? It's evident that there's something going on and I'm supposed to pretend like I don't see or feel it? And you had the nerve to let *her* know before talking to me? After all these years? Got it," Jordyn replied, nodding slowly. She was done playing nice and didn't care anymore.

"Listen. You have been disrespecting me on and off for this entire trip. I've been keeping it cute for Yasmine because this childish behavior is not necessary. We're way too old to be acting like this," Brianna said, releasing fire right back in Jordyn's direction.

Yasmine couldn't even get a word out before Jordyn stood up.

"Guess I'm a child then. Fuck this and y'all. I'm out of here." Not wanting to hear another lie come out of their mouths, Jordyn left seething. For a slither of time, she almost felt like getting along with

Brianna wasn't impossible. But with all of the secrets and lies they were so horribly covering up, it was time to stop pretending.

After Jordyn left, Brianna turned to Yasmine apologetically.

"Yasmine, I'm sorry. It needed to be said. She is so hot and cold with me. I feel like I'm back in middle school and getting bullied off some dumb shit. It doesn't make any sense."

Visibly deflated, Yasmine responded, "I get it, Brianna. I'm not upset at you. This is supposed to be a fun trip. We're gonna all have to figure out how to put our differences to the side and make the best of what is left of it." Yasmine's frustrations were also building and she was unclear whether what she asked of Brianna could be done herself.

When Yasmine and Brianna got back to their suite, the deafening silence was worse than the previous night. No one was talking to each other and with frustrations at an all-time high, there was no point in trying to get on the same page.

Yasmine went out on the balcony to read the book she brought with her on the trip, *Black Girls Must Die Exhausted*.

Truer words have never been written.

Trevor

Good Morning, Beautiful. I hope you had a good night. Me and the guys are heading to the pool this morning. Want to join?

Yasmine

Good Morning! My night was amazing. I'm down, I'll let the rest of the ladies know. See you soon.

Trevor

Looking forward to it.

. . .

The infinity pool he mentioned was in a more secluded area on the resort with less foot traffic, and the girlfriends wanted to go before they left the island.

She didn't want to be a jerk and not update the rest of her friends, despite her irritability.

She sent a text to their group chat saying, "FYI - The guys will be going to the infinity pool we've been talking about around noon. No pressure, but wanted to let y'all know." The message was liked by everyone except Jordyn. Typical.

Jordyn and Amari abruptly left the suite without saying a word, everyone reaching new heights of pettiness.

Yasmine was so enthralled in the book, noon had come and gone without her realizing it. She woke Brianna up from her nap.

"Ready?"

"Yea, girl. Let's do it," Brianna responded.

28. Never Have I Ever
Yasmine

THE VIEW by the pool didn't disappoint when they arrived. Similar to the main pool at the center of the resort, the illusion of its design made the cerulean blue ocean water look like it expanded from right there on the resort. The sunshine was perfect for sunbathing. They still needed to try for a beach day—if their friendships were to get back in order before the trip ended.

When Yasmine brought her eyes to the pool, although a few couples were sprinkled throughout, there was still enough space for everyone in their group to feel comfortable with one another. She noticed Amari and Jordyn laying out on the sunbeds, unbothered. The men were grabbing drinks at the poolside bar.

"We held some seats for you two," Trevor said, walking to the edge of the pool with shots for everyone in the group.

"Thank you," Yasmine responded, grinning from ear to ear.

He got out of the pool and kissed her cheek before asking, "How was your morning? I was wondering why you weren't here yet with the rest of your girls."

"I honestly lost track of time. We were in different locations and we didn't realize they made their way here already." Her spilling the details of the divide in the group didn't seem appropriate and she hoped the rest of her friends would fake the funk also, leaving the drama away from these people who barely knew them.

"You two are nauseating. Let's have some fun. We should play a game," Chris proposed, flicking water at them.

"Let's do it," Jordyn responded, making her way into the pool. Being team players, the rest of the ladies followed suit.

"Let's grab some more drinks and make it fun," David said, walking toward the pool's bar before anyone could object.

"Ok, how about we play 'Never Have I Ever?' Do y'all know the rules?"

"Of course we know how to play the game, David. Who doesn't?" Amari asked flatly.

"My bad, playa. Just wanted to reiterate. I feel like everyone plays differently," he responded, holding his hands up.

"We're good on the rules. I'll start. Never Have I Ever kept secrets from my close friends," Jordyn blurted out. Yasmine rolled her eyes at her friend's blatant shade toward her after the morning's argument. Everyone, men included, took a sip of their drink except her.

"Oh, y'all are starting off spicy. Yikes," Neil acknowledged.

"A little fun shade, no?" Jordyn replied, smirking.

"So, Jordyn, you never kept a secret before? Ever?" Amari asked suspiciously.

"Not from within my friend group, no." She smiled proudly before looking at Neil. "Your turn." Yasmine wanted to wipe the smugness off her face badly, especially since she knew Jordyn shared things with her she never told Amari. *But go off, sis. No need to match her energy. Yet.*

The game continued but was redirected to more innocent statements about skipping work, getting fired, skinny dipping, throwing up from drinking. It was Brianna's turn when she decided to switch gears.

"Ok. Y'all are playing it too safe now. Let's get drunk. Never Have I Ever cheated on a significant other."

Yasmine was surprised to see all the men, except Neil, take sips of their drinks. As far as the women, Amari and Brianna drank from their cups. Trevor intentionally avoided eye contact with Yasmine after taking his sip. Maybe he wasn't who she thought he was. *Are they ever?*

"Brianna, you do know you're not supposed to be the one to say it if you've done it before, right?" Yasmine asked.

"Listen, I know the rules but needed to spice up the vibes in this pool." Her infectious laugh made everyone in the pool lighten up.

Amari went next. "Never Have I Ever been a hater or thought I was better than one of my friends." Ouch. It was evidently "Piss Yasmine Off" Day. She was about to respond when she felt Trevor squeeze her elbow under the water, leading her not to add any more fuel to the ever-building fire. No one drank.

"Never Have I Ever done anything sexual with someone in this friend group," Chris asked, pointing to everyone playing the game.

Yasmine internally gasped when she saw Amari and Brianna take a sip of their drink. At least they were honest.

"Wait. Amari, you did something with someone here? With who?" Jordyn asked, eyeing Yasmine up and down with suspicion.

"Jordyn, does it really matter? It wasn't you, was it?" Amari's annoyance couldn't be hidden.

"See. This is what I be talking about. Y'all have all of these secrets and no one ever wants to include me," she echoed her same sentiments from earlier when it was just her and Brianna. It was a broken record at this point.

"Not that it is anyone's business here, but Amari and I shared our own sexual encounter before. What does it matter to you?" Brianna admitted, unashamed. Amari rolled her eyes, not liking the attention being drawn in her direction.

Jordyn glanced in the ladies' direction.

"Veryyy interesting. And let's be very clear, you don't matter to me at all, sweetie. Moving on," Jordyn said.

The men whose jaws hadn't dropped since Brianna's admission, were now looking back and forth between the ladies, bracing for the argument about to unfold.

Brianna continued. "Oh, I definitely do matter a lot to you, sweetie. I've made you sweat since you met me, which is why you make the snarky statements you do. I told you this morning and I will tell you again, we are way too old to be acting like this. Yasmine can have more friends than you. Grow up."

"Speaking of her, based on her unsurprised face with this info, it seems like Yasmine knew this information and we didn't. How convenient," Jordyn huffed.

Yasmine clapped back with no hesitation. "Jordyn, please don't start your shit. Your head be so far up your own ass, you wouldn't know what was going on if it was happening right in front of you."

"I know Miss-Know-It-All isn't speaking. Look at the pot calling the damn kettle black. Comical!"

"Grow the fuck up, Jordyn."

Trevor made a fruitless attempt to get everyone to calm down, but things were already too far gone. No one listened. Anything bothering the women was coming out right now. The uncomfortable body language from the men left them with no other option than to head to the bar to separate themselves from the mess. How embarrassing.

Seething, Jordyn took the insults further. "Oh, that's what we're doing, Yasmine? How about 'Never Have I Ever' hid my situationship with Xavier when he's literally best friends with my husband?"

Yasmine was stunned to speak, dropping her jaw at Jordyn's untimely reveal.

"Yea, bitch. I know you're still fucking him. And I thought we were friends. Guess I can pull my head out of my childish ass to know some things are happening, now can't I?"

Yasmine's blood boiled. Thank goodness Trevor and the rest of the guys were out of ear's reach, but she was irate. Jordyn knew this whole time? Why didn't she say something? Why would she bring this up in front of everybody?

"Wow, Yasmine. You really have some nerve," Amari said, shaking her head.

"Amari, please. You really have some nerve to speak. Don't you literally sleep around to get ahead in your career? Please step down from the high horse you claim that I'm on and bring yourself back down to reality."

Yasmine regretted her words as soon as she saw the shocked look on her friend's face.

Before another word could be spoken by anyone, Brianna stepped in with her arms extended across the pool. "ENOUGH. Clearly, these conversations are going nowhere right now. We've spent a lot of time together in the past few days, everyone should take a breather and do their own thing." No one uttered a word against her suggestion, walking away without another word. Things went too far.

The pool went from one filled with laughs and drinks flowing to one with awkward silences. The attention from other people watching from nearby made it even worse.

Yasmine missed her friends desperately prior to the trip and wanted to reconnect. Through distance and time, she held tightly to the good memories the most, not the fragmented pieces they created over time. No friend or friendship was perfect. Acknowledging the negative was just as important as the positive, but the bad was weighing heavily on her spirit.

29. Check-Ins
Yasmine

PETTY DISAGREEMENTS naturally happened when people were stuck together for too long. This trip was far different than college when they could go to class, visit home, or spend time elsewhere. Yasmine felt guilty for bringing Brianna into their toxicity. She wouldn't have invited her friend on the trip if she knew it would make a turn for the worst in this way.

She was torn between the idea of leaving the pool to speak with Jordyn and Amari or check in with Brianna. Uncertain with the headspace her longtime friends were in, she chose the path of less resistance first.

"How are you feeling?" she asked, interrupting the conversation Brianna was having with Chris in the middle of the pool. Usually full of banter, he immediately stepped away to give them privacy.

"I'm annoyed..." Brianna paused before confirming. "Not at you, though. Today is a lot. Yesterday was, too. I feel like I'm in the middle of it, but outside of it, too. Y'all seem to have issues bigger than me, though. How are you?"

"Honestly, Brianna, I am not ok right now. You're absolutely right. We've always had little issues, but never erupted to this level, especially in front of other people."

"I agree. But I also don't think you should beat yourself up about it. Give it some time."

"I'm going to try. I'll be by the bar, taking the edge off with a strong drink."

"No problem. I am here if and when you want to talk," Brianna confirmed with a shoulder squeeze.

Yasmine hugged her friend, not allowing the tears to escape her eyes for the umpteenth time this week. She was not an emotional person, but somehow the trip conjured up feelings she couldn't hide from. She thought about how all of the fun moments washed away in one explosive argument.

She needed a distraction and redirected her energy back to Trevor, who was sitting alone in deep thought. She didn't think he noticed her walking over until he slid down one seat when she was still a few steps away.

"How's your spirit?" he asked, prompting her to sit next to him with a tap on the empty seat.

"Honestly, today is by far the worst day of this trip. If I could get on a flight and go home right now, I would. It's too much." Refusing to stay hidden any longer, the water flowing from her eyes betrayed her.

Grabbing a hand, he said, "I understand how you feel. We can sit here for as long as you want. Or you can do whatever. I'm here, though. The guys feel bad about everything, too. We wouldn't have suggested the game if we knew it would open a can of worms in that way."

"It's ok, no one knew. If anything, I want to apologize for putting y'all in our mess. Most days were good, but there were little issues that weren't getting resolved throughout the trip. Today was the boiling point."

"Nothing to be sorry about. It happens. How are y'all going to fix this?"

"I honestly can't think about that right now. I know we have to, and it needs to be done before this trip ends, but I need to process my emotions right now. I understand if you and your boys don't want to hang around us. No need to ruin your vacation because of strangers you just met." Yasmine was not in a mental space to be solution-oriented.

"I know you're not in a good mood right now, but y'all aren't ruining our trip. Look at them joking around right now. Arguments happen. And when y'all are ready to fix it, you will." Glancing over at the other side of the bar, the men were joking around with other guests with not a worry in the world.

Damn. This man knows how to diffuse a situation while also giving the right amount of reassurance, Yasmine thought.

"I noticed that you drank when the cheating statement came up. Anything you want to share?" Yasmine inquired.

"I figured you might have noticed that. The immature version of myself was a dog. That stopped halfway through college. I am not proud of it, but it helped me be the man I am today."

"I noticed you were avoiding eye contact with me. I appreciate how honest you are. Everyone has a past. As long as you take the lessons and apply them to who you are today, that's all anyone could ask for."

"You are one-hundred percent right about that..." he paused before continuing. "I did overhear something about a situation back at home. Jordyn wasn't exactly whispering. Anything *you* want to share?" Yasmine's cheeks heated up with embarrassment since she didn't think he heard or paid close attention after they walked away.

"I recently rekindled with my college ex who moved back to New York. But things really aren't going anywhere with him. I didn't even realize Jordyn knew about us. I fooled myself into thinking I was waiting to tell them when things were official. The honest truth was, I knew deep down he would disappoint me again. I needed to figure it out on my own."

"I understand. Don't beat yourself up for doing what's best for you."

They sat at the bar for a little longer before noticing the rest of their friends left the pool area. Yasmine put her coverup back on and they decided it was a good time to grab a quick lunch, hoping they'd run into their friends along the way.

After Yasmine and Trevor filled their plates, they noticed the guys and Brianna gathered at a nearby table. "What y'all got going on?" Trevor asked, sitting to join them.

David responded, "Nothing much. We didn't want to interrupt your convo so we texted you to tell you where we were."

Trevor looked down at his phone for the first time in a while. "My bad. Didn't see, but we're here now. What are we doing tonight? Still want to hit up the strip club? Taboo?"

"I'm down, we don't have a driver, though. I hit Peter up and he's not available tonight," Chris explained.

"We can ask our driver if he's free to drive y'all. He's been asking us if we need him," Yasmine noted.

"That reminds me. We planned to ask y'all earlier, but do you think you and your girls would want to come, too?" Trevor asked hesitantly.

Yasmine wasn't sure of the answer herself. She and Amari briefly discussed going to a strip club as a very delayed bachelorette experience for Jordyn since she was never able to have one, but things were muddied by their argument.

Yasmine replied, "Under different circumstances, I would definitely say yes. But after the incident earlier, half of us aren't speaking right now. Brianna, would you want to go tonight? No pressure."

"I'm down as long as there isn't any bullshit like there was at the pool. It would also be cool if it were just you and I. Jordyn does too much. And I'm sick of it." Yasmine couldn't blame Brianna for her disdain. If the shoe were on the other foot, she would probably feel the same.

Friendship Fragments

The men were walking Yasmine and Brianna back to their suite, when they spotted Amari with her laptop near the lobby.

Yasmine stopped mid-walk. "It might be a good time to talk to her. Let me nip this in the bud."

Brianna rolled her eyes. "You're on your own. I'll meet you back in the room." She swiftly walked away with Chris following behind her. Amari and Brianna's issues had more layers to it than the rest of the group. They would need their own private moment.

"You need me to wait for you?" asked Trevor.

"You've done more than enough. I'm good. I appreciate you," she replied with a hug.

"Not a problem. Keep us posted on what your driver says. And if y'all wanna come. A fun night out might be what everyone needs." Yasmine nodded her head, but the truth was she really didn't know what would help.

Yasmine sat in the empty chair next to Amari where she noticed her writing. Putting metaphorical pen to paper was more than a profession for her friend. When words failed her verbally, she always chose to express herself in writing even if only for her eyes to see.

Yasmine sat next to her in silence for a little before breaking the ice. "Hey there."

"Hi, Yasmine." Her response was disconnected and monotone.

"How are you feeling?"

"I've had better days. How did things get so fucked up?" Amari kept her eyes glued on her laptop.

"I honestly don't know. We've had little issues in the past, but for some reason, this argument cut deeper. We all went too far." Yasmine felt the lump forming in her throat again.

Amari interrupted, "No. Speak for y'all selves. I didn't go nearly as far as y'all. You're the one keeping secrets. And then you brought up our private conversation about my dating life. I would have never done that to you." Yasmine nervously looked down at her hands, embarrassed.

"You're right. I was completely out of line. Your comments about me acting 'superior' yesterday hurt me and I took things a little far today. In the heat of the moment, I wasn't thinking and I instantly regretted it after it came out of my mouth. I wasn't keeping the secret about Xavier maliciously. I wanted to know if things between him and I were legit before letting y'all in, but they aren't. So there was really nothing to tell. I am sorry about it all."

Amari finally looked at her friend. "I forgive you and I'm sorry, too. I was projecting a bit when you were trying to give me advice yesterday. Now I won't lie. You do get on a high horse to try and tell people how to live their lives while keeping secrets about how you live your own. It's very hypocritical. I do wish you told me about you and Xavier, especially since you gave me a whole speech about not telling you about Brianna. But I can also understand why you did it so it's cool. Speaking of her, we got into an argument in Negril, too."

"Thank you for understanding. And I saw. We've all had our fair share of drama within the last twenty-four hours. I can't keep up at this point. How did that go?"

Amari paused. "...Not well. I feel like we were both upset about things, but it wasn't the time or place for a productive conversation. I actually left more frustrated than I was before we talked."

"Understandable. She did end up telling me about y'all last night. I'm glad she was finally comfortable sharing."

"That's good. At least you provided a safe space for her to share. Regardless of my feelings toward her at this moment, Jordyn pushing for info like that was not ok."

"I agree. And I definitely don't want to speak out of turn, but I can sense there are some strong feelings between the two of you. You should definitely talk about whatever you both are feeling and see how to move forward."

"We will, Yas. I just want to speak from a more rational space instead of in this heightened emotional space I am in right now."

"I understand that," she confirmed before switching topics. "I do have one more thing to run by you."

"Oh goodness. What is it?"

"I know the group really isn't in a space to speak right now, but the guys are going to the strip club tonight. I would hate for the rest of our trip to go to waste because of arguments. Do you think Jordyn would be open to going?"

"I don't know about all of that, Yas. How will we all go while not speaking to each other?"

"That's the thing. I don't know, but don't you also feel like this would add fuel to fire with Jordyn thinking we have this vendetta against her? We discussed doing a strip club night as her faux bachelorette night."

"Well, it was supposed to be a surprise so it's not like she knew about it happening. But let me guess, since you aren't talking to her, you want me to be the one to ask her if she wants to go."

Grabbing her friend's elbow, Yasmine exclaimed, "Would you?!"

Amari rolled her eyes. "I'll ask, girl. But it's only because I want the room to myself tonight."

"Wait, you don't want to come? You were so excited about going."

"That was before all of the bullshit that happened today. I'm going to sit this one out. I need a break from y'all hoes right now."

Her feelings were valid. No one could have predicted a relaxing day at the resort would be more emotionally draining than all of the outside activities combined.

"Thank you so much! I know this drama is a lot for you. I hope we can all get through it, but take whatever mental breaks you need," Yasmine said, reaching to hug her friend.

Amari returned her friend's affection. "I hope so, too. I love you, Yas."

"I love you, too."

30. No More Drama
Yasmine

NO MORE DRAMA, Yasmine whispered to herself before using her key card to enter their suite. She took deep breaths, a fruitless attempt at relieving herself from the angst she felt in the pit of her stomach. The silence upon entry unnerved her even more.

"Why is it so quiet in here?" Yasmine asked, entering her room where she found Brianna scrolling through her phone.

Seemingly aloof to anything going on outside of her rectangular device, Brianna asked, "In here or out there?"

"Well, out there." Yasmine asked, side eyeing her friend. "Is Jordyn here?"

"Oh, she was on the sofa when I got in. Seems like she decided to leave shortly thereafter. I'm not paying her any mind. How'd your convo with Amari go?"

"It went ok. Think we squashed our issue."

"Well, that's good. Are her and Jordyn joining us tonight?"

"Amari isn't, but she said she would ask Jordyn. Despite today's shenanigans, I don't want her to feel left out."

"Got it. Like I said, I am ok if it ends up being us two. That's how it is back home anyway."

"True. I know the group is not in a great place right now, but at the end of the day, they're my friends, too, and we all came here together. I understand your stance, though."

"I hear you, Yasmine. I'm over the bullshit now. Keep me posted on if she decides to join. I want to prepare my energy. I wish I brought some sage to cleanse the energy up in here."

Yasmine laughed. "Honestly, same. I'm gonna do a literal cleansing in the shower to prepare for the night. I'm trying to have a great time, ahkay?!"

"Agreed, sister."

* * *

Yasmine rummaged through her suitcase to find something sexy to wear to the strip club. In the privacy of the shower and finally alone with her own thoughts, she fully surrendered to her emotions, allowing the weight of the day to wash away. The cascading shower water blended in with tears pouring from her eyes. When she finished releasing, Yasmine made a silent promise to herself to enjoy the rest of the trip regardless of what everyone else did.

She heard her phone go off while in the shower and grabbed it immediately as she got out.

Amari
Jordyn said she wants to stay in. Y'all have fun! Don't let today ruin tonight.

Yasmine felt like the decision might be for the best. With Amari choosing not to go, it would be awkward with Jordyn there without their problems resolved. She also noticed a missed text from Trevor.

. . .

Trevor

We're ordering in around 8PM. You and your girls are more than welcome to pre-game here before we go out.

Yasmine

Perfect! Our driver will be here at 10PM. It'll only be Brianna and I. Amari and Jordyn decided to stay back.

Trevor

Ok cool. We're going to have a good night. See you soon!

Yasmine

Indeed we will. See you soon <3

* * *

"Girl, you better wake up and get ready. Aren't we supposed to be ready soon?" Brianna asked, hovering over Yasmine.

Seven p.m. Shit. The stress of the day must have worn Yasmine out.

"Damn, I didn't realize I fell asleep. Let me get it together."

Yasmine's outfit choice of the night was a black cut out bodysuit and a black mini skirt with matching black pleaser pumps. She planned to wear her black Loewe shades and black Jacquemus bag as final touches. The strippers weren't going to be the only ones Trevor had his eyes on tonight.

"Oh bitch, you look the fuck good! That's what I'm talking about," Brianna said, coming out of the bathroom fully dressed.

"You do, too! The girls are not coming to play tonight."

"We sure aren't."

Without discussing what they would wear prior, both friends

opted for an all-black ensemble, complementing one another with their own unique styles. Brianna wore a black vinyl mini dress with black stilettos.

"Them strippers better watch out. We might be the ones walking out with some extra cash in our pockets," Brianna said with a high five to Yasmine.

"Period! We're gonna have a time tonight, sis."

"Facts. Not before we coat our stomachs before drinking. Ready to meet up with the men?"

"Definitely. Let's still take a shot for the road before we meet up with them, though."

"You and these damn shots, Yasmine. Can we ever just chill?"

"Absolutely not. Thank you for asking."

They laughed, walking into the common room and taking tequila shots before they left for the guys' suite. Jordyn was by herself on the balcony and the door to her shared room with Amari was shut. Yasmine almost considered opening the door to show Amari their looks, but it didn't feel right without the tension completely diffused. They exited the suite without interacting with either of them.

The door to the guys' suite was ajar when they arrived, flimsily held open by the security latch. As usual, they looked fine as hell. They were nice arm candy for the night on the town.

Trevor almost choked on his drink when he locked eyes on Yasmine. "Well damn." The men echoed his sentiments by mentioning how beautiful the ladies looked.

"Thanks y'all! Ready to turn up tonight, boys?" Brianna asked, turning to give them a full 360 view of her look. Chris gawked in her direction but fell into his usual routine of joking directly afterward.

"Now how am I supposed to have innocent thoughts when you look like that?" Trevor whispered into Yasmine's ear, sending chills up her spine with flashbacks of their moment the night before.

As they slowly pulled out of their hug, Trevor kept his hands resting above her waist. Yasmine gazed at him seductively. "Who said I wanted you to do that?"

She intentionally walked away before he could answer. Although Chris and David started speaking to him, he kept his eyes fixed on her every move. He scanned her body from head to toe as if he could see what was under it.

They ordered chicken wings, beef sliders, mozzarella sticks, french fries, and pizza. Everyone grabbed appetizer plates before sitting on the sofa for their quick bites.

"Sucks that everyone couldn't be here tonight," Neil noted, breaking the mid-eating silence.

"I know, Neil. I hope you're not too disappointed. I know you and Jordyn bonded in the last few days," said Yasmine.

David interjected, "Honestly, at least there won't be drama. Today was a lot." Trevor shot him a glaring look. "My bad."

"You ladies look amazing so we're in great company. No complaints," noted Chris. The rest of the men nodded in agreement.

"Alright y'all. Hurry up and eat, time to get these shots flowing," Trevor said, heading to their makeshift bar to prepare drinks.

"It's wild how similar you and Yasmine are when it comes to these things," Brianna commented.

"Honestly. I know y'all just met, but I've never seen this man open like this. Keep up the good work," Chris said to Yasmine, dapping her up with his approval.

She smiled at the compliment. No one could predict what the future held, but she was making an effort to live in the moment. Right now, Trevor made her happy.

Passing out shots to everyone, Trevor diverted the conversation.

"Alright, alright. Enough about us. Everyone, grab a drink. Let's get this night really started."

The shots flowed and music blasted. They almost missed the text when Delroy arrived. They took a final shot for the road before going to the lobby. Delroy waved them toward a different vehicle than the one he drove the ladies in earlier in the week.

"New car, Delroy?" Yasmine questioned as he held the door open for them.

"Well, I heard seh wi might hav ah biggah group today. I wanted fi mek sure we had enough space."

"Always such a gentleman," Brianna said, slowly entering the van not to expose everyone to her panty less parts. "These are our friends David, Trevor, Chris, and Neil," she said, pointing to each person as she mentioned their names.

"Nice fi meet unnu. My name is Delroy and I will be di driver. Don't hesitate fi reach out if unnu need anything." The men shared warm salutations while Delroy started the journey to Taboo.

* * *

The men exited the van first at the club to secure a VIP table for everyone to sit at comfortably. With a short window of time before they returned, Delroy turned around to ask, "Unnu need mi fi come inna di club with yuh? Mi will mek an exception if needed. Yuh comfortable wid dem?"

Yasmine appreciated his concern for their safety. "We met them at the resort, but we do feel safe with them. We'll text you immediately if we need you to, though."

"Of course. I'll be close by, text mi when unnu ready. Be safe."

"Will do, Delroy," Yasmine and Brianna said in sync as the men returned to escort them into the club.

31. Lusty Taboo
Yasmine

Taboo was a fairly small club but had enough room to feel comfortable. Although it was not packed, the DJ was playing all the ratchet music the ladies wanted to hear as soon as they walked in. Travis Scott, Juicy J, Drake, and Vybz Kartel. The bands would surely be making everyone dance, not just the strippers. Yasmine and Brianna were dancing with each other before they were settled in their section, already feeling tipsy from the pre-game back at the resort.

The host led the group up to where their table for the night would be and handed out a drink menu. By her flirtatious tone specifically toward him, it was evident she had her eyes set on Trevor. Yasmine wasn't worried because he wasn't her man and it was already clear who he would be leaving with.

The view from the top of the club was far better than it would have been on the main level with the perfect view of the entire venue. There were strippers on the small, platformed stage splitting, bending, and twisting their bodies in ways most women could not do on the ground— much less a twenty-foot stripping pole.

They ordered a few bottles to start the night— one bottle of tequila, one bottle of cognac, and one bottle of champagne.

"I am so happy we decided to do this, Yasmine," Brianna stated, locking their arms together and resting her head on her shoulder.

"I agree. I want to enjoy every moment tonight because who knows what tomorrow will be like."

"My sentiments exactly."

By the time the bottle girls arrived at their section with the sparkler-lit bottles, the club was packed with more dancers walking around to offer private dances. Two of the strippers came into their section after a round of shots and made alluring strides toward Yasmine and Brianna first. Trevor smoothly slid a few stacks of money into Yasmine's hands.

The ladies knew the strategy. Strippers dance on women to turn the men they're with on, leading to more money being spent by both parties. A trick as old as time, but Yasmine didn't mind. With every ass shake and lusty removal of a clothing item to reveal even more skin, she enjoyed the strippers expressing their artistry with every whine and shake while occasionally throwing bills on and around them. Yasmine was as straight as they came, but strippers always turned her on. The confidence in expressing their bodies freely sent her mind racing about...Trevor. She signaled for him to trade places with her on the couch.

"Have fun," Yasmine said, standing up to watch him while he watched the dancer with the more-than-occasional glance in her direction.

In the midst of the club lights and haze of smoke in the air, it looked like more strippers were entering their section. She didn't fully grasp what was happening until she saw the two women hug David and Neil. But it couldn't be. Yasmine looked at her phone and saw a missed message.

Amari

Heads up, Yas. Jordyn decided she wanted to come out. She's dragging me out so she doesn't feel alone. Sorry.

She tapped on Brianna's arm ferociously to get her attention.

"Damn, Yas. What?"

"Look over there." Yasmine nudged her head in the direction she wanted her to look.

Yasmine smiled at her temporarily estranged friends, hoping to diffuse any residual tension for the sake of a good night, but Jordyn intentionally looked past her and settled on the other side of the couch. Amari gave her an apologetic look before sitting down. *Welp, this night is turning into an awkward one quickly.* Did Jordyn genuinely want to have a good night? Or did she want to stir up some more drama?

"Ignore them, sis. Do not let them ruin our night. Let's take more shots," Brianna suggested, trying to keep the energy up.

"You're the one proposing shots this time? I must really look pitiful." Yasmine laughed, following Brianna to grab a cup.

After they threw their drinks back, they sat back on the couch to vibe out to the music and continue enjoying the show. Trevor hastily walked over to Yasmine to check in. "You good, Yas? I saw—"

"I am, Trevor. Thank you. A little shocked is all."

"Yea we all are..." he paused before elaborating. "...except Neil, it seems. I think because it was only y'all two, he was trying to get Jordyn to come out and it worked. I don't think he had ill intentions, but he should have said something to us."

"Yea and we invited them, too, so it's a non-issue. I don't want any awkward vibes. Let's drink our worries away," she said, grabbing another drink to numb her feelings.

"Take your time. It's going to be ok." He grabbed her free hand to squeeze and gently kissed it before walking away.

It was not clear how much time had passed, but Yasmine didn't realize she dozed off on the couch before Brianna tapped her to check in.

"Yo Yasmine, you good?"

"I'm fine, why are you asking me that?"

"Well, let me think. You being asleep on a couch in the middle of the club might have something to do with it."

"Oh shit, I didn't realize. Can you get me some water? I have a piercing headache." Suddenly, the bass from the music felt like it was projecting directly into Yasmine's ear.

She overheard Brianna asking Jordyn to get water since there was no one else around.

Jordyn rolled her eyes before responding, "Sorry, I'm not grown enough to help you with that. And Yasmine is too grown to be as drunk as she is." She proceeded to turn her back and continued dancing to the music.

"What in the fuck is your problem?" Yasmine said.

"What's MY problem? What's yours? You throw jabs and don't expect them to be thrown back at you?" Jordyn stood over Yasmine with her fingers pointed.

Ignore her. Ignore her. Ignore her. NOPE.

"Jordyn, you've been on some different time today. And I am sick of it. Just learn when to shut the fuck up sometimes. There are people who actually want to enjoy their trip, unlike you who chooses misery at every turn."

"Say it to my face."

Standing up to look her in the eye, Yasmine finally admitted what she has kept to herself all these years. "You're a miserable bitch, who is unhappy and blames every person for how their life turned out except herself. And I stay far away because you drain the life out of me."

Jordyn was inches from punching Yasmine in the face before Amari pulled her back by the waist. "We are not doing this. This is not us," Amari said. Jordyn stormed away, crying.

Trevor came to her side when he got back to the section.

"What happened now?" The men had gone to the stage to get a closer look at the dancers, missing the drama unfolding in their section.

Brianna started explaining the situation, but stopped when she saw Amari return with water.

"Thank you," Yasmine said, taking the bottle from her hand without any eye contact, feeling embarrassed about her public display of chaos. Yes, she finally told her truth, but the hurt she saw in Jordyn's eyes was not something she could erase. They had taken it too far again and it was unclear how it would be resolved.

"I've seen all I need to see tonight. How about I take Yasmine back to the resort?" Trevor asked.

"Want us to contact Delroy?" Brianna asked.

"Nah. I think everyone is still having a good time. Y'all can contact him when you're ready. Unless you want to come with us?"

"I do, actually. I don't want to be around any of this bullshit."

"Ok. I'll handle everything. Yasmine, can you unlock your phone for me? I want to contact the driver to let him know the plan."

Before they could find a taxi, Delroy texted back and said he didn't mind doing two trips since he was in the area.

"Everyting alright?" he inquired from the driver's seat as Trevor helped Yasmine into the van with Brianna following right behind them.

"Yea we are. Yasmine was having too much fun and wanted to go to bed," responded Brianna.

"If that's what we wanna call fun," Yasmine said, half asleep on Trevor's arm. By the time she re-opened her eyes, feeling like only seconds had gone by, they were already back at the resort. Her head was throbbing so much, she thought it might explode. She downed the other half of the water bottle still in her hands.

"Feel better, Yasmine. I will pick everyone else up when they are ready."

Trevor shook Delroy's hand to thank him before escorting the ladies into the lobby.

* * *

As they entered the ladies' suite and Trevor prepared to leave, Yasmine kissed him on the neck before asking, "Can I stay with you tonight?"

Shocked by her forwardness, he stuttered. "Oh. Umm. You can. But are you sure?"

"I don't want to be in the same place as Jordyn tonight. It's too much."

Brianna's presence was almost missed before she validated Yasmine's concerns. "It really might be a good idea. She can always come back in the morning."

"I don't mind, but I want to make sure she's comfortable. It's been a long day."

"Thank you for your concern, I am a big girl. Let me just grab my toothbrush and pajamas."

Trevor waited by the ladies' suite door for her to gather some things then walk back to his suite.

With a quick hug, Brianna whispered to her, "Have fun, sis."

* * *

Trevor helped Yasmine take off her heels while she prepared to shower off the night. Drunk or not, she couldn't get in anyone's bed with her outside clothes or a dirty body.

"You want to join me?" she asked Trevor as he passed her a fresh towel and washcloth.

"Join you while you shower?" he replied, confusion filling his eyes.

"Yes, silly. You're capable of looking without wanting to touch, right?" His apprehension made her giggle.

"I am." His words and forcefully stoic body language did not match. Yasmine was purposely dangling a carrot right in front of his face and he looked like he was deciding which approach to take.

"Ok, then hurry and take off your clothes. I'll get started." She removed each item of clothing slowly and deliberately without breaking eye contact with him, watching as his breathing increased with the exposure of each body part. She bit her lips as he watched her enter the shower.

Through the steam glass doors, Yasmine saw Trevor keeping his eyes fixated on hers, taking his own clothes off. She lathered her body with soap and the steam from the shower made her feel less drunk.

Trevor joined her and began soaping himself up, keeping a safe distance between them.

"How are you feeling?" he asked.

"This shower is helping tons. I shouldn't have drank that much. I'm sorry about that."

"Not a problem, Yasmine. You didn't do anything, but I wanted to get you back before things took a turn for the worse." Yasmine wasn't sure if he meant with her drunkenness or between her friends, but either way, she agreed. If Amari had not interfered, fists would have been thrown.

She inched closer to Trevor, allowing the water to rinse the soap off both of their bodies. She slowly backed him up against the glass doors and started giving him slow, seductive pecks to his lips. He returned the gesture, tugging on the back of her braids to fully allow their mouths to pick up from where they left off the night before. The water from the shower was still hitting them, adding more steam to an already heated situation. He immediately stopped to remind her. "You said I can look, but not touch, right?"

"Yes, I said you can't touch me," she said. "But none of that matters now because I changed my mind."

Yasmine grabbed Trevor's hand and moved them slowly past her breasts then back up to her neck, biting her lips at his mere touch. She wrapped her legs around him as he turned her around to press her into the shower wall, kissing her from her shoulder up to her neck while she released a soft moan with each nibble.

He lifted her out of the shower, never taking his lips off hers and slowly placed her on the bed. With him pressed between her legs, Yasmine wrapped them around him to pull him even tighter while softly kissing his ear.

"Are you sure we want to go here tonight? I can wait."

"Trev, you are such a gentleman and I appreciate that. But I don't want you to be one right now, ok?"

Those words unleashed a different side of him. He kissed her with more intensity, moving from her lips down to her collarbone. Yasmine's toes curled, begging for more. He slowly inched farther, giving her breasts the attention they were in desperate need of, gently tugging with every suck of her nipples. With a gentle push of his head, he kissed all the way past her navel down to her toes, putting them in his mouth before moving back to the center of her frame. He teased her, pecking each side of her thigh, enacting full on torture.

"Trevor, please." Smirking at her, he parted her lips to reveal the gushy warmth. Yasmine moaned and curved her body upward in deep ecstasy, unraveling with each stroke of his tongue.

Before she knew it, her body was shaking from orgasming from his tongue alone. He kissed his way back up to her lips and grabbed a condom before completely filling her up. With each cavernous stroke, they emerged themselves in deep rapture, never breaking eye contact. Trevor grabbed her leg to suck her toes again, this time while inside of her. Yasmine came over and over, releasing in ways she had never experienced before. Unable to hold himself together, he collapsed on top of her, releasing all of their built-up tension.

Trevor laid next to her. "Damn, I did not have any of that on my radar tonight at all."

"Was it worth it?"

Kissing both the inside and outside of her palm, he confirmed, "More than that."

32. It's Over Now
Jordyn

JORDYN TOSSED and turned all night, unable to fight back against her restlessness. She felt bad about how things transpired at the club, but at the same time, her suspicions were confirmed. Her friends kept their distance because they felt like she was a burden. At least Yasmine did. The thought of her best friend giving up on her hurt more than anything else.

Jordyn didn't intend for the information about Xavier to spill out like it did during the game, but it shouldn't have been a secret to begin with. When everyone went their separate ways, she didn't even have the decency to check up on her. She stayed back with her new friends.

Yasmine should have found time to speak privately about why she wasn't comfortable with sharing her reignited relationship with Xavier. Sure, Jordyn could have extended the olive branch first, having exposed her in front of friends and strangers alike, but instead Yasmine deliberately avoided her for the rest of the day. Clearly their friendship wasn't more important than the one she shared with Brianna and the new men Jordyn saw her having lunch with. When she saw them altogether eating, seemingly unphased, they were laughing and joking as if the pool didn't almost turn into a WWE Smackdown tag team match. It rubbed her the wrong way.

The only reason she decided to go to the strip club was to enjoy her night. Neil was right; they all deserved to soak up what was left of their trip. But she should've listened to Amari. They needed more time apart.

"I don't know if this is a good idea. It might be best if we all have some space right now and start fresh tomorrow," Amari urged when Jordyn suggested heading out.

"But why do they get to have all the fun? Do we not deserve to?"

"Of course we do. But after everything that went down today, it would be awkward for you to be there alone."

"Oh, I won't be alone because you're coming with me. Duh."

"Jordyn, I'm really tired of dealing with all of you to be honest. I want some peace."

"Amari, I'm not going to cause problems. I only want to get some drinks and see strippers. I've never been to a strip club. C'mon, c'mon, c'mon," she pleaded, dragging her friend out of bed.

"Fine, Jordyn, fine. I'll only go because I know how awkward it would be with you alone. But please, I don't need any more bullshit today."

"All fun, no drama. Pinky promise."

Yet, she broke that very pledge. Walking into the club and seeing the closeness of Yasmine and Brianna instantly enraged her. The pain of the day came rushing back in. The nerve of her to imply Jordyn being self-centered. Everyone had a bit of selfishness to them. Yasmine included. Especially, at times.

She noticed when Yasmine attempted to send a friendly glance in her direction, but it wasn't enough. She planned to ignore them for the rest of the night, just as they had chosen to ignore her throughout the day.

Then Brianna thought it was appropriate to task Jordyn with getting Yasmine water. No. Were there words exchanged between them to garner any generosity? No. Maybe if Jordyn agreed to get the water, things wouldn't have gone left, but they did.

Yasmine had the nerve to curse in her direction, all while admitting what Jordyn knew in her heart of hearts far before the words were spoken. She hated her. If Amari hadn't stepped in, blows would have been thrown for every broken promise, every secret and lie, and for every pretentious moment Yasmine made her feel like she was overreacting. She was right all along.

"You took it too far, Jordyn," said Amari after Yasmine and Brianna left the club early.

"Ok, and what about what she said?"

"Tensions were high and just like in the game, both of you went too far. But you're the one who tried to put your hands on her first. We're sisters. We're supposed to do better than that." Jordyn began to get teary-eyed again.

"I didn't have to do that. I'm pissed at her, but you're right. That was uncalled for." Their friendship might officially be over. It should never have gotten to the point where anyone wanted to put their hands on the other, but there was no way to take it all back. The day worsened. There were two days left with no solution in sight.

"I think with some time and space, y'all can figure it out. Underneath the hurt on both sides is love. You both just need to express your feelings, even the things you've never addressed, not wanting to hurt the other person. It built up to where we are today, but I don't think it's beyond repair."

"You might be right. Guess we'll just have to wait and see."

Day 7: Let's Call A Truce

33. Three Rules
Yasmine

Yasmine awoke to a throbbing headache, paired with confusion about the dark room she was in. It wasn't until she turned to see the beautiful figure laying next to her, she remembered. She kissed Trevor's forehead and he pulled her back closer to his chest, neither still fully awake.

Reminiscing about their moments that transpired a few hours before, she slowly grinded her back on him until he caved and dived back in for another round. Their pre-dawn passion sent them back into a deep slumber.

A glance at her phone some hours later let her know it was shortly after sunrise. She wanted to continue being cradled in Trevor's arms, but the rest of her memories of the day prior flooded her mind. How did everything with her friends become so awful? Why did Jordyn act the way she did at the club?

The trip was meant to fill their cups and instead, completely drained them. Despite every fiber of her being telling her to just spend the day with the guys, then leave in forty eight hours to not deal with the drama, if there was anything left to revive in their friendships, they needed to have a discussion. They were going to need to reintroduce their college solution for conflict—The Sit Down. Brianna would have to participate, too.

There were three rules everyone had to abide by:

Rule Number One: No matter how angry or annoyed anyone in the group might be, once the meeting is requested, everyone must attend. No rebuttals and questions asked.

Rule Number Two: When a person was speaking about their feelings, they must fully have the floor and not be interrupted. If there needed to be a response from anyone, the person must open the floor up for responses to how they felt.

Rule Number Three: Everyone must leave the meeting with all conflicts resolved. It could be an issue no one heard about before, but everything must be hashed out in order to move forward.

The Sit Down was incorporated when conflicts in their group went unresolved. It was used to provide a safe space for everyone to individually speak while also providing a solution for either the group or the specific individuals with an issue. It became an accidental routine after Amari joined the friend group. There was mistrust from Jordyn and Amari after their initial introduction to one another. Yasmine created the rules, knowing Jordyn's alternative solution was to cut people off and forget about their existence.

They continued the trend of The Sit Down throughout the rest of their undergraduate experience. It could be as big as a squabble about leaving a drunken friend on the side of the road or as small as a debate over who ate the last piece of chicken in the refrigerator.

Over a decade later on the island, The Sit Down was very necessary. Yasmine reluctantly decided to be the one to call the meeting. She hoped everyone would follow the rules as they did in the past. Yasmine wanted these issues resolved before nightfall.

Yasmine

Good Morning, Ladies. I am requesting The Sit Down. 3pm. Our suite.

To her surprise, everyone liked the text message to confirm their attendance. Brianna messaged her on the side to ask what it meant and Yasmine was happy to give her the low down, along with the rules to follow.

Despite everyone agreeing they would go, the tightness building in her chest was hard to ignore. She didn't know how everything would unfold, but it was the only way to move forward or be done with each other completely.

She felt like her thoughts were caving in on her and needed fresh air to control her rapid breathing. She barely touched the doorknob when she heard, "Where are you going?" The groggy deep voice reminded her she wasn't alone.

"Oh, good morning, Trevor. I was going to head to breakfast," she responded.

"Damn, was last night so bad that you wanted to sneak out without saying anything?" he asked, sitting up to turn the lights on. The extra baritone of his voice and sleepiness in his eyes made him even sexier.

"Not at all. I feel bad because you're on vacation with your boys. No need to babysit me."

"I don't feel like I am. My boys will always be here. I understand if you want to have breakfast alone. But I can come with you if you want, too." Don't men usually act weird after sex? Yasmine didn't plan to sleep with Trevor on the trip, but the haze of the night led her to. There was no way he would ever take her seriously now, right? What's the point of pretending? All the chaos around her was making her spiral.

"I don't mind if you come. I'm heading to the beach afterward, in case you want to join."

Trevor walked up to Yasmine and gently kissed her collarbone.

"We're actually going to Dunns River Falls today. We still haven't been. But I'll one thousand percent have breakfast with you. Only us two." He disappeared into the bathroom to brush his teeth and put on clothes.

After being on the resort so long, getting breakfast was routine. Trevor and Yasmine quickly maneuvered through the room for the breakfast foods of choice. There was a level of comfort between them, where they didn't need to constantly fill the room with meaningless conversation, just for the sake of talking. Yasmine couldn't believe they recently met each other. She tried to enjoy the moments of solace with him, knowing in a few hours, pandemonium could be on the agenda instead.

They recapped the beautiful night they shared over breakfast. She also gave him the update on her text to the ladies for the afternoon.

"How'd that go?"

"Well, it's something we've done since college, so if one of us calls this meeting, no one usually refuses. This time was no different. Everyone agreed to it thankfully."

"That's good, right? I hope it all works out. Friends are like second families and I can tell there's a lot of love there."

"There seems to be a lot of hurt too, honestly. It is a good sign that they agreed, but I just don't know how things might go. This is also the first time we've done this in years. Everyone seems to be at their wits ends, so I'm more worried than I have been in the past."

"I get it. I say to control what you can and go in with no expecta-tions. It could go horribly, but it could also turn out better than you think. Take it one step at a time."

Trevor's wisdom gave Yasmine a sense of relief she hadn't felt in days. He walked her to the beach before he left for his excursion.

"Everything will work itself out, Yasmine. Ok?" he said, kissing the same hand he held as they walked.

"You're right. Go have fun."

While Yasmine wasn't as sure as he was about how the day would unfold, she also didn't want him worrying about her. They shared one final kiss before he left to go meet up with the rest of his crew.

The sand on the beach welcomed her bare feet with a comforting warmth, not too hot, not too cool—the perfect temperature to be enjoyable. The sound of waves crashing against the shore reminded her of the ocean playlist she sometimes used to help her fall asleep back at home. The sound of real ocean waves— up close and personal — was far better. The beach calmed her anxious spirit, preparing her for the afternoon.

Yasmine found an open beach chair and took a seat under the umbrella. She opened the Kindle app to pick back up where she left off in her book. Without intending to, she fell asleep. She did have a long night, after all. When she woke up and peeked at the time, it was after one in the afternoon, getting closer and closer to The Sit Down. She looked at her phone and saw a slew of texts from Brianna over the last couple of hours.

Brianna
Where are you?

Brianna
Yasmine. Why aren't you responding?

Brianna
Yas, don't play with me. Are you with the guys?

. . .

Brianna

YAS! Where are you?

Brianna

Ok, I texted the guys and they said you're on the beach. If you want space, I will leave you alone. But please text me back at least.

Yasmine felt bad for putting Brianna in a bit of distress and gave a very delayed response back. She quickly gathered her things to grab lunch before going back to the suite to shower.

Brianna was waiting by the door for her, tapping her foot impatiently as Yasmine entered their room. If it were possible, smoke would be coming from Brianna's ears with how mad she appeared. Brianna kept her arms crossed while Yasmine tried to hug her, simultaneously stifling her laughter from her friend's dramatics.

"Sorry, Bri. I was reading then fell asleep on the beach." Not good enough. She stared blankly at Yasmine.

"I'm sorry, ok?! I went to breakfast with Trevor then went to the beach by myself. I couldn't even give you an idea of when I fell asleep. Blame my ocean playlist back at home."

"Yes, I read your texts. I was worried about you. It's also very unsafe to fall asleep alone on the beach like that. Don't do that again."

"You're right. Between the long night we had and the sound of the beach waves, I stood no chance. My bad. How's it been in here?" Yasmine asked, looking in the direction of the room where her other friends were. She did leave her in the warzone alone.

"It's been ok, to be honest. I pretty much stayed in our room all night and morning. I haven't crossed paths with them much."

"Ok cool."

"How do these sit downs usually go? You are all a bit headstrong."

"Definitely. Every one of them has been different, but the end goal usually is the same. We all need to come to a place of understanding and get along afterward. I would personally like to enjoy the last day we have here in paradise."

"Oh, I agree. Let's hope for the best."

34. The Sit Down
Yasmine

THE TENSION in the air could be sliced with a knife. The ladies did their best to avoid one another up until the meeting time. Yasmine sat on the sofa first, three p.m. on the dot. She envisioned several scenarios how things could play out during their sit down, each one more progressively worse than the last. Not helpful at all.

Yasmine didn't realize Brianna sat next to her until she tapped her shoulder and whispered, "It's going to work itself out, Yas." Echoing Trevor's earlier sentiments should have put her at ease, but her accelerated heart rate was telling her a different story.

"I sure hope so."

Jordyn and Amari joined them on the sofa. The silence in the room was deafening. It was unclear if it was due to everyone's shared anxiety, being fed up with each other, or a combination of both.

"Hello," Jordyn said. At least formalities weren't lost.

"Hi," echoed from everyone around the room.

Yasmine spoke first. "Thank you all for joining today," she continued. "We haven't done one of these in a long time and I want to refresh us all with the rules."

"Why doesn't she think we know the rules?" Jordyn whispered loudly to Amari, rolling her eyes.

"We already accomplished rule number one by being here. Rule number two is to make sure the speaker fully has the floor without interruptions. I want to add that this includes side chatter." Yasmine shot a sharp look in Jordyn's direction. "Let's all be respectful of one another. The last rule is, if nothing else, that we can leave here with our problems resolved and getting back on the same page. We love each other way too much to be petty like this. Would anyone like to go first?"

Jordyn huffed as soon as Yasmine mentioned the word love. Hopefully, her theatrics ceased by the time the first person spoke up.

Amari volunteered. "I'll go first. I am sick of this shit. We are way too grown to act the way we have on this vacation. Yasmine, I want to start with you. I feel like you think you're better than us and have this moral compass that can see things better than us. It feels like you think we aren't capable of making the best decisions for ourselves, all while keeping your own secrets from the group. Maybe things aren't done the way you would do it, but that is still each person's individual decision to make, not yours.

"Jordyn, girl. I love you, but you have some inner work that needs to be worked on to have healthy and sustainable relationships. You be doing a lot and you are very territorial. You did the same exact thing you're doing to Brianna to me. After all these years, you still don't want to change?

"And Brianna, I am so sorry that this is your first impression of us as a friend group. We've never been perfect, but this trip has been a true test for our little college group.

"As for us two, I've loved your energy since the moment we met. What we shared was beautiful and I am sorry it was exposed in such a public way without you fully processing it yourself beforehand. There are things we definitely need to discuss, but in fairness, it needs to be on a one-on-one basis. I hope everyone understands why. Thank y'all. Who wants to go next?"

Friendship Fragments

For someone who shied away from drama, Amari's honesty was welcomed in the moment.

Brianna announced. "Ok, I'll go next. This is my first one of these. I hope I get it right. Yasmine, you're my girl. I'm not saying you're perfect because no one is, but ever since we met, you have been nothing short of a friend. You have helped me through some very dark moments and I haven't quite thanked you enough. On the other hand, you do want people to live life in the order you envision. It is not reality and you cannot control the outcome of everything. I love you dearly.

"Amari, I agree there are things we need to talk through separately. But publicly, I would like to thank you for respecting my privacy in regard to us. It was not me being ashamed, but rather working through feelings within myself I didn't realize were there prior.

"Which leads me to Jordyn. This trip is the first time I met you, but Yasmine has always spoken highly of her childhood best friend. I can't speak to your character, but I can say based on my experience thus far, you have not been the person she described. She always mentioned how much I remind her of you, but I don't see how that is possible at all. I would never treat another person the way you've treated me on this trip. It has left a very nasty taste in my mouth. I wish you peace and maybe one day, we can get on the same page. For those two, if not for any other reason," she closed by pointing to Yasmine and Amari.

Jordyn tried to sneakily wipe some tears, but not before Yasmine noticed. As much as her friend infuriated her, she wanted to reach across the sofa and hug her, too.

Jordyn started. "Ok, I'll go. I want to start off by saying I've been thinking about how to approach all of this. I hear what you all have said and it definitely feels like I've put a damper on things during this trip. I feel like since I got married and started a family quickly, you all think I live a perfect life. I am often tired, overwhelmed, and barely see the man who moved me far away from

223

my support system to pursue his dreams. I can't tell if he loves me for me or I only fit into the life he planned long before we ever met.

"Amari, I respect your privacy but I feel like you can be so closed off at times, I wonder if you actually consider me as one of your friends. Or is it a default because of your love and friendship with Yasmine?

"Yasmine, you are my girl, through and through. You have been all my life. I've had quite the jealous streak since you've brought Brianna around. Even when you brought Amari around. It always feels like you want to replace me, especially in recent years where you've become more distant. It took some liquid courage for you to admit it to me last night, which hurt me more than anything else. It hurt even more because I consider you like blood, because as you know, my siblings are much older than me and the bond I share with you is deeper than what I have with them.

"I also want to apologize for airing your business out about Xavier because it was not the time or place to do that. It hurt me you didn't feel comfortable sharing a piece of your life with me. None of this should've gotten to the point where we wanted to put our hands on each other. For my part, I sincerely apologize.

"Brianna, I have not been nice to you at all. I projected many of my insecurities onto you and you didn't deserve that. In the small moments we did get along, I can tell you're a sweet and funny person. You do remind me of myself before kids and I felt envious about that. It makes total sense why Yasmine gravitated toward you. You have no reason to believe me, but I am sorry. There's nothing I can do to change how this trip has gone so far, but I hope we get to start over again one day."

Her voice cracked at her final words. Jordyn's pride often made her admit her faults more privately instead of out in the open. Yasmine reached to hug her friend first and before she knew it, the tears started pouring from her eyes. Amari followed suit and it quickly became a group hug, sealed with Brianna's final touch. It was no secret they were feeling heavy, but somehow this moment made them feel comfortable enough to release their emotions.

Yasmine was the last to go and had to gather herself to speak.

"Ok, so I don't know how to follow up from where all of you left off. Firstly, I love each and every one of you. My life has forever been impacted by you all.

"Amari, you are the yin to my yang. We complement each other, even when we don't always agree. I am sorry for making you or anyone in this room think you should not live life on your own terms. I will definitely take this lesson back to therapy and do the work on it.

"Brianna, you are such a great addition to my life. I do apologize for this uncomfortable position you've been in throughout the week. You didn't deserve the way you were treated and I would never have invited you into our mess if I knew this was how it would turn out. You've handled it like a champ. And I appreciate you even more for that.

"Jordyn, I am sorry you feel abandoned. I love you more than you know. And I do consider you as a sister, too. You mean a lot to me but sometimes I do feel like you don't want anyone else in my life and that isn't fair to me. Or to them. I can be a friend to you and be a friend to others also.

"I admit I have distanced myself over the years. I felt like we grew apart after graduation. I did think of you as the friend with a picture-perfect life. Look at me, I can barely get a man to commit to me. This trip has also shown me that another reason I've separated myself is because of how you react to things. I plan to do better and visit you, call the kids— whatever you need to feel like I am invested in our friendship, too. I'm sorry I made you feel otherwise. I'm also sorry we almost fought. You are like family to me and I never want us to get to a point where we feel like we need to use our hands instead of just saying what's on our minds. Let's never do that again.

"Lastly, I'll discuss one more elephant in the room. Yes, Xavier and I tried rekindling our relationship with his move back to New York. It was casual, even though deep down I wanted more and knew he couldn't provide it for me. I didn't want to share unless it was real this time. And it wasn't. One day, I will get the love I deserve from a man. Until then, I know the love I have from all of you is more than enough."

The tears and sounds of sniffling around the room did not stop after the group hug.

Yasmine tearily concluded. "Wow, well I was hoping for a great outcome, but this might be even greater. I love y'all. Under any other circumstance, things would potentially be awkward for a while, but the rest of our time on this beautiful island is limited. Can we make a promise to enjoy the rest of our time here? Let's make this last night count. What time do y'all think it is?!"

"SHOT O CLOCK," everyone screamed in unison, embracing each other for another teary-eyed hug.

The ladies put on some music and danced their hearts out, letting go of the drama plaguing their trip.

35. A Toast
Yasmine

"So, Yas, where did you end up staying last night? What's the tea? Give us all of the details," Jordyn inquired while they walked to the Italian restaurant in the resort. Yasmine knew this question might come up once everything was mended.

"Girl, I ended up staying with Trevor. Things were awkward in our suite and I wanted a night of peace."

"We figured that was where you were," Amari stated. "Anything exciting happen?"

"Damn, y'all don't want to wait until dinner to discuss?" she responded.

"Thanks for asking. Absolutely not, c'mon tell us," Jordyn pleaded.

"Well, he wanted to take things slow so he gave me my space."

Covering her mouth to stifle a fake yawn, Amari said, "Boring!"

"Well, I wanted a distraction from the chaos and teased him in the shower until he finally gave in and blew my back out, ahkay?!" Yasmine responded, with her friends breaking out into laughter.

"Listen, do you, girl. He seems sweet. Do you see things

progressing outside of the trip?" Jordyn asked the question Yasmine herself feared the answer to.

"Maybe, but I don't know. I'm not trying to get my hopes up too high. We'll see how things unfold. Worst case scenario, I had a great time with him here. Beyond that, I am keeping my expectations low."

"Smart thinking. It's better to live in the moment, you'll figure it out later," Amari confirmed.

"I know you're being cautious with your heart, but have a little faith in him," Brianna whispered to Yasmine as they all entered the restaurant.

The restaurant was much smaller than the other ones they visited during their stay with a cozier family vibe. It was exactly what the ladies needed for the night.

The hostess led them to their table and passed out the menus to peruse. She gave them drink recommendations and the popular dishes served at the restaurant. The ladies started with her drink recommendation called Island Bellini, which combined Italian Prosecco with Appleton and Coconut Cream. After they ordered their drinks, she gave them more time to decide on food options.

Settling in at their table, Yasmine checked her phone and saw Trevor texted her to see how the talk with the ladies went. She gave him an update and asked him how his experience at Dunn's River was. Afterward, she scrolled her phone until it was her turn to order.

"Rasta Pasta on any menu is my type of carrying on," Brianna exclaimed, reviewing the options on the menu.

"I'll have the same. No need to look for anything else," Yasmine followed up, placing her menu down.

"There's so many good options to order from here. I wish we came sooner," noted Jordyn. Italian had always been her favorite cuisine.

"Everything happens for a reason. This might be perfect timing for us to get up close and personal after everything," said Amari. "I wouldn't have believed this was possible this morning." The friends nodded in agreement. As if on cue, the waitress showed up with another round of drinks.

"I'd like to propose a toast," said Jordyn, raising her glass. "Cheers to forgiveness and new beginnings. I hope we fully enjoy every remaining second of this trip." Everyone followed suit, reaching their cups toward the center of the table, echoing her sentiments.

They talked about random things from what was going on in their favorite reality TV shows to not wanting to head back home already. They were finally having a genuine moment, enjoying one another's company just as it should have always been. There was one more full day left at the resort and they needed to make the most of it. They planned to go to the beach during the day, then potentially go to one last party to wrap things up for the night.

"Do y'all want to get changed after dinner then come back outside to enjoy the night?" asked Brianna.

"That sounds like a good idea, I'm down," Amari replied.

"Let's do it!" exclaimed Jordyn, making Yasmine happy to see everyone willing to be together again for the night.

After they finished their meals, they put on comfortable clothes and snuck out a bottle of liquor for more drinks. They kept the night chill, people watching and guessing the life stories of the various other guests passing them by. It was the perfect way to reconnect with their inner child. And with each other.

"Y'all wanna hit the guys up?" asked Amari, a sharp contrast to her hesitation with their presence earlier in the trip.

"Eh, we've spent a lot of time with them. I think we're in need of some girl time tonight," Yasmine responded.

"Fair enough."

Trevor also texted her to see if she wanted to spend quality time with him, but she was exactly where she needed to be. With her girls.

Day 8: Soak It All Up

36. Shifting Gears
Yasmine

AFTER A ROLLERCOASTER OF EMOTIONS, the final day arrived. Yasmine was torn between feeling relieved and sad at the impending departure from her friends she desperately wanted to see nine days prior. She was beyond her capacity for social interaction, but also wanted to soak up the last moments with them, especially with everyone finally getting along.

"Now y'all know we have to get extra drunk on our last day. Shot 'O Clock!" she exclaimed, entering the common area.

Through some excitement and groans, the ladies each took one before heading to breakfast for their normal routine. They divided and conquered between the several stations for pastries, omelets, and fruit then joined one another at a table in the far left corner of the dining room. As they sat down, they noticed the men entering the food area, walking in their direction where a table opened up.

Trevor arrived at the table first, hugging each friend, saving Yasmine for last to lift her into a big hug. "Good morning! I'm so happy to see you." His words harmonized perfectly with Yasmine's internal feelings. She closed her eyes, soaking in the beautiful woody aroma radiating off his skin. She noticed the favorite scent she loved on him was Bleu de Chanel when she saw it on his nightstand. It had only been a day since they saw each other, but it felt like forever. She would need to find time to spend with him on their last day.

Pushing his table next to theirs, he chose the seat nearest to Yasmine. When the rest of his friends joined, they hugged each woman to greet them also. Everyone ate and shared laughs about random happenings in the past couple of days.

"It is nice to sit down and joke around together again after these last few days," Chris said.

"Definitely. We're really sorry about that," noted Brianna.

"No worries at all. It happens. It's y'all last day, though. Let's make it a memorable one," he responded.

"What's on the agenda today for y'all?" asked Neil.

"Yea, what are you getting into?" David followed up.

Amari responded. "Well we're probably heading to the beach now, but no other concrete plans afterward. What do y'all have going on?"

"We heard about this boat party happening around two o'clock. I know it's the last day, but we don't mind if y'all want to join. It's up to you, though." Trevor squeezed Yasmine's hand under the table, confirming he wanted her to join. She remained quiet, letting the rest of her friends make the final decision. She wanted everyone on one accord before sharing her own opinion.

"I'll leave that decision up to the rest of y'all. I'm down for whatever," said Amari, turning to the ladies.

"I don't mind going on a boat again but would still love to head to the beach now for a few. We haven't gone there yet," Jordyn stated.

"I agree. I'm down to do both. Let's try to do everything we can today!" Brianna exclaimed.

After holding her breath waiting for everyone's response, Yasmine was finally able to exhale with relief and squeezed Trevor's hand back. With new plans on the horizon, they opted to leave the men at breakfast to bask in the sun.

* * *

"We don't have to go anywhere with the guys if y'all don't want to, you know?" said Yasmine as they found shaded seats in the sand. Even at ten in the morning, it was already scorching outside.

"What makes you think we don't want to?" Jordyn asked.

"After everything we've been through in the last few days, I want to make sure it's something we all want to do," Yasmine explained.

"We appreciate your concern, but I think we're good, unless anyone else feels differently. Let's make up for the time we lost and go out with a bang!" Amari declared.

"Yes, let's turn up!" Brianna followed up with an equal level of excitement.

Although together, everyone was in their own world by the beach. Yasmine read her book, Amari was writing, and Jordyn and Brianna did their own bonding, taking pictures in the water.

* * *

"Time to get ready," Jordyn said, tapping Yasmine's shoulder to wake her up. The combination of reading and the sounds of ocean waves put her right to sleep— again. Yasmine made a mental note to try a different sleeping playlist before her next vacation.

"My bad, my bad. Let me get up. Wait, where's Amari and Brianna?" asked Yasmine, looking over at the two empty chairs while putting her coverup back on. They wiped the sand off their bodies before exiting the beach.

"They left to go have a private conversation. Or whatever else they want to do, I don't know. I still can't believe they had sex."

"I was in shock when I first saw it, too, but I think they actually care about each other. They need to figure it out so I am happy they're talking."

"Seeing them in the act must have been an experience for you, too. But if Brianna makes Amari happy, I am more than happy for them both. It might disrupt this little friend group we're trying to build, though." Jordyn looked bashfully in Yasmine's direction.

"It definitely could. Do you see Brianna as a person you could actually be friends with?"

Jordyn pondered for a moment. "I do. She really does remind me of myself in a lot of ways, despite how I acted at the start of the trip. The pre-mom me. I was intimidated by the reminder because I feel like I've lost that a bit. If I allow myself to be more vulnerable, I think it could be a good friendship. She just wants to have a good time and I love that. Based on how I treated her, I am not sure if she's open to the idea, though."

"I'm not sure where her head is at, but I do know that she's a nice person. If your actions align with your words, I think she would be more than willing to have a friendship with you, too."

"Good to know."

Brianna and Amari were already dressed for the boat by the time they returned to the suite.

"We were wondering when y'all would show back up," said Amari.

"Yasmine was in the deepest sleep. I didn't want to disturb her, but with the clock ticking, eventually I did. We should have enough time since y'all are ready."

Yasmine stated. "Agreed. Let me hurry up and get it together."

37. Bon Voyage
Yasmine

THE VAN to the boat party included thirty minutes of drinks, jokes, and dancing. It was as if no time had passed and old friends were catching up on a fun adventure. Several groups of people were gathering near the boat as they pulled up to the dock. The boat was triple the size of their catamaran. Unlike their private experience earlier in the trip, this one would be filled with people, gathered for an afternoon to remember.

The dancehall music was bumping through the speakers as the boat eased into the deep, blue ocean waters. Everyone grabbed a shot and mixed drinks to enjoy while they became awestruck by the views.

It was evident when the liquor took over the ladies' bodies. They found themselves dancing nonstop, even when they didn't know the words to the music. After some tumultuous days, it was nice to dance and laugh again. Brianna and Jordyn. Brianna and Amari. Amari and Yasmine. Yasmine and Brianna. Jordyn and Yasmine. It was the perfect way to spend their last day.

The men were never too far away and although the boat was multiple levels, they were always within eyes' reach. They were all strangers prior to the trip, but quickly seemed like they formed long-lasting friendships with one another. The men supported and watched over the ladies as if they were their personal bodyguards. Men having fun with the opposite sex while simultaneously keeping them safe was the right type of carrying on.

Yasmine noticed a few women walk up to Trevor flirtatiously, trying to get him to dance with them. She felt a bit jealous, although she knew she shouldn't. Her mind was scrambled, not wanting to have expectations but also beginning to form feelings for him. Intrusive thoughts began seeping in, replacing the joy she should have with the day they were having. She left her friends still having a blast on the dance floors and decided to look out at the water instead. Pensive.

When Amari asked if she was ok, she smiled it off to hide the truth. It was unclear how much time passed or what song was playing, but without looking, she knew whose hand was at the small of her back.

"You good?" The deep voice that made her heart jump questioned.

Fighting back what she could not determine were happy or sad tears, Yasmine responded, "Yes. Why do you ask?"

"Well, I noticed you standing alone in the middle of a party and you seem to be deep in thought. What's going on? Did something happen with one of your friends?"

"No, no. Nothing like that. I am in my head, but I need to stay in the moment."

"Want to talk about it?"

"Not really. I want to enjoy tonight."

Trevor placed a delicate kiss on her forehead. "If not now, then later. Or when we get back home. I'm here for you, Yas. I am not going anywhere."

Before either of them knew it, unaware of anything going on around them, they shared a sensual kiss temporarily dispelling any fears Yasmine felt just a few minutes ago.

"Here you lovebirds go again. We're in the middle of a party and y'all are here tonguing each other down? Yuck," Chris noted.

"You're not wrong, Chris. Let's turn up," Yasmine responded.

They re-joined the group and danced the evening away. Everyone was having so much fun. When the boat made its way back to shore, the friends were disappointed.

"Thank y'all for inviting us out today, it was exactly what we all needed," said Amari. The confirmation was clear in everyone's eyes.

"You are more than welcome, Amari. I know y'all have your own thing to do tonight, but if you end up wanting to chill, let us know. If not, that is fine, too. We can find y'all in the morning to say goodbye," Trevor explained.

The ladies hugged each of the men before parting ways. The reality of their nearing departures seeped in like a thief in the night.

38. The Pact
Yasmine

DRESSING up for the final night of a trip was almost as important as the first, if not more. It represented transitioning back to reality, ending on as much of a high note as the start, bringing any trip full circle. The ladies made a reservation at the only restaurant they had yet to try at the resort— the steakhouse. They agreed to dress up a little more than they had the rest of the trip.

While getting ready, Yasmine helped Jordyn sort through some of her outfit options.

"Jordyn, the first orange halter dress you showed me would look beautiful on you!"

"Even with all of these back rolls I've accumulated after giving birth?"

"Girl, please. You look amazing. And the color would complement your sun-kissed skin, too. Trust me."

Yasmine's outfit choice of the night was a bold red to complement her Hershey complexion. Tonight was a bon voyage to her girls, but she also planned to give Trevor one last glimpse to remember.

"It's twenty minutes to eight, y'all. We really have to go," Brianna urged.

Yasmine and Jordyn walked into the common room where Brianna was already pouring up a round of shots. She looked wonderful, wearing a cream mini strapless dress with the tan lines from the week adding a glowing illusion of straps. Amari kept true to her style with a twist. She chose to go into the night wearing a blue two-piece pant set. The top was a button-down vest with a smidge of cleavage revealed.

"Ok, Amari! I see you tryna be sexy tonight. Don't hurt 'em," Jordyn bantered.

"Aww stop it, y'all. I can switch it up when I feel like it," Amari responded.

"I hate to break up this moment y'all are having, but we only have ten minutes. We gotta go," Brianna said, passing last minute shots around.

The steakhouse was different from the hibachi and Italian restaurants the ladies already experienced during their stay. As they entered, the kind staff escorted them to their seats. The aroma of perfectly cooked steaks filled the air. The menu displayed a variety of steak options, from juicy ribeyes to tender filet mignons.

While looking over the menu, the waitress walked over to fill each of their glasses with water and asked what other beverages they would be interested in ordering. Champagne was the only option on the agenda for their night of celebration.

Amari cleared her throat and raised her glass. "Tonight, I'd like to be the one to make a toast." Everyone except Yasmine followed her lead.

"We can totally do this now, but I have a last surprise for later that I think everyone will love," noted Yasmine.

"Damn, Yas. What a way to burst my bubble," Amari stated.

"No, no. I don't want to do that to you. You're right. Let's do a toast now and we can still do one later," Yasmine explained.

Amari continued. "Thank you! Since Yasmine is up to some of her usual shenanigans, I'll save the good speech for later. I'd like to make a toast to us all being beautiful and thriving. And especially for us having a great day, one of my favorites of the entire trip."

Everyone raised their glasses, recorded an obligatory boomerang for social media, and sipped on their drinks. It was unclear how much time passed, but their food came out quickly. After the "oohs" and "aahs" from looking at each other's main dishes, the ladies savored their meals while the live steel pan band played Caribbean music in the background.

"Yasmine, are you going to see your man tonight?!" Jordyn asked.

"Not my man, but I may spend some time with him. I'm not entirely sure yet. This trip was about us women reconnecting and that's my focus for the night. Speaking of, after this, can you all head to the beach and I will meet you there? I need to grab something from the room."

"Sis, I have on some expensive shoes. I'm not going in the sand with these," noted Brianna, pointing at her Christian Louboutin shoes.

"I have my big mom bag here; would you be ok putting them in here?" Jordyn offered.

"That works! Sorry y'all. This is just the first time I'm wearing them."

"Totally understandable, I was only trying to limit the extra walking in the heels to begin with. I'll be right back," Yasmine said before leaving the table.

"Need any help?" Amari asked.

"Nah, but can you help find a good spot for us all?" Yasmine requested.

"Definitely, see you soon," she confirmed.

After dinner, Yasmine nervously grabbed the bag she packed earlier in the evening. At the rate the trip was initially going, she wasn't convinced this last piece she planned would happen, but she was glad everything shifted back for the better.

* * *

It was the perfect night for the beach. It wasn't too windy and felt warm enough, where the rush from the waves didn't make outside feel too cold. The ladies were so deep in laughter and conversation, they didn't notice when Yasmine showed up behind them.

"Woah, when did you get here?" Jordyn yelped, startled by the gentle touch to her shoulder.

"Got what you needed, Yas?" Brianna asked.

"Sure did," Yasmine responded, pointing at a big bag over her shoulder. Her idea seemed good in theory, but she hoped the execution would match the way she envisioned it.

As she laid her bag onto the sand and pulled out the items, Jordyn asked, "Ooh, are those fire lanterns?"

"Way to give away the surprise," Amari joked.

With a playful side eye in Jordyn's direction, Yasmine responded, "Yes, they are. As we conclude this trip, I want each of us to express our favorite part and set any other personal intention before releasing it into the sky. Fire lanterns are said to carry good luck and bring hope for the future. With the emotional ride we have been on, I feel like it's the perfect way to end our trip."

"Ooh this sounds fun!" Brianna screamed.

"Does anyone want to go first?" Yasmine asked.

The gentle sound of the waves accompanied the ladies as they met closer to the beautiful ocean water, each carrying a fire lantern to be lit.

"I'll go," said Amari. "It is no secret that I tend to tip toe past drama and avoid being in the midst of it, but I was involved in some messy moments this time around, too. I know this trip had some bumps along the way, but I do feel closer to all of you.

"I want to be open with all of you that Brianna and I decided earlier that we would rather be platonic friends than romantic partners. We decided this not only for us two, but for the sake of the friendships we have here, too. I want to release the fear of speaking my own truths and be more vulnerable in sharing my feelings without the fear of being judged."

Brianna helped her light the lantern then Amari released it into the night's sky, symbolically lifting burdens off her shoulders. Brianna went next.

"When Yasmine invited me on this trip, I didn't know what to expect. Amari and I had some flirty exchanges through social media and texts. Jordyn, I had only heard about. It is always a risk going on a trip with people you don't know. In the beginning, I felt like an outsider because the love between all of you is so apparent.

"There were some great moments where I felt like we've all known each other for years. I want to be clear that I do not want to replace anyone in this group. I am just happy to be here. There's still things to learn about one another, but I do think if we try, we could all be great friends. I want to release any negativity that happened on this trip so we can start fresh as a group, if you will all have me."

As she helped Brianna light her lantern, Jordyn said, "Well, I hope you didn't think it all ends now. You are our sister now, too." With those words coming from Jordyn, who was involved in much of the week's conflict within the group, everyone's eyes filled with tears.

"Well, I was at the center of some drama on this trip, huh?" Jordyn joked, nervously playing in her hair. "Seriously, I know we went through our apologies already during The Sit Down, but I do want to express those same sentiments again. I apologize.

"Being married with kids, I can't always relate to what everyone is going through, which makes me feel left out at times. This was my first time away from my little family and I didn't realize some of the wounds I still carried, which made for some ugly moments here. I want to release my insecurities and territorial behavior. I do have a sweet spot for all of you and yes, Brianna, I would love to start fresh and get to know you on a deeper level." Brianna tearily helped Jordyn release her lantern into the sky.

Yasmine went last. "I am thankful I was able to reconnect with all of you and strengthen our relationships. I know we had some rough moments, but I think it made us stronger as a unit. I can agree about the good times being amazing. I want to release any feelings of doubt and focus on strengthening all of our bonds when we get home. I also want to release feeling the need to try to steer how each of you live your lives, it's not my place and I am happy to be here for the journey. I love y'all. Forever and always."

The group, now in routine with lighting the lanterns, joined forces to send the final lantern soaring into the night, its glow adding to the ethereal dance above with the rest. They held hands, tears streaming down their faces, and stared at the visual representation of their fears and insecurities being released into the night's sky.

Friendship wasn't easy. It demanded the same level of dedication as any other relationship. It could become distant and fragmented. Through age and different seasons in life, everyone's individual path may align differently than it did when initially introduced. Allowing space for friends to grow, to make mistakes, to grow apart, and to come back together, was the truest testament of all.

Yasmine didn't want the feeling of renewed connections to end. "I know we haven't made it back home yet, but can we make a pact to do this every year? For real, this time?" she asked.

Epilogue

2 Years Later

AFTER THEIR VACATION TO JAMAICA, the ladies became far more consistent in their communication with one another. They set aside the third Wednesday of every month, where it was mandatory to catch up over a video call, with Brianna included. Of course, there were times where they needed to speak more, but having a set date on their calendar held them accountable to being there for one another consistently.

Yasmine's life changed drastically after their trip. She left her corporate job to finally pursue her real dream of becoming an interior designer. It was an interesting journey, but nevertheless an exciting experience. She recently helped a popular influencer decorate her home, boosting her popularity and bookings.

After months of courting post-vacation, Trevor made things official with her during the holidays after their summer rendezvous. Despite them meeting being a happenstance situation, he was consistent and intentional since the day they met. After dating for a year, they decided to get a three-bedroom apartment together to confirm if they were compatible in all aspects— so far, so good.

Jordyn started individual therapy after their trip. After another bout of couples' therapy, Malik took heed to her concerns and found a way for his schedule to slow down a bit, giving them more time to spend together as a family, which did wonders for her mental health. Individual therapy helped her heal some inner child wounds and work through her triggers. Was it working? The jury was still out.

Amari was still roaming the world, finding inspiration for her books. She recently moved to London to immerse herself in the community for her next book release. She also met a woman named Laila, who was the love of her life. After less than a year of dating, she made plans to propose to her, finally feeling the level of partnership she was seeking romantically.

Brianna still lived in the building in Brooklyn where she and Yasmine first met. She was still a traveling nurse, but also started an esthetician business on the side as a supplement to her income. This allowed her more freedom to give the girls whatever beauty enhancements they desired. Romantically, she was still single and mingling, figuring things on her own time.

Despite all the changes in their lives, the ladies kept their promise to one another for an annual vacation. To make things easier, they decided to take a vacation together around the same time every year in mid-July. Last year, they went to Cabo. They went the full week with very minor hiccups here and there, but it was eons better than their first trip. Yasmine was more than excited for their next adventure of choice in Saint Lucia.

After months of being excited to book their travels, they suddenly flaked on her, giving excuses about work or other life commitments. Not wanting to cause any unnecessary contention in the group, she couldn't express to them how much it hurt her.

If it weren't for Trevor, she would have ditched the vacation idea altogether. He insisted on her keeping the promise to herself and to go with him instead. Yasmine reluctantly agreed but knew it wouldn't be the same without her girls.

Most of that was forgotten when they landed. Saint Lucia was one of the most gorgeous places Yasmine had ever laid eyes on. Its picturesque beauty could only be described as a painting. She felt like she was in a piece of art with the bluest skies and greenest trees, roads winding to discover more of its lushness at every turn.

"Babe, we have to hurry to make our reservation at nine," nagged Trevor. They were compatible in most ways, but he loathed her commitment to running behind.

"I'm coming, I'm coming," insisted Yasmine, rushing to put the final touches on her makeup.

Yasmine didn't have many requests for the trip, but she did want one night at a restaurant at Jade Mountain Resort. The view of the majestic Piton Mountains in the background as they ate was a sight she wanted to see. Although they were fully booked when she called, Trevor called incessantly and somehow was able to get them to squeeze the couple in on the requested night.

* * *

Upon entering the restaurant, the cordial waiter led them up some steps to the terrace. As they reached the top, Yasmine's jaw immediately dropped. There were red rose petals beneath her feet, their vibrance contrasting the miniature candles leading them to the edge of the terrace where a giant heart made of white rose petals displayed the LED sign with the words, "Will You Marry Me?'" She looked at her sneaky boyfriend, eyes tear-filled with disbelief and kept nodding her head as they stood in front of the sign.

"You didn't?!"

"I did," he responded, getting on one knee.

"My life has been forever changed since the day I met you. I knew when I met you, I could never let you go. You have proven me right every single day since then. I am a better man because of you and hope we can continue to build a lifelong legacy with each other. Yasmine Imani Hughes, will you do me the honor of marrying me?"

"Yes. Yes! Ten thousand times, yes." As he placed the ring on her finger and kissed her, she noticed it was a gorgeous emerald cut with accented baguettes on the band. *He must have spoken to my...*

Before she could complete her thought, her closest family and friends ran toward her out of nowhere.

Wait, they're here? They're here! Cue more waterworks.

"Congratulations!" She heard echoes all around her, but still was wrapping her brain around how her man planned this. Her friends didn't cancel on her after all. They were in on everything.

"I can't believe y'all made me think you were canceling on me."

"We would never break our promise, sis," Amari said with a hug.

"When Trevor came to us with the idea, we were worried. But also knew surprising you in this way would take you out," Jordyn confirmed.

"Are you happy?" asked Brianna.

"I am beyond happy. Not only do I get to marry the love of my life, but my friends were a part of the entire process. I don't know what I would do without y'all."

They sealed her words of affirmation with the friend group hugging, full of tears and laughter.

Discussion Questions

Please do not read any further if you have not finished reading the novel

These questions are meant to be used as a guide for discussion, whether individually or amongst a broader group of people. I highly recommend discussing with a group of friends open and honest dialogue

1. Have you experienced fragments in any of your past or current friendships? How did you address those difficulties?
2. Do you believe that friendships evolve over time? Which part of the story resonated the most to you?
3. Who was your least favorite character in the story? Which character in the story can you relate to the most? Why?
4. What were your thoughts on the section titles being presented as an itinerary of the trip? Did they add an element of suspense about what each day would bring?

Discussion Questions

5. Yasmine and Jordyn have been friends since childhood. Do you have a childhood friend? How have you navigated major life milestones together? Did those experiences strengthen your bond or create distance?

6. Yasmine, Jordyn, Amari, and Brianna each handled conflict differently during their vacation. How do you typically navigate challenges in your friendships? Are you more communicative or inclined to avoid confrontation? Have you ever held back your true feelings to keep the peace?

7. Jordyn felt threatened by new friends joining her group, fearful of being replaced. Have you ever felt territorial in a friendship or been on the receiving end of it? What was that experience like, and how did it impact the relationship?

8. Yasmine kept her renewed relationship with her college beau, Xavier, a secret from her friends. Have you ever hidden something from a friend out of fear of being judged? Did you eventually share the truth? How did it affect your relationship?

9. Brianna joined the friend group as a newcomer during their Jamaica trip. Have you ever been the "new friend" in an established group or introduced someone new to your own circle? How did it affect the group's dynamic?

10. Yasmine was accustomed to Xavier's avoidant communication style. How do you think that shaped her feelings when meeting Trevor? Do you believe our past relationships influence how we approach new ones?

11. The tension between Yasmine and Jordyn built up to the point where they nearly had a physical altercation in the "Lusty Taboo" chapter. Have you ever experienced such intense tension with a friend? How did you manage it, and were you able to de-escalate before it went too far?

Discussion Questions

12. Which character left you wanting to know more about their life? Who would be your pick for a follow up story?

Acknowledgments

This book means the world to me—it's the tangible proof of me taking a leap of faith on myself. Writing and publishing a novel was a dream I held onto for years, but it wasn't until I pushed past my fears that I could finally bring it to life. *Friendship Fragments* is my debut, and I'm proud to say it's the first of many to come.

This story is my love letter to my friends—old and new—who have left an indelible mark on my life. But more than that, it's a dedication to every version of myself that has existed along the way. Each of my main characters carries traits of who I've been, whether those parts have stayed or been outgrown. Writing this novel gave me a space to honor it all.

None of this would have been possible without the incredible people in my life:

To Skylar, Callie, Nate, Maya, Ruth, and Laila: Thank you for being my beta readers and first eyes on the book. Your thoughtful feedback brought these characters to life in ways I couldn't have done alone.

To Talia: Thank you for reading an early draft during our DMV weekend and for your encouraging words when you didn't know how much I needed them.

To my editor, Khloe: As a first-time author, I was intimidated to dive into the editing process, but you made it approachable, constructive, and even enjoyable. Thank you for suggesting the title change—I can't imagine the book with a title other than *Friendship Fragments*.

To my cover designer, Denise: You brought the vision to life with patience and even more creativity. Thank you for working with me to ensure every detail reflected the heart of this story.

Tiara: Thank you for constantly asking, "When are you going to write that book?" I finally did it, sis.

Big up, Janette! Mommy, thank you for supporting me, even when you're still figuring out exactly what I'm accomplishing.

Chanae: Thank you for being the best big sister and for encouraging me to intern at the *Philadelphia Daily News*. That opportunity shaped my love for storytelling.

Samantha: Thank you for sharing my passion for reading and for sisterly bookstore trips to hunt for new releases.

Diamond: Thank you for being the best little sister anyone could ask for. Your light and laughter brighten my world.

To all of my friends: Without our shared experiences, this story wouldn't exist in its truest form. Thank you for being the chosen family I will forever treasure.

And finally, to you—the reader: Thank you for taking the time to read *Friendship Fragments*. I hope the story resonates with you and inspires you to take a chance on yourself, just as I did for myself. Your support means everything, and I can't wait to share more stories with you in the future.

About the Author

Chantal Bookal has always been captivated by the magic of storytelling, particularly tales that explore topics such as friendship, love, and suspense. A lifelong reader, she now brings her own voice to the page, sharing stories that leave a lasting impact. Her debut novel, *Friendship Fragments*, delves into the intricate bonds between friends, weaving together heart, tension, and emotion in a way that only she can.

Outside of writing, Chantal thrives in the corporate world as a Sourcing Manager. When she's not working her nine-to-five, you can find her at the gym, enjoying a fun brunch with friends, or binge-watching her favorite shows.